PRA...

*Allergi...*

"The meals that Gigi Fitzgerald makes may be low in calories, but author Peg Cochran serves up a full meal in her debut book."

—Sheila Connolly, *New York Times* bestselling
author of the Orchard Mysteries

"A delicious, de-liteful debut. Gigi is a heartfelt protagonist with calories to spare. Tasty food, a titillating story, and a spicy town and theater, rife with dramatic pause. Add a dash of romance, and you have the recipe for a successful series."

—Avery Aames, Agatha Award–winning
author of the Cheese Shop Mysteries

"Full of colorful characters, delicious diet foods, a rescued dog, and an intriguing mystery, *Allergic to Death* is tasty entertainment."

—Melinda Wells, author of the Della Cooks Mysteries

"Mouthwatering gourmet meals and a scrumptious mystery—a de-liteful combination!"

—Krista Davis, *New York Times* bestselling author
of the Domestic Diva Mysteries

"A delicious amateur-sleuth tale . . . Culinary cozy fans will take De-Lite with Peg Cochran's first recipe."

—*Genre Go Round Reviews*

"An absolute delight . . . A super fun read."

—*Cozy Mystery Book Reviews*

*continued . . .*

# Iced to Death

Peg Cochran

BERKLEY PRIME CRIME, NEW YORK

**THE BERKLEY PUBLISHING GROUP**
Published by the Penguin Group
Penguin Group (USA) LLC
375 Hudson Street, New York, New York 10014

USA • Canada • UK • Ireland • Australia • New Zealand • India • South Africa • China

penguin.com

A Penguin Random House Company

ICED TO DEATH

A Berkley Prime Crime Book / published by arrangement with the author

Berkley Prime Crime Books are published by The Berkley Publishing Group.
BERKLEY® PRIME CRIME and the PRIME CRIME logo are trademarks of
Penguin Group (USA) LLC.

For information, address: The Berkley Publishing Group,
a division of Penguin Group (USA) LLC,
375 Hudson Street, New York, New York 10014.

ISBN: 978-0-425-25254-3

PUBLISHING HISTORY
Berkley Prime Crime mass-market edition / March 2014

PRINTED IN THE UNITED STATES OF AMERICA

10  9  8  7  6  5  4  3  2  1

Cover illustration by Teresa Fasolino.
Cover design by Sarah Oberrender.

# Chapter 1

Giovanna "Gigi" Fitzgerald ladled a generous serving of mushroom barley soup into each of the open containers lined up on her kitchen island. Once filled, they would go into white boxes with *Gigi's Gourmet De-Lite* written on them in silver script. She glanced out the window of her small cottage where fat flakes of snow drifted past. According to the radio, accumulation was less than an inch so far, and she trusted her bright red MINI Cooper would make it through okay. She had several hungry customers waiting for the diet gourmet food she delivered for each of their meals.

Reg, her West Highland white terrier, was asleep right next to the heating vent. Gigi smiled. Reg knew how to make himself comfortable. And when she was cooking, he was never far away. If a piece of food happened to hit the floor, his eyes would fly open immediately and he would be on it so fast there would be no time to invoke the five-second rule.

Right now he was snoring softly, his right ear twitching in time to his breathing, a bluish-gray beam of weak sunlight slanting across his belly. Gigi smiled at him. She'd taken Reg on in a spur-of-the-moment decision, but he had turned out to be a wonderful companion.

Gigi put the containers of soup into her signature boxes along with a piece of crusty whole-wheat bread, a small salad and a fruit compote for dessert.

"Come on, Reg, we're going for a ride."

She didn't have to say it twice—the small dog jumped to his feet immediately, both eyes open and bright. It was hard to believe he'd been asleep seconds earlier. He paced impatiently in front of the back door as Gigi reached for her coat. She carefully loaded her containers into the back seat of the MINI and held the passenger door open for Reg. Reg always rode shotgun, staring through the front window as if he, not Gigi, was responsible for driving the car.

Gigi put the car in gear and slowly backed down the driveway. The wheels slid, then gripped again, and they were on their way. She switched on the windshield wipers, and the snowflakes, which were now coming down faster and harder, were briefly whisked away.

The roads were covered with a fine dusting of snow, but here and there ice lurked beneath the surface. Gigi gripped the wheel as she negotiated the narrow, winding road leading toward the small downtown area of Woodstone, Connecticut.

Gigi made her delivery rounds as quickly as she could. Flurries of snow continued to fall, and the roads became even slicker. She'd spent most of the previous years living in New York City, where she'd hardly ever needed to get behind the wheel. She breathed a sigh of relief after she delivered the last Gourmet De-Lite container and was able to turn around toward home.

She rounded the corner onto her street, and her spirits rose as her cottage came into view. It was white with a bright red door, dormer windows and a picket fence.

With a red, white and green Ralph's Pizza delivery truck in the driveway.

There must be a mistake. She didn't order a pizza. Not that she didn't love it—especially the wonderfully aromatic pies Carlo and Emilio used to make at Al Forno—but Ralph's was pedestrian fare, full of calories and laden with fat, and something she tried to stay away from.

It had to be a mistake.

A young man in a bright green ski cap and a zip-up plaid jacket was standing at Gigi's front door, an expectant look on his face.

She pulled into the driveway and stopped. She opened the door to let Reg out of the car and he ran ahead of her, jumping around the young man's legs and sniffing furiously at the pizza box. Gigi was about to call out to the delivery boy when her front door slowly opened.

"What on earth . . . ?" Gigi was so stunned she stopped in her tracks.

A woman stuck her head out the door. She was tall and thin with dark hair styled in a pixie cut. She exchanged some cash for the pizza box in the delivery boy's hands and was about to shut the door when she noticed Gigi standing in the driveway, still openmouthed.

"Surprise," she yelled, waving the pizza box toward Gigi.

"What . . . when . . . how did you . . . ?" Gigi stammered as she approached her own front door.

"You didn't lock it," the woman said, making it sound like Gigi's fault. "Well? Aren't you glad to see me?" She threw her free arm around Gigi's neck and hugged her.

"What are you doing here?" Gigi looked her younger sister up and down. Pia was a little thinner than the last time they'd seen each other, and the pixie haircut was new. Gigi liked it. Pia's eyes were enormous, and the cut accentuated them beautifully. She hadn't seen or heard from her sister in over a year—not since she had taken off for some artist's commune in the south of England where they made their own paper and paint and grew their own food.

Pia waved the pizza box under Gigi's nose. Gigi had to admit, it did smell good. She just hoped none of her clients had seen Ralph's delivery truck in her driveway! She tried to set a good example by eating healthily herself.

"What are you doing here?" Gigi asked again.

Pia made a face. "Let's get comfortable first, and I'll tell you everything. I've brought a bottle of plonk—cheap red wine," she explained, obviously noticing the look of bewilderment on Gigi's face.

Gigi followed her sister to the kitchen, still half stunned by Pia's sudden appearance. A battered suitcase and stuffed backpack had been tossed willy-nilly into the living room. Gigi felt her jaw clench. She cherished her cottage and took the time to keep it neat and tidy.

"Got any paper plates?" Pia pulled open drawers and cabinet doors and then slammed them shut. She opened the red, green and white pizza box, which she'd placed on the counter, and pulled out a slice. "Sorry, but I can't wait. I've been dying for some decent food ever since I left the States. It was all roasted root vegetables and dandelion salads in

that commune. I've been pining for some good junk food."
She took an enormous bite of the pizza.

Gigi grabbed plates and napkins from the cupboard and
set them out on the island. The pizza really did smell good.
She hesitated, and then finally helped herself to a piece.

"To answer your question," Pia said around a mouthful
of pie, "there was this guy."

Gigi groaned. With Pia, it was always some *guy*. Gigi
carefully blotted her slice of pizza with some napkins and
then took a tiny nibble from the end. It wasn't as bad as she
expected. As a matter of fact, it tasted heavenly.

Pia twisted the top off the bottle of red table wine she'd
brought and waited while Gigi fetched wineglasses.

Pia filled a glass for each of them. "You have no idea how
wonderful this is. In the commune, we each had one ugly,
handmade brown mug that we used for everything. Even the
elderberry wine ended up tasting like coffee." She shuddered. "I did do some amazing work there though." Pia
helped herself to another slice of the pie. "And it was good
with Clive while it lasted."

"What happened?"

Pia heaved a dramatic sigh and rolled her enormous green
eyes. "I thought I had found my happily ever after, but it
turned out he was cheating on me with that witch Blythe,
whose family owns the property the commune is on."

"I'm sorry." Gigi looked at her sister. Somehow she didn't
seem particularly brokenhearted. "How . . . how long are
you staying?" The words stuck in Gigi's mouth, and she took
a big glug of her wine. It went down the wrong way, and she
began to cough.

Pia shrugged. "Don't know really. Until I'm on to the

next good thing." She pouted prettily. "You don't mind do you?"

"Er, no. No. Of course not." Gigi said insincerely.

Gigi's cottage was small, but she'd always found it more than roomy enough for her needs. After only four days with her sister in residence, however, the space was beginning to feel terribly cramped. There was only one full bathroom and a tiny powder room, and Pia thought nothing of leaving her wet towels draped over the bath or her dirty clothes strewn across the floor. Gigi's tiny guest room was already awash with Pia's things. Her sister didn't seem to feel the need to put anything away or to make the bed. Whenever Gigi passed the room, the sheets were in a tangle and the comforter was in a pile at the foot of the bed.

Gigi was working on boxing up her Gourmet De-Lite lunches when she glanced at the clock. Surely Pia would be up soon. Gigi had saved her something for breakfast, but it was already nearly lunchtime.

"Good morning," Pia called suddenly, startling Gigi.

She was dressed in a pair of black leggings, over-the-knee suede boots and a long, hand-knit-looking tunic.

"I've got some breakfast frittata left for you if you want," Gigi offered.

Gigi looked at Pia's long, thin legs and wondered, not for the first time, why she couldn't have gotten some of the same genes.

"Thanks, but I'm going out. I have a lunch date." Pia smiled enigmatically.

"Really? Who?" Pia seemed to attract men like magnets attracted metal.

Pia grabbed her coat, which she'd left draped over one of the kitchen chairs, and began to put it on. "I'll tell you when I get back." She winked at Gigi. "This could be the real deal, but I don't want to jinx it."

"Oh," was all Gigi could manage.

"Do you need anything while I'm out? I'd be happy to stop by the grocery store."

"That would be great." Gigi jotted a few things down on a list and handed it to Pia.

"Ta-ta," Pia headed out to the ancient, pea green Volkswagen van she'd bought from someone on Craigslist the day after her arrival. She'd assured Gigi that she was leaving soon and making her way across country to California, but so far, she hadn't showed any signs of imminent departure. And now with romance in the air, Gigi was beginning to wonder if she'd ever get going.

Gigi sighed. She loved her sister, and it was fun having her around, but she really wanted to have the cottage back to herself.

Gigi put on her own coat, and Reg, who was asleep on top of the heating vent, snapped to attention.

"Yes, you're coming, too." Gigi grabbed Reg's leash while he did an animated dance around her ankles.

Gigi drove down High Street, past all the shops that had become so familiar to her. Someone was leaving the Book Nook with two shopping bags. Sienna must be pleased, Gigi thought. She and Sienna, the bookstore's owner, had been best friends since college, and Sienna had convinced Gigi to move to Woodstone and open her business when Gigi's marriage came to an end. Gigi passed Declan's Grille and felt hot color rush to her face. The owner, Declan McQuaid, was extremely attractive, and she always felt slightly awkward around him. He'd made it quite clear he found her attractive as well, but she'd sworn not to get involved. Declan himself had admitted to being the "love 'em and leave 'em" type, and Gigi didn't want to take a chance on ruining the budding romance between her and Detective Bill Mertz.

Gigi continued down High Street to her last stop, the law firm of Simpson and West. Madeline Stone, one of her newer clients, was waiting in the small wood-paneled lobby when Gigi got there. She was wearing a slim pencil skirt and a big smile. She had recently become engaged to Hunter Simpson, the son of one of the firm's partners. She held out her left hand as Gigi approached. Gigi dutifully admired the large diamond solitaire that adorned Madeline's ring finger.

"It's beautiful." Gigi couldn't help but recall that she'd had one very much like it, but she'd sold it and purchased her MINI after her divorce from Ted. She hadn't regretted it for a minute.

"I'm so excited about the engagement party Mr. Simpson is throwing for us Saturday night." Madeline's eyes glowed as she stopped herself and giggled, "I guess I should call him Bradley now that he's going to be my father-in-law." She blushed again. "I can't quite picture myself calling him . . . Dad." She ducked her head.

A young woman in a pantsuit brushed past them and gave Madeline a strange look.

"Everyone is so jealous," Madeline whispered to Gigi as she watched the other woman push open the heavy front door. "They were all hoping to snag Hunter themselves." A second, very becoming blush colored her cheeks pink. "I still can't believe he proposed to me!"

Gigi patted Madeline's arm. "Hunter is the lucky one if you ask me."

Madeline's blush intensified.

The elevator doors pinged open, and a tall, attractive blond woman rushed out, stomping past Gigi and Madeline, an expensive leather handbag swinging furiously from her arm. Her black suede stilettos clacked loudly against the marble floor. Her cheeks were flushed bright red, and her cashmere coat swung wide open despite the frigid temperatures awaiting her outdoors.

"Hold my calls. I'm going out," she barked at the secretary sitting behind the polished wooden reception desk. The girl jumped and nodded her head, but the woman had already swept past in a cloud of expensive-smelling French perfume. She charged through the front door, heedless of the half inch of snow that had collected on the sidewalk.

"That's Tiffany Morse," Madeline said in an undertone to Gigi. "Rumor has it she's in line to become the first female partner at Simpson and West."

Moments later they heard a car engine start up, and then a bright red Mustang streaked past the front window of the building, fishtailing slightly on the slick road.

"I wonder what's got her in such a tizzy?" Madeline stared out the window. She turned toward Gigi. "I heard her arguing with Bradley earlier." This time she barely stumbled over the name. "I was surprised the two of them were fighting. She's Bradley's . . ." She hesitated. ". . . Pet. If you know what I mean." She rolled her eyes at Gigi.

Gigi nodded.

"Don't get me wrong, she's a good lawyer. One of the best. It's just that Simpson, West, Donahue, Flanagan and Moskowitz—that's the firm's full name but obviously it would never have fit on the sign out front or on the letterhead so we just go with Simpson and West—has never had a female partner before." She frowned. "Mr. West once said he wouldn't have a woman partner unless it was over his dead body, but I guess Mr. Simpson"—she blushed again—"I mean Bradley, managed to change his mind."

Gigi supposed Madeline must be right. But if Bradley had changed Mr. West's mind, it sure made her wonder what Tiffany Morse had done to change Bradley's mind.

Gigi had just returned home from making her dinner deliveries when she heard the knocking sound that heralded the arrival of Pia's beat-up old VW van. The car hissed loudly as the engine was turned off. Gigi couldn't imagine Pia attempting to drive that thing to California—if she ever left, that is, now that she had apparently found true love or, at least, romance.

Pia came in through the back door carrying two bags of groceries. Her cheeks were flushed from the cold, and moisture glimmered in her short, dark hair.

"Snowing again," she said as she dumped her purchases on the counter. "I didn't think Sparky was going to make it up the hill."

"Sparky?"

Pia gestured with her shoulder in the general direction of the cottage's driveway. "I decided to name that beastly van." She sighed. "At least it's getting me around."

Gigi thought of mentioning California but decided that

perhaps this wasn't the best time. "What did you buy?" she asked instead.

"I'm sorry." Pia made a sad face. "I forgot some of the things on your list. Just the parsley, lettuce and chicken stock though."

*Those were the only things on my list*, Gigi thought as she watched Pia unpack the groceries. "What did you get?"

"Twinkies!" Pia held up the cellophane-wrapped package triumphantly. "And some of that buttered movie popcorn in case we want to watch a flick on television." She dug deeper. "Hot dogs for dinner." She laid them on the counter. "Chocolate chip cookies, marshmallow fluff and salt-and-vinegar potato chips," she finished triumphantly. "Do you know the Brits call chips *crisps*?"

Gigi shook her head. She was in shock over the contents of her sister's shopping spree. Surely Pia didn't think Gigi was going to eat that stuff?

"How was your lunch date? It must have gone well." Gigi glanced at the clock. "It's almost dinnertime."

"Oh, I spent some time setting up a small studio I found to rent by the week. It's out by that industrial park on the edge of town. Nothing fancy, but it will allow me to get some work done." Gigi was relieved. The thought of Pia bringing in paint or clay or whatever she used for her artwork to the cottage gave Gigi the shivers.

"My lunch date was dreamy though." Pia perched on one of the stools around the island and popped the top off a can of soda—not sugar-free, Gigi noted—and took a huge gulp. "I sat at the bar and kept him company."

Gigi felt something in her chest freeze. "Sat at the bar?" she repeated.

Pia shook her head. "Yeah. He runs this place downtown. A lot of English cuisine but nothing like the stuff we had in that commune. His food is good."

Gigi's mouth had dried up. "What was the name of the place?"

"Declan's Grille. I never thought I'd fall for another Englishman, but Declan McQuaid has to be one of the dreamiest men I've ever met." Pia stared into space, a rapturous look on her face.

"Oh," Gigi said in a very tiny voice.

# Chapter 2

Gigi was filling containers with her clients' lunches when Pia wandered into the kitchen. A piece of hair stood straight up on the top of her head, and her face was still creased with sleep. She had Gigi's robe wrapped around a pair of faded long johns.

She must have noticed Gigi glancing at them.

"From Marks and Sparks," she said as she poured herself a mug of coffee from the thermos on the counter. "Otherwise known as Marks and Spencer. That commune was so flipping cold, I had to wear them under everything to stay warm." She yawned loudly and settled down at the kitchen island, cradling her cup and watching as Gigi finished loading her containers.

Fortunately for Gigi, Pia had been spending most of her time at her new studio, often working into the wee hours of the morning and only slipping into the cottage as dawn was beginning to break. Gigi, on the other hand, was up with the birds and in bed by ten o'clock more often than not, so they were like ships passing in the night. It definitely made for a better relationship.

"I stopped by Declan's for a bite yesterday," Pia smothered another giant yawn. "I rather think he does fancy me."

Gigi froze momentarily. "Are you . . ."

Pia ran her hands through her short hair, making her cowlick even more pronounced. "Oh, he hasn't asked me out yet or anything. But give me time . . ." She let the sentence trail off enigmatically.

Gigi didn't know how that made her feel. On the one hand, she was dating Detective Bill Mertz and enjoying their budding relationship. On the other hand, she couldn't help going weak in the knees every time she saw Declan McQuaid. And the thought that he might take her sister Pia out made her feel . . . slightly jealous.

"Well, I'm off to deliver these." Gigi gestured toward the stack of filled containers on the counter. "Eggs and bacon are in the fridge. Help yourself." She pulled her scarf off the hook by the door and wound it around her neck. "Come on, Reg."

Reg immediately jumped to his feet, despite the fact that he'd been snoring softly seconds before.

Gigi was slipping into her coat when the telephone rang. She glanced at the clock on the wall. She was five minutes behind schedule and was tempted to let the call go to voice mail, but perhaps it was a client with a change of delivery plans. That happened at least once a week.

Gigi reached for the phone, and Reg lay back down, his head on his front paws, his expression clearly one of disappointment.

"Hello?"

A man's voice came across the line, deep and lilting. Gigi felt her face begin its telltale burn. It was Declan McQuaid. The sound of his voice never failed to bring a rush of heat and color to Gigi's cheeks. She glanced at Pia, and Pia looked back at her curiously.

"Gigi. I'm glad I caught you." Declan's normally smooth voice had a slightly panicked edge to it.

"Oh?" Gigi was intrigued. She plunked down on the stool next to the telephone and swiveled so that her back was to her sister. She heard Reg give a deep sigh from his post by the back door.

"I need your help desperately."

Gigi frowned. She couldn't imagine what Declan would need her help with. Unless he was in trouble. She had helped solve two murder cases recently, although she had no illusions about her sleuthing abilities.

"My chef just threw down his apron and walked out the door."

"You mean he's quit?"

"Yes." Declan's furious exhale came over the phone line loud and clear. Gigi could picture his strong, dark brows lowered over his bright blue eyes.

"But why . . . how?"

"We had a small argument, nothing serious. I didn't think . . ." Declan paused. "Anyway, he's gone. I tried to persuade him to stay and help with tomorrow night's party, but he refused."

Gigi had heard that chefs could be temperamental, but behavior like this was unprofessional.

"I can handle dinner tonight myself. Most of the

preparations are already done," Declan continued, "but I really need help with this big engagement party. They've booked the restaurant for the whole evening. I gather that Simpson guy is rolling in dough. It's his son who's getting married."

"Yes. I don't know the son, but I know the bride-to-be. Madeline Stone has been a client of mine for a couple of months. Unfortunately I don't know how I can help. I don't know any professional chefs. Perhaps you could try an employment agency?"

Declan snorted. "That would be fine if I wanted someone to sling hamburgers." He paused. "I was hoping you would be willing to help me."

"Me?" Gigi squeaked. While she might prepare delicious diet food for upward of twelve people a day, she was far from a restaurant chef. "I'm not sure . . ."

"I know it's an awful lot to ask. You've probably been invited to the party as a guest."

Gigi thought of the new dress hanging in her closet that she'd bought to wear to the event.

"I'm just not sure how much help I'd—"

"I've pared down the menu," Declan hastened to reassure Gigi. "I really just need another set of hands. My sous chef is something of an idiot and needs lots of direction. I don't know anyone else who has as much experience in the kitchen as you do. Cookery is becoming a lost art—it's all micro-wave or take-away these days."

Gigi was flattered. And she had to admit, working side-by-side in the tiny restaurant kitchen with Declan was a very attractive proposition.

"Please?"

Gigi couldn't resist. "Okay. But I can't promise I'll be all that much help."

"You've saved my life. You have no idea."

By the time Gigi hung up the phone, Reg had rolled on his side in front of the back door and was sound asleep again.

"Who was that?" Pia asked.

Gigi felt her face burn. "Oh, no one. No one, really." She glanced at the clock in alarm. All of her deliveries were going to be late now. She buttoned her coat and grabbed Reg's leash.

"Come on, boy, we've got to get going."

Reg scrambled to attention immediately and looked at Gigi as if to say *it's about time*. He managed to convey the impression that he, personally, had been ready for hours.

Gigi was conscious of Pia's curious look as the back door closed behind her.

For the life of her, she couldn't imagine why she hadn't admitted to Pia that it had been Declan on the phone.

Now she had two problems, Gigi realized as she drove through downtown Woodstone. Although it was only early afternoon, the dense cloud cover made it feel much later. The streetlights were on and so were the lights over the shops.

Gigi was going to have to eventually admit to Pia that not only had she been talking to Declan on the phone, but she was going to be working with him on Saturday night. Pia was going to wonder why Gigi hadn't told her right away. Gigi felt a trickle of sweat make its way down her side despite the blowing snow.

Worse, she was going to have to tell Mertz that she couldn't attend the party with him. That was bad enough, but when he found out it was because she was helping

17

Declan . . . To say he wasn't going to be happy was an understatement. The trickle of sweat threatened to become a torrent as Gigi thought about her situation.

She would have to tell him that night. Mertz was coming to dinner, Pia would be at her studio, and they would have some time alone. Gigi slowed in front of Bon Appétit, Woodstone's gourmet and cookery store. Perhaps a good bottle of wine was in order. She'd wine and dine him, and hopefully, soporific with food and drink, he wouldn't protest about the change in plans for Madeline's engagement party.

Yeah, right.

Delicious, rich smells permeated Gigi's tiny kitchen. She was making chicken cacciatore and had an antipasto platter of olives, provolone cheese, prosciutto, eggplant caponata and marinated mushrooms ready to serve along with some artisanal bread. The expensive bottle of wine Gigi had splurged on sat on the counter *breathing*. Surely all that would put Mertz in a receptive mood . . . right?

With dinner prepared, Gigi was able to indulge in a lavender-scented bath before leisurely dressing and doing her hair and makeup. She was ready and pacing the hall ten minutes before Mertz was due to arrive, but even so, his sudden knock on the door, quickly followed by Reg's excited barking, startled her.

The open door let in a blast of cold air along with a smattering of snowflakes.

"It's snowing again." Mertz said, handing Gigi a large paper-wrapped bouquet of assorted flowers.

"These are lovely, thanks."

Mertz ducked his head. "Glad you like them." He motioned toward the door. "I'll clear the walk and driveway for you before I leave."

"You don't have to—"

"It's no problem. I don't want you out there trying to do it yourself." He brushed the melting white flakes of snow off his coat before handing it to Gigi. "Roads are fine fortunately." He took a deep breath. "Sure smells delicious in here."

Reg was dancing in and out between Mertz's legs, demanding his due, so Mertz reached down and scratched him between the ears. He gave Gigi a peck on the cheek, and the coldness of his touch made her shiver briefly.

Mertz rubbed his hands together briskly. "What smells so good?"

"Chicken cacciatore," Gigi answered as she hung his coat in the closet.

"Chicken catch-a-who?"

"Cacciatore. It means hunter or hunter-style, either chicken or rabbit, with onions, tomatoes, herbs and wine. In southern Italy it's usually red wine, while in the north they use white."

"If it tastes half as good as it smells . . ."

"Oh, it does, don't worry."

He followed Gigi out to the kitchen, where she rummaged in a cabinet for a vase. It had a small chip on the rim, but it wasn't visible when she placed the flowers in it. She added some water and placed it in the center of the kitchen island.

"There." Gigi moved the vase a bit to the left. "That looks perfect."

"Glad you like them." Mertz cleared his throat and looked down at his feet.

Gigi got out two wineglasses, poured them each a glass of the Syrah the clerk at the wine store had recommended, and pulled the antipasto platter from the refrigerator and placed it on the counter.

Mertz accepted his glass of wine and helped himself to the delicious treats on the platter.

"I'm really looking forward to tomorrow night." Mertz selected a Kalamata olive and popped it into his mouth.

Gigi paused with her wineglass halfway to her mouth. She made a noncommittal noise. She could feel heat rising up her chest to her neck and toward her face. Perhaps it would be better to feed Mertz first before breaking the news to him.

Gigi had opened up the small gate-legged table in the living room that served as a dining table on occasion, and Mertz helped her carry out the platter of chicken, along with the bottle of wine and their glasses. She had a fire going in the fireplace—not exactly roaring, and it had taken her the entire Sunday edition of the *Woodstone Times* to get it going, but the logs glowed brightly in the shadowy room.

Mertz wasted no time in tucking into the meal. "I'm starved," he said around a mouthful of chicken. "Lunch was a bag of chips from the vending machine."

"What do you think?" Gigi watched him as he chewed.

Mertz gave a deep sigh. "Delicious. Absolutely delicious. What did you call this again?"

"Chicken cacciatore."

"Best meal I've had in a long time." He forked up another bite of the stew. "I was about to run down to the diner for lunch when a call came in. Those potato chips didn't quite fill the void, I'm afraid."

Gigi raised her eyebrows questioningly.

"Someone stole Mrs. Nottingham's garden gnome." Mertz rolled his eyes. "That's the second yard ornament to go missing in as many days. Someone also swiped one of those old-fashioned jockeys the Yarboroughs had beside their driveway."

"What on earth would anyone want with them?"

"Beats me." Mertz sighed and finished the last bit of chicken on his plate. "My guess is some kids are pulling a prank. I'm sure they think it's funny, but I don't appreciate their wasting my time."

Mertz shrugged and tossed his napkin onto the table. "That fire looks very inviting. Why don't we take the rest of our wine over to the sofa?"

"Okay."

They sat side by side on the couch, a careful two inches separating them. Mertz placed his left arm along the back of the sofa, the tips of his fingers lightly brushing Gigi's shoulders.

The warmth of the wine and the cozy crackling of the fire relaxed Gigi, and she found herself leaning against Mertz's shoulder.

He moved his hand to the back of Gigi's neck, his fingertips brushing her skin lightly. "What time should I pick you up for tomorrow night's party?"

Gigi stiffened, all sense of relaxation gone. "About the party . . ."

"Hmmm?" Mertz turned toward her slightly.

Gigi's fingers twisted together in her lap. Guilt pricked at her skin like a thousand porcupine quills. How was she going to break the news to Mertz?

"What about the party?" Mertz turned further around so he could see Gigi.

She closed her eyes. "Something has come up."

"Oh, no. I hope nothing's wrong." Mertz's blue eyes crinkled with concern.

"Not wrong, no. Not exactly."

"What is it then?"

Gigi twisted her sweater between her fingers. "It's like this. Declan's chef quit—"

"The party's cancelled?"

"No. But Declan needs help in the kitchen, and I . . . I . . ."

"Volunteered?"

"Yes," Gigi said meekly. "I didn't want to, but he persuaded me."

"Persuaded you?" Mertz jumped to his feet. "I have heard the fellow is terribly persuasive so I'm not surprised.

"I'm sorry." Gigi got to her feet, too.

"I was looking forward to going with you." Mertz's mouth quirked downward.

"You can still go," Gigi said although she knew that would be scant consolation.

"Forget it." Mertz opened the closet by the door and retrieved his coat. He slipped into it briskly. "Thanks for dinner."

The slam of the door on his way out told Gigi everything she needed to know.

# Chapter 3

Gigi woke up on Saturday morning feeling as gray as the skies outside her window. By agreeing to help Declan, she'd upset Mertz—and just when their relationship was starting to take off. Would he forgive her or just move on? She felt a nagging sense of loss as she dressed to go about her day—her usual jeans, comfy sweater with the sleeves that were a little too long because they'd gotten caught on the agitator in the washer, and a pair of warm, thick-soled shoes. She thought briefly of the pretty dress waiting in her closet . . . would she ever have the chance to wear it now?

Reg watched intently as Gigi cracked eggs for scrambling. She would top them with some salsa and a dash of grated low-fat cheese and roll them in a low-fat tortilla. Her clients' dinner had simmered overnight in her slow cooker—delicious, warm and hearty chili that she would serve over half a cup of brown rice. The scent of cumin and chipotle peppers had wound its way into her senses during the night, prompting a dream of backpacking through some foreign, exotic country where the landscape was richly colored in brilliant jewel tones. It had been a disappointment to wake up to such a gloomy day.

Gigi was spooning scrambled eggs into the tortillas when the back door opened. She jumped.

"It's just me," Pia said, unwinding her scarf and hanging it over the hook next to the door.

"I thought . . . I assumed you were . . ."

"I spent the night at the studio."

Gigi noticed the dark stains under her sister's eyes.

"I was really on a roll. This new piece is going fantastically. Besides, I didn't want to interrupt you and your detective." She gave a wicked grin and opened one of the cupboards, pulling out a ceramic mug. "Is there any coffee?"

Gigi jerked her head in the direction of the coffeemaker and turned toward her sister. "I feel badly. You didn't need to stay out overnight on my account. Bill left early."

"Oh?" Pia paused with the coffeepot poised over her cup. "What happened?"

Gigi hesitated. She wasn't totally comfortable confiding in her sister. Pia had never been good at keeping secrets. Gigi remembered telling her about a crush she had had on a boy in sixth grade. Pia had gone to school the next day and told all her friends about her big sister's infatuation. By lunchtime, half the school had known Gigi's secret, and the boy in question had taken to avoiding her in the halls.

But that was then. Pia had grown up. Surely she knew how to keep a confidence now? Besides, Gigi really did need to tell her about helping Declan out. She didn't want Pia to find out from someone else and assume that there was a reason Gigi had kept it hidden. Because there wasn't. Gigi had made up her mind. Declan was one of those dazzling, fascinating objects that it was best to look at but not touch.

Gigi closed the last of her containers and added it to the stack on the counter. She rinsed out her coffee mug and poured herself another cup. She was stalling, and she knew it. She sighed and eased onto one of the stools in front of the island.

"We had a disagreement," she began, "about our plans for tonight." She took a sip of her coffee. It was hotter than she'd expected, and tears came to her eyes.

"But I thought you were going to that party. You showed me your dress and everything." Pia opened the freezer and pulled out a box of raspberry toaster pastries.

Gigi shuddered as Pia slid one of the frosted cakes into the toaster.

"I was. But Declan asked me to help him in the kitchen. His chef quit, and he's short-handed." The words came out in a mumbled rush.

"Declan? I don't understand. Why you? I mean . . ."

"I'm the only person he knows who can find her way around the kitchen. Not that I'll be doing much more than peeling and chopping and stirring."

Pia rounded on Gigi, her eyes glittering. "You fancy him yourself, don't you?"

"No!" Gigi said with as much conviction as she could muster.

"I hope not." Pia clutched her coffee cup to her chest. "Because *I* fancy him." She poked her own chest with her index finger. "A lot. He's absolutely dreamy, and I just know we were meant for each other." She sniffled and wiped at her nose with her sleeve. "You have your fellow; why can't you let me have mine?"

And she flounced from the room.

Her exit was punctuated by the ping of the toaster as it shot the finished pastry into the air.

Gigi made her deliveries with a heavy heart. She'd agreed to help Declan because it seemed like the right thing to do, but now she'd upset two very important people in her life. She would have to figure out a way to make it right.

Meanwhile, she had to drop Reg off at Alice Slocum's. Alice had offered to take him for the day since he wouldn't be allowed at the restaurant, and Gigi hated to think of him home alone since she had no idea what Pia's schedule for the day was. Alice had been one of Gigi's first clients. She'd wanted to lose weight for her daughter Stacy's wedding, and she'd been very successful. She and Gigi had become friends, and she sometimes helped Gigi out. The fact that she worked part time as a secretary in the police department made her an invaluable source of information.

Alice was waiting at the door with a dog treat when Gigi got there.

"So, you're spending the afternoon with Declan," she said, with what could only be described as a wicked smile.

Gigi frowned. "It's not what you think."

"I'm sure. I just wonder what Bill Mertz will think about it."

"Wonder no more. He made it quite clear he doesn't like the idea."

"Maybe it will spur him on." Alice ran her hand through her tumble of gray curls.

"To what?" Gigi unclipped Reg's leash and placed it on Alice's hall table.

"You know. Pop the question."

Gigi's mouth hung open. "But we've only been dating a few months. It's not even serious yet."

Alice shrugged. "You've never heard of a whirlwind romance?"

Gigi laughed. "Somehow it feels like Bill Mertz and whirlwind romance don't quite go together."

"You never know." Alice smiled enigmatically and bent down to scratch Reg behind the ears. She looked up. "Don't worry. He'll be fine." She gestured at the dog.

Gigi knew he would, but he looked so forlorn peering out the glass panes beside Alice's door as Gigi drove away. Once again, she cursed herself for saying yes to Declan.

Gigi drove down High Street and turned into the parking lot between Gibson's Hardware and Declan's restaurant. She parked toward the back, leaving the other spaces for the guests who would be arriving later that evening. Gigi glanced at her watch. She was right on schedule.

"You are a lifesaver," Declan said as he answered the door immediately after Gigi's knock. His dark hair was slightly disheveled, and his chin was covered in fine stubble. Gigi wondered how late he'd been working the night before. He was wearing jeans, an apron and a T-shirt that said *Declan's Grille* and showed off his strong biceps. Gigi knew most chefs earned their muscles in the kitchen, not the gym. Lifting heavy pots and pans all day long was a strenuous workout.

The restaurant itself was in shadowed darkness. An expectant hush hung over the room and the tables were bare, awaiting the napery and silverware that would magically transform them. The scent of garlic simmering in olive oil hung in the air.

Gigi followed Declan to the galley kitchen, where pots were already steaming on the stove and a cutting board was piled high with chopped onions. She looked around but there was no one else in sight.

Declan ran a hand through his hair, disheveling it further. "Armand is taking a break. He should be back soon," he said as if reading Gigi's mind.

Gigi hoped Armand would hurry back. Being alone with Declan was making her nervous. Her glance kept straying toward his strong back and arms and the way his jeans fit—tight but not too tight.

"What's on the menu?" she asked to distract herself.

"For starters, I'm doing pea and mint soup," Declan lifted the lid on one of the pots and invited Gigi to have a sniff.

It smelled heavenly. She shuddered to think of how much butter and cream must have gone into creating such a delicious mixture.

"Then there's sirloin steak with green peppercorn sauce, fried potatoes and a gratin of marrow."

"Marrow?"

Declan frowned and bit his lip. "Don't know what you Yanks call it." He reached for the handle of the refrigerator, pulled it open, rummaged briefly, then turned around and held out a green vegetable toward Gigi.

"Oh, we call that zucchini."

"Zucchini it is then." He smiled and some of the shadows

disappeared from his blue eyes. "And for afters, there'll be cake, of course, with a serving of Eton mess."

Again, Gigi marveled at how the English and Americans both considered themselves to be speaking English, but so many of the words and expressions were different.

"Eton mess is basically berries layered with whipped cream and meringue." Declan explained.

"Sounds delicious."

Declan shrugged. "Let's hope so." He glanced at his watch. "I can't think where Armand has gotten to." He shrugged. "We'd best get to work without him."

Gigi's nervousness around Declan dissipated with each onion she chopped and pot she stirred. He was strictly professional, keeping watch over everything on the stove and in the oven. She didn't want to admit to herself that she was just a teeny bit disappointed.

The missing Armand finally slunk in an hour later, smelling of cigarette smoke and beer. Declan gave him a stern look, and the sous chef immediately set about chopping a large batch of fresh mint, a sulky set to his mouth.

Gigi was barely aware of the passage of time as she provided Declan with his extra pair of hands. They worked together seamlessly and mostly wordlessly, efficiently putting together the feast for Bradley Simpson's engagement party for his son and future daughter-in-law.

Gigi had just finished washing and hulling an enormous batch of strawberries when the back door opened and one of Declan's waitresses bustled in. Several more followed, along with three busboys who immediately got to work setting the tables. The men shouted back and forth about the previous week's sports scores, drowning out the women's high-pitched chatter as they readied Declan's Grille for the party.

An hour later they heard the front door open. Declan wiped his hands on his apron and went out into the main dining room. Gigi heard the murmur of masculine voices combined with the occasional softer tones of a woman's. She was sweeping the discarded strawberry tops into the garbage can when the door to the kitchen burst open.

"Simpsons are here," Declan said economically. "The rest of the guests will be arriving shortly." He gestured toward the stove. "Let's get the first batch of bacon-wrapped scallops into the oven."

Although Declan's expression was bland, Gigi sensed his nervousness. The success of this party meant a lot to him. The Simpsons were very influential in town, and if they were displeased, it wouldn't be long before there was a *For Sale* sign on the front door of Declan's Grille.

Armand slid a tray of the hors d'oeuvres in question into the oven while Declan unwrapped a large piece of pinkish-red fish.

"Salmon?" Gigi asked.

Declan nodded as he carefully removed the layers of plastic wrap. "Gravlax. I made it myself." He smiled self-deprecatingly. "I used to date this Danish girl. She was a model," he threw out offhandedly, "and she taught me how to do it."

Gigi wasn't surprised. Declan was definitely the tall, blond, Danish model type, not the average, everyday-girl type. Gigi immediately thought of Pia. Fortunately, her sister was anything but average.

"The name means grave salmon and refers to the medieval practice of curing the raw fish by burying it in the sand above the high-tide level." Declan smiled and the dimple in his cheek deepened. "Which I most certainly didn't do. Nowadays, you cure the salmon with salt, sugar, plenty of fresh dill, a bit of lemon peel . . . " He stopped suddenly. "But then I imagine you already know that. But there is my secret ingredient." He winked at Gigi. "A dash of the finest Irish whiskey—Kilbeggan—from the oldest distillery in the world."

Declan took a long, thin-bladed knife and began to cut slivers off the piece of salmon. He placed them on a tray alongside neatly arranged squares of buttered toast.

The noise level from the restaurant had risen considerably. "Sounds like the guests are arriving." Declan frowned and ran a hand through his hair, leaving his curls standing on end. "I feel terrible." He touched Gigi's shoulder. "You should be out there, dressed to the nines, enjoying yourself."

Gigi looked down at her faded jeans. She was a mess, and she knew it. She'd run her hands through her tangled auburn curls countless times during the course of the day. Even without looking, she could tell that her nose was shining, and her lips were pale since she'd bitten off the bit of colored lip gloss she'd put on long ago that morning.

"Why don't you go have a wee peek at the crowd. I imagine you'd like that."

Gigi smiled. Declan had guessed correctly—if she couldn't be part of the party herself, she at least wanted to see who was there and what they were wearing.

"Okay." She took off her apron, balled it up and tossed it on the counter.

"I expect a full report." Declan grinned as his sharp-bladed knife slid through the piece of salmon.

"Aye, aye, sir."

Gigi headed for the swinging door to the restaurant. She would hover in the back and spend a few minutes taking it all in.

Most of the gathering had crowded into the bar area or stood, drinks in hand, between the artfully set tables. Waitresses circulated with trays of hors d'oeuvres, and the bartender, a seasoned-looking pro in his fifties, wielded a silver cocktail shaker as if it were a percussion instrument.

Madeline looked radiant in a crimson wrap dress with a deep-V neckline and cap sleeves. Gigi had never met Hunter Simpson, but she picked him out easily enough. He had one arm around Madeline, and in the other, he brandished a glass of what looked like sparkling water. He was slim, with a halo of light brown curls, and bore a slight resemblance to his father.

Bradley had the paunch and the smug, self-satisfied look so common to men of his age and stature. He was wearing a double-breasted navy blazer, gray slacks and a crisp white shirt open far enough to reveal the gray hair on his chest. Gigi recognized his wife Barbara Simpson because she had recently had a consultation with Gigi about becoming a client. Barbara hoped to start the plan as soon as the party was over, with the aim of losing twenty pounds before her son's wedding. She had dark hair, cut short up over her ears, and she clutched a pashmina wrap that almost hid her stocky middle. Gigi thought she must have been quite attractive at one point in time, but now she looked like the typical middle-aged woman—slightly overweight and a touch masculine.

The woman Madeline had identified earlier as Tiffany Morse, potential Simpson and West partner, stood in front of the bar, surrounded by a cadre of admiring men. Her black dress most decidedly deserved the term *little*—it had a hem so high and a neckline so low that they threatened to meet in the middle. Someone must have said something funny because she tossed back her head and laughed, exposing a long, white column of a neck that was accented by the sparkling sequins edging her plunging neckline.

Gigi noticed Bradley Simpson glancing in her direction more than once. The third time he did it, she saw Barbara Simpson frown and whisper in his ear.

Bradley threw back his shoulders and put his hands to his mouth creating a megaphone.

"Hello, everyone," he shouted above the din of voices and clinking glasses. "Hello."

Someone took a fork from one of the tables and began banging it against a water glass. Bradley smiled and waited as the chattering voices slowly came to a halt. He cleared his throat and puffed out his chest.

"As you all know, we're here tonight to celebrate the engagement of my son"—he nodded curtly toward Hunter, who looked frozen, his eyes wide and his arm tight around Madeline's waist—"to . . ." Bradley hesitated just long enough that a few people in the back began to murmur softly. "To Madeline Stone!" He finished triumphantly, a satisfied smile on his face. He looked around as if trying to determine which of the women in the restaurant was, indeed, his son's intended.

Gigi glanced at Madeline. A stiff smile was plastered on her face, and Hunter had tightened his grasp on her waist and was whispering in her ear.

"My son"—Bradley waved his glass of amber-colored

whiskey in the air—"has done me proud." He glanced at his wife, but it was obvious he didn't really see her or he might have noticed the anxious look on her face. "I chose the noblest profession of all. The law." He glanced down at his highly polished Gucci loafers. "Like my father before me, and his father before him." He looked up and his glance swept the assembled crowd.

Everyone was quiet—no ice tinkling in glasses, no whispered conversations or clearing of throats.

"But Hunter," Bradley gave a nod toward his son, whose face was darkening by the second, "chose medicine." He annunciated the world carefully as if it left a bad taste in his mouth. "Surgery." He laughed softly and shook his head. "Do you know who the original surgeons were?" He scanned the crowd as if looking for someone with the answer. He shook his head again, tilting his chin upward. "Barbers. Barbers were the original surgeons. The red-and-white stripes on the barbers' poles were meant to signify their craft of bloodletting." He looked down at his shoes again. "My son eschewed the noble profession of the law for . . . bloodletting."

Deafening silence greeted Bradley's pronouncement and was quickly followed by a rustling sound as Hunter Simpson broke away from Madeline's embrace and began making his way toward the exit. No one said a word until the echo of the slammed front door had died away.

Madeline's face crumpled, and she quickly pushed her way through the crowd toward the restrooms. Several people put a hand on her arm, but she brushed them off. Gigi hesitated, then went after her.

"Oh, I hate him!" Madeline cried, her hands balled into

fists, when Gigi joined her in the sanctuary of the ladies' room. "He's mean, despicable, and absolutely horrid, and I'll hate him as long as I live." She grabbed a tissue from the box on the counter and blew her nose. "He's always resented the fact that Hunter wasn't interested in *the law*." Madeline imitated Bradley's snooty tones to perfection. "He should be proud of his son. He's a trauma surgeon, and he helps people." She gave a loud sniff followed by a hiccup. "He's been working at Woodstone Hospital teaching the doctors there a new technique he pioneered."

Gigi just let Madeline talk. The best thing for her would be to get it all out. Then it would be time to powder her nose and join the crowd with her head held high. Gigi could hear the sound of voices swelling outside the door. There was an occasional laugh mingling with the tinkling sound of silver on china.

The party would go on, with or without Madeline and Hunter.

# Chapter 4

Gigi helped Madeline blot her tears and dash some powder over her reddened nose. She was about to suggest that Madeline apply a little more of the crimson lipstick that matched her dress when someone pushed open the door to the ladies' room.

"Oh, my dear, I am so sorry." Barbara Simpson grabbed both of Madeline's hands in her own. "It's just that Bradley is so disappointed that Hunter has decided not to follow in his footsteps. He had so hoped that his son would take over as partner someday." She smiled benignly. "Frankly, I am so proud of Hunter I could burst."

That brought a brief smile to Madeline's lips.

"But you must come back out and join us, or Bradley will be furious. All of his colleagues and friends are here, and it's bad enough that Hunter went off the way he did. Bradley is most upset with him. It's all very embarrassing."

Barbara turned toward the mirror with a small cry of dismay. The light in the ladies' room glinted off her sequined top, making her look heavier than she was.

"I really must powder my nose and refresh my lipstick. Bradley expects me to look my best."

Gigi had a good idea of what she'd like to say to that so-and-so Bradley, but she kept her mouth shut and gave Barbara a tight smile. She was relieved to see that Madeline was rummaging around in her own beaded handbag for her compact.

They waited while Madeline freshened up, and then Gigi reached for the door.

Barbara was about to follow her when she stopped suddenly. "Now where did my wrap get to?" She looked around her, and both Madeline and Gigi also scanned the counter and floor.

Barbara shrugged. "I must have left it on my chair." She turned toward Madeline with a rather forced smile. "Chin up, dear. We mustn't spoil Bradley's party."

*Bradley's party?* Gigi thought to herself. She wondered if Madeline knew what she was getting herself into with a father-in-law whose ego was bigger than the state of Texas.

Barbara and Madeline headed back to their tables, and Gigi made her way toward the kitchen.

"What in the blinking hell else can go wrong?" Declan spit out as Gigi pushed open the swinging door to the kitchen. The room was hot and steamy and the harsh overhead lights glared off the metal of the hanging pots and pans.

"What's wrong?" Gigi reached for her apron and began to tie it around her waist.

"Stacy's spent more time in the bathroom being sick than waiting on tables." Declan cocked his head toward the employee restroom off the kitchen. He ran both hands through his hair distractedly. "I've sent her home so now we're short-staffed in the restaurant as well as in the kitchen." He grimaced. "The steak and peppercorn sauce will be a disaster if it gets cold."

"I can help. I waited tables in college." Gigi hoped Stacy wasn't seriously ill. She was Alice's daughter, and Alice would be devastated if anything happened to her only child.

"I couldn't possibly ask you. You've already done so much to help—"

"I don't mind. Really."

Declan gave Gigi a grin that threatened to melt her knees. "If you're sure you don't mind?"

"Not at all."

"If you're game—Armand!" Declan snapped his fingers toward the sous chef, who was slumped on a stool next to the counter, his eyes at half-mast. "Start plating the entrée."

Gigi was suddenly regretting her impulsive offer. It had been years since she'd waitressed. It would be just her luck to spill something on one of the guests. But there was no getting out of it now. With Declan's help, Armand had already prepared two trays.

They had barely finished when Rita burst through the swinging doors, her jaws going a mile a minute, snapping and popping a large piece of pink gum.

All the waitresses at Declan's wore old-fashioned barmaid's uniforms with a full skirt, a low-cut, puffed-sleeve white blouse and a frilly apron. Stacy filled hers out to perfection, but Rita was rail thin, and the whole ensemble hung on her like a flag on a pole with no breeze. Her face was pinched and hard, her skin roughened from too many hours spent in tanning parlors.

She grabbed the first tray and hoisted it to her shoulder with the ease of a seasoned pro. She gave her gum one last good crackle and pop and was through the swinging doors, off to deliver the food.

Gigi was immediately intimidated. It was all she could do to pick up the tray with both hands. None of this carrying-on-her-shoulder stuff for her. She knew her limits. She gave Declan a weak smile as he held the door open for her.

They were to start serving from the back, the first course, or "starters" as Declan called it, having been brought to the customers in the front first.

Gigi slid the first plate in front of a man whose suit smelled faintly of mothballs and was of a cut and color reminiscent of the fashion from a decade earlier.

He seized his knife and fork eagerly, turning to the woman beside him, whose dress fit as if she'd been ten pounds heavier the last time she wore it. He cut a chunk of steak and forked it up eagerly. "At least my brother-in-law isn't going to make us wait for our entrée." He stuffed the bite of steak into his mouth. "It's bad enough we're sitting all the way back here. We're family after all."

The woman with him, who Gigi assumed was his wife, smiled wanly and accepted the plate Gigi placed in front of her. Gigi served the rest of the table and began to head back toward the kitchen, her tray now empty. She was making her third trip from the kitchen, and starting to feel more confident, when she noticed a bit of a commotion at the front of the restaurant.

The woman who had been sitting next to Bradley's brother-in-law was helping Barbara Simpson to a seat by the front door. Bradley followed close behind with an annoyed expression on his face. Barbara swayed slightly, and the woman quickly put out a hand to steady her. Barbara slumped onto the proffered seat, her chin coming to rest on her chest.

"Can you give us a hand?" Bradley grabbed Gigi's elbow as she went by.

"Certainly. What can I do for you?"

"We need a taxi. My wife has . . . taken ill . . . and needs to go home. I can't seem to find my cell at the moment. Never can find the darn thing when I need it." He scowled, his thick, graying brows drawn together over eyes as black and as cold as coal.

"I'd be glad to. There's a land line in back." Gigi hurried toward the kitchen.

She called Woodstone's only taxi service—two ancient Lincoln Town Cars obviously purchased second- or third-hand and run by two equally ancient drivers who rarely got the speedometer up past thirty miles per hour. She wondered why Bradley couldn't run his wife home himself. He certainly didn't seem very concerned.

Gigi was helping Armand fill the final tray when Rita stuck her head into the kitchen. "Who called for the taxi?"

Gigi stopped with a plate halfway to the tray. "I did. For Mrs. Simpson. She's not feeling well and wants to go home."

Gigi hastened out to check on Mrs. Simpson and the taxi. Her sister-in-law was attempting to put Barbara's coat around her shoulders.

"My wrap," Barbara said. "I've lost it."

"We'll find it later," the thin, mousy woman said consolingly.

Gigi hastened to reassure them that Declan's would call if the missing wrap turned up.

Barbara let herself be led out to the waiting Lincoln Town Car, and Gigi hurried back to the kitchen.

"It certainly has been quite a night." Declan turned a chair around and straddled it, briefly leaning his forehead against the chair back.

The dishes, silverware, glasses and dirty linens had all been collected, and the dishwasher was humming. Armand had already left, pulling his beret down over his forehead and his scarf up to his chin.

"I'll be going if there's nothing else." Rita poked her head into the kitchen. She was zipping up a dark blue parka with a fake-fur collar.

Declan waved a hand wearily. "Good night. And thanks."

"I should be going." Gigi started toward the hook where she'd hung her coat.

Declan put out a hand. "Don't go yet. Let's just relax for a minute." He unstraddled the chair. "Wait right here."

Gigi felt her stomach do something strange and queasy. She ought to leave. She really should. But she felt rooted to the spot like Lot's wife. Hopefully her fate would not be as drastic.

Before she could move, Declan returned with a bottle of brandy in one hand and two glasses in the other. Gigi started to protest, but he was already uncorking the bottle and pouring them each a snifterful.

"Just one drink." He gave Gigi the same smile he had earlier—the one that made her knees buckle. He pulled two stools next to each other and patted one of them. "I can't thank you enough for saving my bacon tonight. I don't know what I would have done without you."

Gigi didn't know what to say so she just smiled and took a sip of the brandy. It was excellent—smooth and mellow, much like Declan himself—but she was tired, and she was afraid it was going to go to her head. Then she, too, would be calling the Woodstone Taxi Service for a ride home.

"This place"—Declan gestured around the interior of the kitchen—"means the world to me. I've sunk the lot into it, as you can imagine." He peered at Gigi over the rim of his glass. "My folks ran a pub back in Manchester. Just a place where the locals grabbed a pint after work and whiled away a Saturday afternoon playing darts. Mum did butties and a decent ploughman's lunch." He took a sip of his brandy. "But I wanted to go one better." He scowled. "A bit egotistical of me, don't you think?"

Gigi shook her head. "No, I think it's normal."

They talked some more, Gigi taking cautious sips of her brandy. She was conscious of the time passing. She nibbled on the edge of her thumb. What was Pia going to think if she caught her coming home so late?

But Declan was telling her about his childhood and growing up as the youngest of three sisters, and Gigi became caught up in the story. She told him about her father dying when she was little more than a toddler, and how the Fitzgerald brothers had enveloped Gigi, her sister and her mother and made sure they never lacked for anything.

Before Gigi knew it, her glass was empty and the hands

on the clock pointed to one A.M. She jumped off her stool. "Oh. I'd better be going. It's terribly late."

"Pia—that's your sister isn't it?" Declan said suddenly. Gigi nodded.

Declan shook his head. "She's quite a character. I enjoy our chats when she comes in." He scanned Gigi's face. "She doesn't look all that much like you, but I can see a bit of a resemblance." He winked at Gigi. "Frankly, I'd rather have the real deal, if you know what I mean."

Gigi's heart began to pound strangely. "Yes, well, good night." She grabbed her coat and struggled into it, wrapping her scarf securely around her neck.

"If you wait while I turn the lights out, I'll walk you to your car."

"No, no, I'll be fine." Gigi twisted the door handle. "I've got to get going."

Declan looked at her quizzically and shrugged. "Okay, then. Are you parked right outside?"

"Yes. At the end of the row, toward the back." Gigi gestured in what she thought was the right direction.

"You should be safe enough. Hopefully there are no boogeymen lurking in the alley. I'd feel better if you'd let me walk you, but I'll keep the light on until you get to your car. Just give me a honk as you go past, okay?"

Gigi nodded. She pulled open the door and slipped outside. The temperature had dropped, and the brisk wind felt like an icy slap against her face. Snowflakes drifted down from the inky sky, were picked up by the wind and swirled in circles. Gigi felt a cold sting as they melted on her face.

The parking lot was filled with shadows and pockets of darkness. Gigi made her way carefully, her eyes on the ground, searching for the black icy patches that lurked treacherously underfoot. Something winked in the darkness, a mere speck, caught in the light from one of the lamps. Curious, Gigi bent down for a closer look. It was a silver sequin. It must have come off one of the women's dresses. Without thinking, Gigi tucked it into her pocket and continued on her way.

The bulb in one of the old-fashioned light stanchions was out, leaving a large section of the parking lot in total darkness. Gigi was inching her way forward along the slick macadam when her foot suddenly struck something soft and yielding yet strangely solid at the same time.

"Oh." She couldn't help crying out.

She looked down to see the outline of a darkish shape that looked like a bundle of clothes. She leaned over and peered at the obstruction. When she realized it was human, she began to scream.

# Chapter 5

Gigi's scream came out in a puff of vapor, rending the frigid and silent evening air. Her teeth began to chatter almost immediately, and she clapped a hand to her mouth to stop the second scream that rose in her throat.

She couldn't have just tripped over a . . . body. There was some mistake. It was a heap of old clothing, not a . . . a . . . person. Gigi forced herself to open her eyes and take a second look.

It *was* a body—a man—and he was lying on his stomach, his right arm trapped beneath him. The falling snowflakes mingled with the bright red blood that had pooled alongside him.

Before Gigi could move, the door to Declan's opened and slammed against the side of the building.

"Gigi!" Declan ran across the parking lot toward her,

slipping and sliding on the ice and nearly falling at one point. "What is it? Are you okay?"

Gigi nodded mutely and pointed at the body sprawled at her feet.

"What the bloody . . ." Declan knelt on the icy ground and put his fingers against the man's thick neck.

He stood up slowly, shaking his head.

"Is he . . ."

"I'm afraid so." Declan stuffed his hands in the pockets of his jeans. He shivered slightly and pulled the edges of his shirt closer together.

"What should we do?" This wasn't Gigi's first encounter with a dead body, but she still felt at sea as to how to handle it. She supposed you never did get used to it unless you were a policeman, and it was part of your job. The thought of the police brought Mertz to mind. She desperately wished he were there at the same time that she dreaded the thought of his arrival. A shiver racked her body. What was Mertz going to think of her being at Declan's so late at night? She pushed the thought from her mind and tried to concentrate on the situation at hand.

"We have to call the police." Gigi began to dig in her handbag for her cell.

"Absolutely." Declan rubbed his hands together and then up and down his arms where the snowflakes were melting slowly on his shirt. He stared at the body at their feet. "That coat looks familiar, doesn't it?" It was gray wool with a black velvet collar. "It's quite posh. Must be someone important."

Gigi risked a quick glance at the corpse. There was something familiar about the man—even in death there was an air of authority about him.

"Think we ought to turn him over?" Declan's teeth had begun to chatter.

Gigi shook her head. "No, we need to leave him this way until the police get—hello? Hello?" Her 9-1-1 call had gone through. The woman on the other end spoke calmly and briskly. Gigi explained the situation as succinctly as possible.

"Hold on one moment, please."

Gigi glanced at Declan. "Why don't you go inside and get your jacket? I'll be fine."

Declan headed toward the darkened restaurant at a trot. "Just give me a sec. I'll be right back."

Within minutes the lights from a Woodstone patrol car swept the darkened parking lot, catching Gigi in their glare. She quickly stepped out of the circle of bright light, but the brief exposure had left her as blind as a mole. She blinked furiously, trying to decipher the face of the policeman behind the wheel.

The patrolman was shutting his door when another car pulled into the lot, skidding on the icy pavement. Gigi had no trouble recognizing the driver—it was Mertz.

"Thank goodness the police are here," Declan said as he joined Gigi again. He had on a black peacoat with the collar turned up.

Gigi was of two minds. She was glad that Mertz was there to take over. On the other hand, she really didn't want to face him right now. How was she going to explain what she was doing at Declan's at one o'clock in the morning? She thought of Pia again, and hoped she'd gone off to her studio like she normally did and wouldn't be there when Gigi slunk home in the middle of the night.

The patrolman stood aside, his hands stuffed into his

pockets, as Mertz approached the scene. He circled the body twice before looking up at Gigi and Declan.

"You must be freezing. Why don't you go inside? I'll talk to you when I'm done."

He managed to make it sound like a threat, Gigi thought, as she followed Declan back to the restaurant. Her teeth were chattering, and the tips of her fingers felt numb.

They let themselves back into the kitchen, which was cooling quickly since Declan had turned the heat down for the night. Gigi decided to unbutton her coat but keep it on.

Declan glanced at her. "You're cold. Why don't I put on some coffee? I doubt any of us is going to get to sleep anytime soon. And I imagine the coppers out there"—he jerked his head toward the door—"would appreciate a cup, too."

Gigi nodded. She thought of phoning Alice to say she'd pick Reg up in the morning, but knowing Alice, she had already come to that conclusion. She and Reg were most likely tucked into bed keeping each other warm.

Declan swung a battered, metal coffeepot under the tap, filled it with water and put it on the stove to boil. He looked over his shoulder at Gigi. "I imagine it's some homeless person who succumbed to hypothermia." Declan shivered. "Poor sod. I feel terrible for him."

"But his coat. It was obviously expensive."

"Picked it up at a thrift store perhaps?" Declan opened a cupboard and took out a handful of mugs.

"His hair was neatly trimmed." Gigi closed her eyes and tried to bring the scene back in her memory. "His shoes. They were good quality and well polished." She thought for a moment. "And there was blood . . ."

"I suppose the police will figure it out soon enough."

Declan held the coffeepot over the mugs and began to fill them with the rich-smelling brew.

Gigi had a strange feeling in the pit of her stomach. The man had seemed familiar, even though she'd only been able to see his back.

Before she could give it any more thought, the door to the kitchen opened, and Mertz stepped in. His nose was red from the cold, and snowflakes were melting in his hair. His eyes lit up when he saw the mugs of coffee sitting out on the table.

"Help yourself. There's a cup for the other fellow, too."

The cold stare Mertz had been giving Declan softened slightly. He helped himself to a mug and held his hands around it. "Thanks. He's guarding the scene. Crime scene guys should be here soon, too. Mind putting on a few more cups? I'm sure they'd appreciate the java. It's freezing out there." He took a sip of his coffee and sighed appreciatively. "Want to tell me what happened?" He sagged against the wall.

Declan pushed a stool toward him with his foot. He and Gigi looked at each other.

"As you know, I was helping Declan in the kitchen tonight." Gigi carefully avoided looking at Mertz's face. "I was just leaving when . . . when I all but tripped over the . . . body."

Mertz made a big show of glancing at his watch. "This would have been, what? A little after one?"

Gigi nodded, knowing her face was doing a slow burn.

"Did you recognize the man?" Mertz looked from Gigi to Declan and back again.

Both Gigi and Declan shook their heads.

"I thought perhaps he was homeless and had wandered into our parking lot." Declan picked up one of the mugs of coffee and held it to his lips.

"We found his wallet and identification in his jacket pocket. It seems he was the host of tonight's party—Bradley Simpson."

Gigi gasped. "What . . . what happened?"

"Was it hypothermia?" Declan stopped with his mug halfway to his mouth.

Mertz gave Declan a strange look as he shook his head. "No, as a matter of fact, it wasn't." Mertz had crossed his arms over his chest, and Gigi thought he looked terribly forbidding.

Declan put his mug down and leaned back in his chair. "What was it then?" He didn't sound particularly interested in the answer.

"We found an ice pick protruding from his head." Mertz glanced at Gigi quickly, as if to make sure she was okay. "It looks like murder."

"How awful," Declan said.

Gigi was unable to find her voice.

Mertz looked at Declan. "Do you happen to know," he said very casually, crossing one leg over the other, "how an ice pick with the name *Declan's* carved into the wooden handle ended up in Bradley Simpson's temple?"

It was nearly three A.M. Sunday morning by the time Gigi turned into the driveway of her cottage. The place was completely dark—Pia hadn't even left the light on over the front door. Was she in bed asleep or had she gone to her studio? Gigi slipped out of her shoes by the back door and tiptoed past the guest room. The door was cracked, but it was too dark to see inside. Besides, the way Pia always left the bedclothes in such a tangle, it would be impossible to tell if there was a body in the bed or not.

Gigi undressed without even turning on the light and slid beneath the covers. She groaned. She was tired from her head down to her very toes. Her eyes, however, refused to stay shut. The scene in Declan's parking lot kept running through her mind. She missed Reg's cozy warmth, and although she hugged her pillow to her chest, it was no substitute for his comforting presence. The thought that if she had a husband, she'd have a warm body to snuggle up to ran across her mind like a blip on a radar screen. No use in thinking about that now. She had the feeling that it was going to take a while for Mertz to come around . . . if ever.

Gigi hardly slept all night and was almost glad when it was finally time to get up the next morning. She padded out to the kitchen and measured coffee and water into the pot, leaning her elbows on the counter, her eyes closing, as she listened to the machine gurgle and spit. The aroma began to revive her, and she retreated to her bedroom to pull on some clothes.

She filled a travel mug with the freshly brewed coffee and headed out the door toward her car. She scraped some fresh snow off the MINI's windshield and began the short drive to Alice's house.

Alice was in her bathrobe and holding a cup of coffee when Gigi rang her bell a few minutes later. Reg was right beside her, giving excited yelps.

"I hope I didn't wake you." Gigi bent down so Reg could lick her face.

"Nope. I've already made my coffee." Alice gestured to the mug in her hand. Her eyes twinkled. "So, it was a late night, was it?"

Gigi nodded. "Stacy wasn't feeling well so Declan sent her home. I lent a hand with the waitressing."

"Stacy wasn't feeling well?"

Gigi heard the alarm in Alice's voice. "Nothing serious, or I'm sure she would have called you. Seemed like some kind of stomach bug. She couldn't keep anything down."

Gigi looked at Alice and was surprised to see the sparkle in her eyes.

Alice clapped her hands. "That's wonderful." Her face was lit and glowing.

Gigi failed to see how Stacy having a stomach virus could be termed wonderful.

"Don't you see?" Alice asked.

Gigi shook her head. She most certainly did not see.

"Stacy must be pregnant! I'm going to be a grandmother." Alice brushed at a tear that had formed in the corner of her eye.

Gigi thought Alice was jumping to conclusions, but how to let her down easily?

"Let's not say anything just yet." Alice put a finger to her lips. "I'll let Stacy tell me in her own time." She winked at Gigi. "In the meantime, tell me about your evening with Declan."

Reg had given up jumping on Gigi's leg—his way of saying *let's go*—and had curled up in a sunbeam that slanted across the braided rug in Alice's foyer. "I didn't spend the evening with Declan," Gigi corrected. "I was working. And it was terrible." Gigi hesitated for a second, but Mertz hadn't said anything about not telling anyone about Bradley's death. Besides, the news would be all over town before the noon whistle blew.

"As I was leaving, I found Bradley Simpson's body in the parking lot."

"Body?" Alice squeaked. "As in . . ."

Gigi nodded. "Yes. He was dead."

"What on earth happened?"

Gigi shrugged. "I have no idea." She shivered, even though the sun coming through the window was warm against her back. "Someone had stabbed him with an ice pick. Murder." Gigi didn't see any need to broadcast the fact that Declan's name was on the murder weapon.

Alice gasped. "What are things coming to? Although from what I've heard, there are plenty of people who won't be sorry to hear that he's gone." She folded her arms across her chest. "How his poor wife can stand him, I don't know. My neighbor"—she jerked a thumb to the right—"does a bit of housework for them. She said Barbara Simpson has resorted to . . ." She made the motion of holding a glass to her mouth and drinking. "Not that anyone can blame her."

Gigi thought back to the previous evening and Simpson's obnoxious speech. No, she didn't think anyone could blame Barbara Simpson at all.

Gigi spent the rest of Sunday—a bitterly cold day with a ferocious wind that picked up the newly fallen snow and tossed it around—curled up on the sofa with a book, Reg nestled in at her feet. She felt incredibly weary from all the work and strain of the evening before. She really needed to run the vacuum and throw a load of laundry in the washer, but she couldn't bring herself to move from her cozy nook.

Every time the floor creaked or a window rattled, she jumped, thinking it was Pia coming home from wherever she was. Even though Gigi was relishing the time alone in her own cottage, she was worried about her sister. Pia's studio wasn't in the best part of town, and Pia wasn't known for being cautious.

Gigi's real fear was that Pia had somehow learned about Gigi's late departure from Declan's on Saturday night. Her sister was known for jumping to conclusions, and Gigi had a strong feeling she knew what conclusion Pia would arrive at.

Pia appeared just as Gigi was heating up a bowl of lentil soup for her dinner. Although she was sorry to have her dinner interrupted—she was going prop her book up and continue reading—she was relieved to see that Pia was okay. She did look tired, though, and there was a smudge of blue paint on her right cheek.

"Want some soup?" Gigi opened the cupboard and began to reach for another bowl.

"What is it?" Pia peered into the pot on the stove.

"Lentil."

Pia shuddered. "No, thanks. I had my fill of that when I was in the commune. Ghastly stuff. Looked like dirty water with a handful of lentils thrown in." She opened the cupboard, took out a can of processed cheese Gigi most definitely hadn't purchased, and sprayed it directly into her mouth.

Gigi cringed. Suddenly her sister looked more like a lost child than the grown-up woman she was. She remembered their childhood and tiptoeing into Pia's room to comfort her after a nightmare when their mother was too occupied with her grief over losing her husband to do much of anything.

Pia stretched her arms overhead. "I'm beat. I think I'm going to go to bed. I worked all night."

"I know," Gigi said more sharply than she meant to. "I was worried about you."

Pia rolled her eyes. "Oh, please. You sound like Mom."

"Maybe I do, but I don't enjoy spending my day thinking something might have happened to you."

"Look, if you'd rather I left, just say so."

"That's not what I meant at all," Gigi said, although a small part of her did wish her sister would at least find her own place. "It's just that I worry when I don't hear from you for so long."

Pia sighed. "Sorry," she said begrudgingly. "I didn't mean to worry you. But I am being careful." She shivered. "I heard there was actually a murder in downtown Woodstone on Saturday night. Declan told me about it when I stopped by." Pia gave a slightly hysterical laugh. "The guy had been truly iced. Stabbed with an ice pick."

"I know." Gigi tried to block out the image that rose to her mind.

"How did you know about it?"

Gigi looked down at her feet. It was now or never. Pia would find out anyway. "I was there. I . . . I found the body."

"How horrible." Pia rushed to put her arms around her sister. "But wait." She pulled away. "Declan said it was really late. What were you doing there?"

Gigi spread her hands out. "We started talking and . . ."

"And?" Pia demanded.

"And nothing. We just talked, and I lost track of time."

"Oh, sure." Pia poked Gigi with her index finger. "You won't admit it, but you do fancy Declan for yourself. Well, you can't have him."

And for the second time in the short span she and Gigi

had been living together, Pia flounced from the room, slamming the door to the guest bedroom so hard that it bounced back open again.

A subdued air hung over Simpson and West when Gigi arrived with Madeline Stone's breakfast on Monday morning. The receptionist sported a grim expression, and people scurried about with their eyes focused on the ground. Gigi had the feeling, though, that underneath the surface things were bubbling and boiling like a witch's cauldron. She sensed an aura of smug satisfaction hanging over the place. If Bradley treated his staff like he treated his family, then odds were he wasn't very well liked, and he wasn't going to be missed.

Gigi took the elevator up to the third floor, where Madeline toiled in a small cubicle amidst a sea of similar cubes along with the other staff who didn't yet rate a windowed office on the hushed confines of the second floor. Gigi remembered her meetings with Mr. West and the impressiveness of his wood-paneled, antique-filled corner office. It was what everyone at Simpson and West aspired to.

The elevator jerked to a stop, and the door slowly opened. A small huddle of men in pin-striped suits hovered near the entrance to the break room, coffee cups in hand, voices low in conversation. A similar group of women in short skirts and variously colored sweaters stood around the water cooler, occasionally throwing glances over their shoulder, looking ready to scatter like a flock of birds if someone with authority came along.

Gossip buzzed like electricity sparking along high-tension wires.

Gigi noticed that Madeline's eyes were puffy and red-rimmed as she handed over the breakfast Gourmet De-Lite container. Her cubicle was, as usual, piled high with folders, papers and various files. A silver-framed picture of Hunter Simpson, his light curls blowing in the wind, a smudge of blue water just visible in the background, stood in pride of place on Madeline's desk.

Madeline pulled a handkerchief from her sleeve and dabbed at her eyes. "It isn't as if I knew . . . Bradley . . . all that well," she confided to Gigi. "But I feel so badly on Hunter's account." She gave a loud sniff.

"He must be terribly upset." Gigi couldn't help wondering how Hunter really felt about his father's death. She doubted there was much love lost between them. She remembered Bradley's hurtful comments, and Hunter's abrupt departure on Saturday night.

"He's devastated," Madeline said, dabbing at her nose with the tissue. "And he's worried about Barbara and what this is going to do to her. Bradley took care of everything. Barbara hardly had to lift a finger."

*Must be nice,* Gigi thought but then changed her mind. She much preferred being a capable woman and running her own business than being dependent on a man for everything.

"Hunter must have found his father rather . . . difficult . . . to get along with," Gigi hazarded.

Madeline's eyes widened. "Hunter adored his father. He would have done anything to please him."

*Except become a lawyer,* Gigi thought. It seemed as if Madeline was protesting just a little too much.

"When is the funeral?"

"I don't know. Hunter is helping his mother with the arrangements right now." She glanced at her watch. "They're meeting with Father Stephens in half an hour over at St. Andrews Episcopal Church. They've been members since they moved here from the city when Hunter was a baby."

"Is that where you're being married?"

Madeline gave a loud sniff. "Yes. Although we've decided not to go through with a big wedding under the circumstances. Just a small reception with a few family and friends."

Gigi nodded. She thought it was a shame that Madeline was going to be cheated out of a proper wedding—surely every girl's dream. She thought back to her marriage to Ted. Perhaps she'd been too taken up with the excitement of the planning and should have paid more attention to his potential—or lack thereof—as a husband.

"Have the police told you anything?" Gigi said as delicately as someone putting a toe in frigid water. She hadn't heard a peep out of Mertz and wondered what was going on.

Madeline shook her head, a sob turning into a hiccough. "They said"—she lowered her voice and leaned closer to Gigi—"that he was stabbed with an ice pick. I can't get over it! Things like that aren't supposed to happen in Woodstone."

# Chapter 6

Gigi's mind was going as she left Simpson and West. Madeline had been quite determined to convince Gigi that Hunter and his father got along just fine. What Gigi had witnessed on Saturday night suggested something altogether different. Was Madeline afraid that Hunter might somehow be involved?

Walking briskly, Gigi headed toward where she'd parked the MINI. Reg was asleep on the package shelf above the backseat and jumped down when he heard her put her key in the lock. He took his accustomed spot in the front passenger seat, yawned widely and shook.

"A few more deliveries, and then we can go home," Gigi reassured him as she pulled out onto High Street.

Gigi's last delivery was to a new development on the edge of town. The builder had razed all of the trees and replaced them with enormous brick Georgian-style homes. A few anemic-looking maples had been planted in the front yards, and a fancy wrought-iron gate separated the exclusive enclave from the rest of the world. Gigi's newest client, Penelope Lawson, had been referred by Madeline. Her husband, George, worked at Simpson and West and had just been promoted to a small office on the hallowed premises of the second floor.

Penelope came to the door in a pair of baggy sweatpants and an oversize T-shirt advertising a 5K race to raise money for the local animal shelter. Penelope wasn't particularly overweight, but she was determined to lose the final ten pounds she'd gained after her last baby.

She took the container of food from Gigi and frowned. "Have you delivered Madeline's yet? How is she holding up? George got a call last night from Mr. West. I can't believe Bradley's dead."

"I guess Madeline is doing as well as can be expected under the circumstances," Gigi said.

"I should probably give her a call."

"I think she'd like that."

Penelope shook her head. "It's still so hard to believe. Mr. West had to repeat it to George twice before he was able to take it in." She played with the frayed edge of her T-shirt. "I wonder what this means for the partnership? I mean, will they be replacing Bradley? George hopes he eventually—"

The wail of a baby from the back of the house cut her short. "Sorry, that's Hughie. I've got to go."

Gigi reluctantly turned away from the now-closed door and headed back to her car, where Reg was waiting, his attention caught by a fellow checking his mailbox across the street. Bradley's death was obviously going to shake things up at Simpson and West. Had someone from the firm been determined to free up a partnership?

Gigi noodled on the idea as she pulled away from Penelope's house and headed back toward town. She needed to make a stop at Bon Appétit. Woodstone's gourmet and cookery store. Evelyn Fishko stocked items Gigi couldn't find anywhere else—truffle oil, fresh pâté, interesting cheeses and other delectable goodies.

"You'll have to stay here," Gigi said to Reg as she closed the car door. Evelyn loved dogs, Reg especially, but the Board of Health made the rules, and she had to abide by them.

Evelyn's rather long face looked even longer when Gigi pushed open the door to Bon Appétit. She had her usual cardigan draped around her shoulders, and her glasses were pushed up on top of her head, holding back her thick, gray bob.

"Good morning," Gigi said as she approached the counter.

Evelyn's greeting sounded more like a grunt than her usual cheery hello.

Gigi looked at her. "What's the matter? You seem awfully down in the dumps today."

Evelyn grunted again. "I am. Have you heard about that new shop that's opening in town?" She jerked her head toward the right. "It's going into that place where the old Clip and Curl used to be."

The Clip and Curl had been one of the many casualties of the changing times. Most of the Woodstone residents went to the chain place that was out at the mall, and the Wall

Streeters who owned the big houses in Woodstone still went to their favorite salons back in the city.

"What kind of shop is it?"

Evelyn leaned her elbows on the counter. "That's the thing. It's going to be some super fancy gourmet store." She swept a hand around her own establishment. "I'm afraid they're going to put me out of business."

"But people have been coming here for years."

Evelyn raised an eyebrow. "You saw how fast everyone deserted Woodstone Opticians when that chain eyeglass place opened at the mall. Apparently they're putting a ton of money into the place. It's owned by two guys from the city." Evelyn waggled her eyebrows at Gigi. "They already have a shop on the Upper West Side, and they wanted to expand. Why Woodstone?" she added glumly. "I heard they're going to do wine and cheese parties, give cooking classes, the whole shebang. Who's going to want to come to this dusty old place when they can go there?"

Gigi glanced around Bon Appétit. She loved it the way it was, but looking around with an unbiased eye, she supposed it could use a little updating. Dust had collected on some of the cans, and more than a few of Evelyn's signs had faded into invisibility.

"You've always had whatever I needed," Gigi said reassuringly. "Surely that will count with the citizens of Woodstone."

Evelyn's mouth turned down at the corners. "But wine and cheese parties and cooking classes? I'll never be able to compete with the likes of that."

Gigi raised her chin. "Well, maybe what you need is a battle plan."

Evelyn tilted her head to one side and looked at Gigi with narrowed, but curious, eyes. "A battle plan?"

"If they can throw wine and cheese parties, so can you. When are they opening?"

Evelyn glanced at the calendar behind her with beauty shots of Connecticut. "It's February now. I heard the grand opening festival is to be in April sometime."

"So you have almost two months. A little fresh paint, some rearranging, and no one will recognize this place."

Evelyn's expression lifted slightly. "You know, I think you're right. It's been an age since I've done any sprucing up. Hey"—she put a hand on Gigi's arm—"maybe you can give a cooking demonstration."

Gigi thought for a moment. "Branston Foods is supposed to debut my line of frozen Gourmet De-Lite dinners soon. Perhaps they would hold the launch party here." Gigi started to get excited. "And give you at least temporary exclusivity in carrying them."

"That would be splendid!" Evelyn's eyes had brightened considerably. "Now that we've got that settled, what can I get you?"

Gigi pulled out her shopping list.

"I don't suppose you were at that party at Declan's Saturday night?" Evelyn said as she plunked a bottle of aged balsamic vinegar down on the counter.

"Actually, I was." Gigi said.

Evelyn shook her head. "I wonder if Barbara Simpson finally snapped and offed him."

"I don't think so. She left the party early because she wasn't feeling well."

"You mean she'd had too much to drink." Evelyn reached

for a jar of capers on the shelf behind her. "She's been to some fancy rehab place twice now. For exhaustion." Evelyn made air quotes. "One of those joints where you get your meals prepared for you, spend all day talking about yourself and have massages and do yoga. Sounds like a vacation to me." Evelyn snorted. "Doesn't seem to have done her any good though."

Alice had hinted at something similar, Gigi remembered. But she was pretty certain Barbara had been sick the night of the party, not drunk.

Gigi pulled away from the curb in front of Bon Appétit and waved good-bye to Evelyn, who was standing in the doorway looking slightly happier than she had when Gigi arrived.

Gigi was half excited for and half dreading her next appointment—the same sort of feeling she remembered having in second grade before her first ballet recital. Victor Branston, founder and CEO of Branston Foods, had decided to run a series of radio commercials, and he wanted them to have a personal touch in keeping with the concept of Gigi's Gourmet De-Lite—meaning he wanted Gigi to record the commercials herself. She had never done anything like it before, but the marketing manager for Branston's, a very slick young man who bore a slight resemblance to a less down-home version of Elvis, assured her that there was nothing to it. Gigi wasn't so sure about that, but she was in no position to disagree.

As she drove toward a small strip mall on the outskirts of Woodstone, she reminded herself that trying new things was good for you—it stretched you and made you grow.

Still, if she hadn't already agreed to it, she would have turned tail and run straight home.

The building she was looking for turned out to be a converted shop front with a small printed sign in the window that read *Keith's Recording Studio*. Gigi pushed open the door reluctantly, Reg sticking close to her heels. Dusty album covers adorned the walls, and the carpet was faded and threadbare. A receptionist sat at a nicked and dented metal desk, her back to Gigi, the telephone clutched between her shoulder and her ear.

She turned around when she heard the door open and motioned Gigi toward one of two orange, molded plastic chairs. Gigi recognized her from Madeline Stone's engagement party as the woman who had helped Barbara Simpson after she'd taken ill. Today she was wearing skintight jeans and a stretched-out brown T-shirt with *Keith's Recording Studio* barely visible on it.

Reg hunkered down next to Gigi's chair, and Gigi had just picked up a two-year-old copy of *Rolling Stone* when the door opened and the manager from Branston's came in. Gigi watched as he hung his coat on a metal coat rack. He was handsome, if you liked the type, but there was something smarmy about him that set her teeth on edge.

"Alec Pricely." He held his hand out. He was wearing a brown suit, a dark brown shirt and a silver tie.

Gigi shook his hand gingerly. It was quite cold. Before she could say anything, the door to the recording area opened and a young man popped his head out. He had dark hair that stood on end and the tattoo of a fleur-de-lis on his right wrist.

"I think we're about ready," he said.

Gigi felt her heart do a slight tap dance in her chest.

"There's nothing to be nervous about," Pricely said, as if reading her thoughts.

Gigi just smiled at him.

"You can leave your pooch with me," the girl behind the desk said. "I'll be glad to keep an eye on him. We've got three strays ourselves." She reached into her desk drawer and pulled out a dog biscuit.

Reg was happily nibbling away as Gigi and Pricely went into a windowless room dominated by a control panel with all sorts of dials and buttons. A young man who introduced himself as Geoff sat down in front of it in a worn-looking swivel chair. He faced a wall of glass and a smaller room beyond, where Gigi could see a narrow podium and a microphone.

Pricely handed Gigi a piece of paper. "Your part is written right there." He pointed a rather stubby finger at several lines of text.

Gigi took the paper and read over the words. She hoped she could get through them without flubbing.

It took her ten tries to nail it. It felt strange talking into the microphone while wearing a set of headphones.

"Pretend you're talking directly to your audience," Pricely said, sounding slightly exasperated after the fifth take.

Gigi could see him through the window turning his gold-and-diamond wedding band around and around.

She tried again. "From my house to your house . . ." she began, when Geoff tapped on the glass, and she heard the click of the mic coming on.

"Sorry about that. I wasn't quite ready." His voice came through the glass.

Gigi started over. By the time Geoff and Pricely were both satisfied, perspiration was running down her sides, and she'd finished the glass of water the receptionist had brought her.

"Great job," Pricely said, clapping her on the back.

Gigi gave a weak smile.

"About the music," Pricely said, slumping back into his seat. "Something upbeat, I would think."

Gigi hesitated.

He waved a hand at her. "Thanks a million. I'll take care of the rest of this."

Gigi nodded gratefully and headed toward the reception area.

She was wrapping Reg's leash around her hand when the receptionist looked up at her. "Didn't I see you at Hunter Simpson's engagement party?"

Gigi nodded. "Yes. I was meant to be a guest, but Declan, the owner, needed my help in the kitchen."

"I thought you looked familiar, but I couldn't place you. It was driving me crazy." She stuck her pencil behind her ear. "Quite a do wasn't it?" She looked down at her nails briefly. "Until that sod Bradley had to cut into Hunter the way he did." She quirked a smile at Gigi. "Jimmy—that's my husband—is Hunter's uncle. Not much love lost between him and his brother-in-law, as you can imagine."

Gigi tried to look interested without looking too interested. In her experience, an overly obvious show of interest tended to remind people that they were spilling their secrets to a near stranger, and it would often staunch the flow of information.

"I'm Cheryl, by the way." She held out a slim hand. The skin on the back of it was pale and thin and dotted with a handful of brown spots. Cheryl was a lot older than she wanted people to think. "I felt badly for Barbara. First Bradley going off the way he did, and then her coming down sick. Barbara's a good egg."

Gigi nodded. "Are Barbara and Jimmy close?"

Cheryl made a back-and-forth motion with her hand. "They used to be, but ever since Barbara and Bradley got married . . ." She rolled her eyes. "Bradley is such a snob. Didn't want to associate with us."

"That's too bad." Gigi tried to inject just the right note of sympathy into her voice.

"Yeah. Well, Jimmy may not be a lawyer, but he does all right considering. Runs a body shop just outside of town. Nowadays they would have diagnosed him with a learning disability, but back then . . ." She shrugged. "But like I said, he does all right, and I bring in what I can working here at Keith's." She fiddled with the hoop in her right ear.

"It's not easy nowadays," Gigi said, injecting even more sympathy into her voice.

"You're telling me!" Cheryl snorted. "If I hadn't needed that operation . . . Keith can't afford to offer us health insurance, and the same with the body shop where Jimmy works. Barbara"—she looked at Gigi as if to see if she was following the story—"is a decent sort, and when she heard the trouble we were in, wrote a check right on the spot."

Gigi nodded, again trying to present the appropriate level of interest without scaring Cheryl off.

"Bradley insisted on drawing up some papers to show that we'd pay up as agreed. I know Barbara could care less about stuff like that." Cheryl wiped her nose with the back of her hand. "Of course now with Bradley dead maybe it won't make any . . ."

The unfinished sentence hung in the air between them. Gigi cleared her throat and made noises about getting her coat and moving on.

Cheryl smiled and held out her hand. "Nice to meet you."

Gigi smiled, nodded and shook the proffered hand.

She fastened Reg's leash, said good-bye again and went out the door. She couldn't believe it—Cheryl had just admitted to a very, very good reason for murder.

# Chapter 7

"How are things going with your sister?" Sienna poured Gigi a cup of steaming coffee. They were settled into the coffee corner, as it was known, at the Book Nook.

"Okay. I don't see much of her given the hours she keeps."

"How long does she plan to—"

"She said she has an appointment to go look at some apartments. I feel a little guilty, but I can't wait to have the cottage all to myself again."

"That's perfectly understandable." Sienna stirred her cup of herbal tea. "I was really sorry to miss the big party and all of the excitement. Oliver's mother called up out of the blue wanting to see Camille"—she smiled at the baby gurgling happily in the bouncy seat next to her—"and she offered to pay our airfare and everything. I must admit it was heavenly to get away to Palm Beach at this time of year." She wiped a bit of drool from the baby's mouth.

"Although we think poor little Camille is cutting a tooth, don't we pumpkin?" She cooed at the infant. "The first evening she had us up almost all night."

Gigi glanced at her goddaughter. She seemed perfectly content now, rocking in her bouncy chair, trying to stuff her fist into her mouth.

"We were invited because Oliver's friend, George Lawson, is an associate at Simpson and West. I think the whole thing was less of an engagement party and more of a business affair for Bradley Simpson." A slight frown crossed Sienna's face. "I'm sorry. I shouldn't be speaking ill of the dead, as my mother would say."

Gigi cupped her mug of coffee. "It seems there were plenty of people willing to speak ill of him while he was alive."

Sienna cocked her head. "Really? I didn't know him at all well. Oliver said he was a hard-driving lawyer and an incredible rainmaker for the firm."

Gigi told Sienna about her recording session earlier that day. "Cheryl told me that she and her husband had borrowed money from Barbara Simpson. They seem to think that with Bradley out of the way there won't be any need to pay her back."

"She said that?" Sienna looked up from wiping another blob of drool off of Camille's chin. She gestured at the cloth in her hand. "They say all this drooling means she's teething, although we can't see anything yet."

"She didn't come right out and say it. She sort of left it hanging." Gigi wondered if she could have misunderstood Cheryl. She didn't think so.

"Sounds like you've found the perfect suspect." Sienna grinned, and Gigi knew she was thinking of some of their past detecting adventures. "What do the police think?"

Gigi slumped in her seat. She still hadn't heard from Mertz. "I don't know. Mertz and I had something of a falling out. He didn't want me helping Declan out the night of the party although I assured him I'm not attracted to the man in the least." Gigi remembered some of the feelings she'd had while sitting in the kitchen with Declan, after everyone had left, and a flash of heat rushed to her cheeks.

Sienna glanced at her quizzically. She'd taken Camille from her bouncy seat and had the baby cradled against her shoulder. "Why do I think there's something you're not telling me?"

"There isn't." Gigi protested a little too fiercely. She had to force herself not to squirm.

"So the police haven't identified any suspects yet?" Sienna shifted the now-sleeping Camille slightly. The baby's hands were tangled in Sienna's long mane of golden hair, and her tiny, rosebud mouth was partially open.

Gigi shook her head. "Not that I know of, but I imagine Declan is going to be at the top of their list." The thought made her shiver again, and she clutched her coffee cup more tightly.

"Mertz wouldn't do that just because—"

"Oh, no. Not just because he's jealous. Mertz would never do that." Gigi looked into the depths of her steaming mug of coffee. "It's because of what they found at the scene."

"Something that traces to Declan?"

"Yes. The ice pick that was used to kill Bradley had Declan's name carved into it."

Sienna drew in her breath sharply, and Camille gave a muffled cry before settling back down to sleep. "That doesn't look good. But someone could have taken it from his kitchen."

"True. But how is he going to prove that?"

"What reason would Declan have for killing Bradley Simpson? Did they even know each other before last night?"

"I don't know. I don't think so."

The bell over the front door tinkled, and a blast of cold air drifted toward the coffee corner. Sienna stood up briefly. "Madison's behind the register. She'll keep a lookout."

Gigi was refilling her coffee cup when the newly arrived customer suddenly appeared around the end of one of the shelving units. She had on a strange assortment of ill-fitting clothing—red-and-white-striped socks, clogs that looked to be about an inch too long, wide-legged trousers that ended well above her ankles, and a corduroy car coat with sleeves that hung down past the tips of her fingers. She rounded the corner and headed toward the back of the store.

Gigi looked at Sienna with her eyebrows raised. Sienna glanced over her shoulder quickly.

"That's Janice Novak. I've heard she gets most of her clothes out of the Dumpsters around town," she whispered.

"That's so sad."

Sienna nodded. "She used to work for Simpson and West in their accounting department." Sienna glanced around and lowered her voice even further. "Apparently she embezzled some small sum of money from the firm." She mouthed the words *gambling problem*.

"Too bad."

"The firm decided not to press charges, but the partners refused to give her a reference, and she can't get much of a job anywhere else. Besides, just about everyone in Wood-stone knows about it—Bradley Simpson was apparently quite vocal when it happened. I heard she was working at the Dollar Store in that strip mall on the edge of town, but when her register didn't add up one night, they let her go."

"That's a shame."

"It's made her a little . . . off."

Gigi also realized that it made her more than just a little *off*, to use Sienna's expression.

It also made her another perfect suspect in Bradley Simpson's murder.

Gigi was surprised to see Pia sitting at the kitchen island nursing a cup of cocoa when she got up the following morning. Her sister's face looked thinner than usual and was ashen with fatigue. Pia poked at the marshmallows in her cup with her index finger.

"Good morning," Gigi offered tentatively. It was obvious from the stiff set of Pia's shoulders that something was bothering her.

Pia didn't respond, just lowered her face into her mug of cocoa.

Gigi sighed and began measuring coffee into the coffeemaker. She added water, pushed the button, and the machine gurgled to life. It was equipped with an automatic timer, but she never seemed to remember to set it up the night before—although the few times she had, it was heavenly to wake up to the smell of freshly brewed coffee instead of the usual racket from her alarm clock.

Pia made a small noise—to Gigi it sounded halfway between a squeak and a suppressed sneeze. Was Pia crying? Gigi glanced at her sister again and saw her shoulders were shaking.

She was.

"What's wrong?" Gigi asked with a sense of resignation. Pia regularly got into scrapes that ranged from almost nothing to practically illegal.

"I went to Declan's last night," Pia said with a hiccough. "We had a wonderful chat. I've really missed having a man in my life."

By Pia's own account, she had said good-bye to the philandering Clive barely a few weeks before, so her love life had hardly been akin to the Sahara desert.

"He asked me to stay for a nightcap." She glanced up at Gigi. "It's wonderful to find someone who *understands* you."

Anyone who could understand Pia was exceptional indeed, Gigi thought. Gigi had hoped that Pia's infatuation with Declan would have passed by now. Obviously it hadn't. She had to figure out a way to let Pia know that Declan wasn't serious . . . but without hurting her feelings. Somehow Gigi didn't think that was going to be possible.

"We had such a lovely chat." Pia drained the rest of her cocoa and put the mug down. It had already left a series of wet rings on Gigi's countertop. "And then the police came in! Said he was wanted for questioning." She turned large, imploring eyes on Gigi. "For that murder in the parking lot!"

Gigi was reaching for the carafe of coffee, and her hand jerked, sloshing hot liquid onto her bathrobe. She stared at the spot and sighed. The robe was due for a wash anyway.

"You have to do something." Pia knitted her fingers together as if she were praying.

"Me?" Gigi pointed to herself. "There's nothing I can do. I'm sure that the police will soon sort it out and realize they've made a—"

"You can call that detective of yours. Tell him he has to let Declan go. He had nothing to do with the murder. It's not fair!" She ended on a wail.

"We're somewhat on the outs at the moment," Gigi admitted.

"Then you have to make up with him. Come on," Pia pleaded. "You know you want to."

Gigi had to admit her sister was right. She missed Mertz.

"Just call him and see what you can find out." Pia slid off her stool and grabbed the phone from the cradle. "Here." She held it out toward Gigi.

"I can't just call him and . . . demand an explanation." Gigi insisted.

Pia's face fell, then almost immediately brightened. "Have him over for dinner. Wine him and dine him. That ought to do the trick."

Gigi was surprised to find herself actually considering the idea. She'd always done whatever was necessary to take care of Pia. Was this any different?

Pia waved the phone at Gigi.

"Oh, all right." Gigi took the receiver from Pia's hand and quickly dialed the Woodstone Police Station. Her mouth went dry. What if Mertz refused to talk to her? What if he hung up on her?

She glanced over her shoulder at Pia, who was making encouraging gestures.

Gigi slammed the phone down. She couldn't do it.

"You have to." Pia grabbed the phone and handed it back to Gigi.

Gigi dialed the number again with trembling fingers. She turned her back on Pia and listened as the phone rang. She

79

closed her eyes, hoping that by some miracle no one would answer. But of course that was impossible.

The receptionist's voice came on the line.

Gigi managed to find enough breath to ask for Mertz. Once again she closed her eyes and prayed that he was out on a case somewhere.

No such luck.

"Mertz," he said economically. Gigi could hear the rustling of papers in the background and muted voices.

"I . . . I hope I'm not disturbing you," Gigi managed to squeak out, ready to hang the phone up immediately if he said he was busy.

"Gigi!"

Gigi had thought Mertz might sound annoyed, exasperated, angry, distant, but instead he sounded . . . pleased.

Gigi gulped hard. "I was wondering if . . . if . . ." She turned around to see Pia urging her on. "I was wondering if you'd like to . . . um . . . come over for dinner." Again Gigi hesitated, and Pia waved her on. "Tonight."

"I'd love to." Mertz sighed. "But I'm going to a meeting out of town, and I'm not sure when I'll be back. If it's not too late, maybe I can just stop by, and we can have a cup of coffee?"

"Sure. That would be fine." Gigi heard voices in the background.

"Listen, I've got to go. I'll call you later and let you know how things are panning out, okay? Maybe I'll be able to get away earlier."

"Great. Fine." Gigi hung up the phone.

"What did he say?" Pia demanded immediately.

"He said he'd stop by if he can." She explained about the out-of-town meeting.

"You'll need to be prepared." Pia paced up and down the kitchen, an anxious look on her face. "What are you going to make?" Before Gigi could answer, she continued. "It would look odd if you had a complete dinner waiting for him . . . just in case. It might be best to have some ingredients on hand so you could whip up something simple like . . . I don't know. You're the chef."

"I think I can handle it," Gigi said dryly.

"And wine. Don't forget to get a bottle of wine to relax him."

"It's already on my mental list."

Pia threw her arms around her sister. "You're the best."

Gigi sighed and returned the hug.

Later that afternoon, as Gigi was driving through the darkening town after having delivered her dinner meals, a commercial came on the radio. She had tuned to a rock station she liked—if asked, she would deny it, but she had a penchant for cheesy pop songs and had been known to sing along at the top of her lungs while piloting the MINI through Woodstone.

She'd just finished a rousing rendition of one of Britney Spears's earlier songs when the music ended and the advertisement came on. Gigi had her finger on the button and was about to change the station when a familiar voice caught her attention. *Her* voice. Advertising Gigi's frozen Gourmet De-Lite dinners. She nearly drove into a light post on High Street, she was so surprised. She supposed Branston was running the commercials now to create excitement over the launch of his new product—Gigi's frozen diet entrées.

It was strange hearing her voice emanating from the radio. Reg obviously thought so, too. He tilted his head, listening, occasionally turning to look at Gigi with a curious look on his face. He gave a confused howl as the commercial came to an end.

"That's okay, boy." Gigi reached out and patted him on the head. "I'm here and not inside the radio."

He gave her another strange look and then, with a sigh, hunkered back down on the front passenger seat.

As Gigi pulled into the driveway of her cottage, a feeling of relief swept over her. She'd left a few lights on, and they glowed warmly through the front windows. Pia had assured her she would be at her studio, so Gigi knew she would have the place to herself.

Reg raced ahead of her as Gigi headed toward the front door. She picked up the spill of mail that was fanned out across the wood floor of the foyer and stacked it on the kitchen table. She'd go through it later.

Gigi hadn't heard from Mertz yet. Most likely his meeting would run late, and he wouldn't be stopping by. She sort of hoped that would be the case. As much as she wanted to see him again and mend the rift that had opened between them, she wasn't anxious to bring up the subject of Declan's possible guilt in Bradley's murder.

Gigi made herself a cup of tea and curled up on the sofa with a book. A sense of peace settled over her as she listened to the blissful silence broken only by the occasional exhale from Reg, who had staked out a spot at her feet.

Gigi was enjoying her book, but soon her eyes grew heavy. There was no harm in closing them for a few minutes, she thought. She stretched out on the sofa, displacing Reg, who retreated to the furthest end, and pulled up the throw she had tossed over the arm of the couch. When she woke two hours later, she was cold and cramped. The clock read nine o'clock. Mertz was certainly not going to be stopping by at this hour, so she might as well change into her pajamas, make some cheese toast for her dinner—she wasn't particularly hungry—and have an early night.

Gigi slipped into her favorite pajamas—the ones with the reindeer on them that her mother had given her when she was a senior in college. The hems were ragged and the pattern was nearly worn off in spots, but they were soft and comfortable.

She was heating water in the kettle when the doorbell rang.

Note to self, Gigi thought as she flung open the front door. Always, always, peek through the window before opening the door.

Mertz stood on her front steps, his collar turned up around his ears, and his hands stuffed into his pockets. Snow was falling, and flakes were melting in his hair.

"Oh," was all Gigi was able to muster.

He glanced at her reindeer pajamas and a smile briefly crossed his face.

Gigi held the door wider. "Come . . . come in," she stammered. She could already feel her face flushing crimson. Why, oh why, hadn't she left her jeans and sweatshirt on?

"I hope I'm not too late. The meeting was positively interminable."

Other than a fleeting smile, Mertz didn't seem to mind Gigi's unconventional attire or even notice it much. Gigi really liked that about him. Ted had been hypercritical of everything she wore, how she did her hair, what perfume she chose, even going so far as to tell her what shoes to put with her outfit. It was a relief to be with a man who accepted her the way she was.

"Come on in. Please."

Mertz followed her into the living room, where he stood awkwardly, not even unbuttoning his coat.

"Let me take your coat."

"I wasn't going to stop, considering the hour," Mertz blurted out. "But as I was driving along, all of a sudden your voice came on the radio." He smiled. "I almost hit the light post outside of the Silver Lining."

*That makes two of us,* Gigi thought.

Mertz took a deep breath. "I'm really sorry about Friday night. I guess I was . . ." The words stuck in his throat. ". . . jealous of Declan."

Gigi noticed that the tips of his ears were bright red.

She shrugged. "That's okay." She fiddled with the loose button on her pajama top.

Mertz reached into his coat pocket and handed something to Gigi. "Here, this is for you. I know Valentine's Day isn't until next week, but . . ." He trailed off, his whole face turning almost as red as Gigi's had earlier.

"Oh . . . my . . ." Gigi didn't know what to say. She accepted the gaily wrapped box and stood looking at it.

"Go ahead. Open it."

Gigi moved over toward the sofa and perched on the edge. Mertz joined her, watching eagerly as she undid the white ribbon and tore off the glossy red paper. Gigi held her breath as she lifted the lid of a dark blue box with Woodstone Jewelers written in elegant gold script across the top.

"Oh." She lifted out the pin nestled inside. It was a gold whisk with a ring of dark blue sapphires circling the handle. "Oh," she said again, not quite able to speak.

"I hope you like it." Mertz frowned, his eyes darkening. "I had them make it especially for you."

"I love it," Gigi said, tears rushing to her eyes. It was the most thoughtful gift anyone had ever given her.

She could feel Mertz relaxing beside her. She thought about some of the extravagant jewelry Ted had bought her. None of it had ever really suited her. They were pieces he liked. Not like this pin. This was perfect.

Gigi looked up in time to see Mertz dash a hand across his eyes.

"Happy Valentine's Day."

Before Gigi could answer, he leaned toward her and enveloped her lips with his. It was several minutes before they broke apart. Gigi tried to catch her breath.

"Have you eaten? Did they feed you at your meeting?" Gigi put the pin carefully back in the box. She looked up to see Mertz roll his eyes.

"Not unless you count an Almond Joy bar, a bag of Cheez Doodles and a bottle of water."

Gigi laughed. "No, I'm afraid that doesn't count. I don't know what I have in the fridge, but I'm sure I can rustle up something." She crossed her fingers behind her back, knowing full well she'd spent an hour in Shop and Save trying to decide what to buy in case Mertz showed up for dinner.

Mertz followed her out to the kitchen, where he straddled a chair and watched as she rummaged in the refrigerator.

Gigi pulled out a packet of Black Forest ham, a jar of coarse, grainy mustard, a chunk of butter still in the wrapper, several slices of Gruyère cheese and two eggs. She lifted the lid of her ceramic bread box and rummaged around until she found half a loaf of white bread.

"What are you making?" Mertz sounded bemused.

"The French call it *croque monsieur*. Basically it's a fancy grilled ham and cheese sandwich."

"Sounds delicious."

"It is." Gigi swung a frying pan onto the lit burner on the stove and added a smear of butter. She hardly ever used butter, given that her recipes were all low calorie, but you couldn't make a croque monsieur without at least a dab of it.

She assembled her sandwiches, dipped them in a mixture of beaten eggs and a few spoonfuls of water, then added them to the butter already sizzling in the pan. When they had turned golden on one side, she flipped them over.

"You have no idea how good that smells."

"The French also do a *croque madame*, which is a similar sandwich but with a fried egg on top."

"The French sure do know how to eat. We thought adding marshmallow fluff to our peanut butter sandwiches was the cat's meow, as my mother used to say."

While Gigi prepared the meal, she directed Mertz to get out placemats, napkins and silverware. When Gigi looked up from plating the sandwiches, she discovered Mertz had folded the napkins into a pyramid shape.

He looked embarrassed when Gigi stared at them, her mouth slightly open.

He shrugged, the tips of his ears coloring again. "I spent one summer working as a busboy in the Poconos. About the only thing I learned was how to fold napkins. That and that I don't like borscht." He shuddered.

Gigi laughed as she put the plates on the table.

Mertz had obviously been very hungry. He devoured his *croque monsieur* in record time. Finally, Gigi was finished as well. She'd completely forgotten she was wearing tatty old reindeer pajamas and that her red hair was pulled back haphazardly with a twist tie from a loaf of bread. She felt utterly relaxed.

Mertz glanced at his watch as he swiped his napkin across his mouth. "I'm sorry, but I have to be getting back to the station."

This was the moment Gigi had been dreading. She had to ask him about Declan before he left.

She handed Mertz his coat and watched as he put it on and wound his scarf around his neck. Gigi tried to find the words, but they weren't coming.

Mertz stood at the front door, looking down at his hands as if he suddenly found them fascinating. "I don't know how to tell you this—"

"What!" Gigi looked at him, alarmed.

"We've brought Declan McQuaid in for questioning."

"I know. My sister told me. She's very upset. She's taken quite a liking to him."

Mertz closed his eyes briefly. "You know that ice pick they found in the vic's body was his?"

"Yes. You said his name was carved into it."

"It's not just that. Someone might have lifted the pick from the kitchen when he wasn't looking." Mertz looked down at his hands again.

"Yes?"

He looked up at Gigi with sad eyes. "His were the only fingerprints found on the weapon." He sighed. "And several witnesses heard him arguing violently with Bradley Simpson at one point during the evening."

# Chapter 8

Gigi half expected to find Pia waiting in the kitchen when she got up the next morning, but the room was empty. She peeked into the guest room, but even with the bedclothes in their usual tangle, she could tell the bed was empty.

She breathed a sigh of relief as she measured coffee into the coffeemaker. She wasn't up to facing Pia just yet. And certainly not before her first cup of coffee.

Mertz made the evidence against Declan sound fairly damning, but Gigi was quite convinced that Declan was innocent, and she had confidence that in the end, truth would prevail. How she was going to convince Pia of that, she had no idea.

Gigi readied her clients' breakfasts and carried the Gourmet De-Lite containers out to her car. Reg wove in and out between her legs, nearly tripping Gigi.

"It's okay," she reassured him. "You're going, too."

He settled down with a relieved sigh, and she was able to finish loading the car and slip into her coat and boots.

As Gigi drove past Declan's Grille on the way back from Simpson and West, she was half afraid she'd see a big *Closed* sign on the front door. There wasn't, and there was actually a glimmer of light visible through the window.

Rather impulsively, Gigi turned into the parking lot and pulled into the space. "I'll only be a minute," she told Reg as she got out.

She tried the kitchen's back door first. It opened easily, and she stepped inside.

The kitchen was dark and empty without pots simmering on the stove or dishes baking in the oven. The smell of cooked food hung heavy and stale in the air. Gigi pushed open the door to the restaurant proper. The room was shadowy, with a bright pinprick of light coming from the tiny lamp clipped to the hostess desk. It was the only fixture that had been turned on. Declan was seated on a bar stool, slumped over the bar, his head in his hands. He jumped when he heard Gigi clear her throat.

"Gigi." It came out sounding more like a groan than a greeting.

Gigi slipped onto the stool next to Declan's. Declan looked at her with shadowed eyes.

"You've heard."

Gigi nodded.

"Someone's been nicking things from my kitchen. That's why I carved my name into anything I could. Look." He glanced up at Gigi, a pleading look in his eyes. "Anyone could have taken that ice pick. Anyone! It was pandemonium in here on Saturday night." His eyes cleared slightly. "Or maybe someone nicked it earlier in the week. Planning ahead so to speak."

"That could be. Mertz said much the same thing."

Declan's face brightened. "He did?"

"Unfortunately the only prints found on the pick were yours."

Declan jerked as if he'd just touched a live wire. He slapped the bar with his open palm. "They had to have worn gloves then, hadn't they? It's the middle of February. No one would have thought it strange." Declan gripped the edge of the polished wooden bar with both hands. "Besides, I didn't even know the fellow until he called me about hosting his party. Why in the blinking heck would I have murdered the man?"

Gigi looked into her lap as if she would find some sort of solace there. She didn't believe Declan was the murderer, but how to prove it?

"Mertz said that someone has come forward . . . a witness," Gigi said haltingly. "They claim to have heard you arguing with Bradley the night of the party. Violently arguing, was how they put it."

Declan went very still for a few seconds. He turned slowly to look at Gigi before his glance darted away. "We did have a bit of a row. But it wasn't something I'd have killed the man over." He clenched his fists. "The arrogant so-and-so tried to stiff me on the tip for the waitresses. Said it was standard to include eighteen percent to cover the gratuities. I told him it might be standard in his book, but that I hadn't done it. We went back and forth over it." He gave an abashed smile. "I'm afraid I did raise my voice a bit. Fine thing for someone who's constantly drilling it into the staff that the customer is always right." He looked Gigi in the eye. "We settled the whole thing amicably enough."

Gigi was quiet.

"You do believe me, don't you?"

Gigi nodded yes, although somehow she knew in her gut he was lying.


Gigi hit the gas a little too heavily as she drove through Woodstone. She knew in her heart that Declan couldn't have killed Bradley. She didn't know why, but she was certain. But she was also positive that he was lying to her. Was he protecting someone else? Was he afraid it would make things worse for him with the police?

She didn't have time to think about it. She needed to get home and work on lunch prep for her clients. Gigi reached out and gave Reg a scratch behind the ears. He sighed softly and leaned against her hand, directing her caress to underneath his chin.

"You'd have me scratch you all day if you could." Gigi gave him a final pat and put her hand back on the wheel.

A weak, pale sun was struggling higher in the sky. The snow alongside the road, which had been white and new the other night, was mixed with grit now, and Gigi's tires swished loudly on the wet street. She was heading past the last of the downtown shops when she remembered her dry cleaning was ready. There was a space outside of Abigail's, only four doors down from the Sweet Kleen Laundry. Gigi pulled over, lined up her car and swiftly backed into the space. She remembered her earlier attempts at parallel parking, and a hot flood of color washed over her face. Mertz had caught her attempting to maneuver the MINI into a space that would have fit an eighteen-wheeler. She could still see the look of amusement on his face. Fortunately, he'd subsequently given her a few tips, and now Gigi was quite confident in her parking skills and didn't have to circle downtown Woodstone looking for a place to leave the car that didn't involve parallel parking.

Reg looked at her hopefully when she opened the door, but she shook her head and he settled back down on the passenger seat.

"Not this time, buddy. But I'll only be a sec, and then we'll be heading home."

Gigi locked the car and pocketed her keys. She was stepping away from the curb when she collided with someone coming out of Abigail's. The woman had a shopping bag in each hand and was struggling to put on a pair of oversize sunglasses.

"I'm sorry," Gigi said automatically.

"All my fault," the woman said. "I wasn't looking where I was going." She lowered her glasses and peered at Gigi. "You're the Gourmet De-Lite girl, aren't you?"

"Yes." Gigi suddenly recognized the woman as Barbara Simpson, Bradley Simpson's widow. Words of sympathy rose to her lips, but Barbara was already talking.

'I still need to do your program if you have space for me." She gestured with her chin toward the shopping bags. "I've just bought a new outfit for Bradley's funeral, and it seems I've gone up a size again." Her chin wobbled, and a tear snaked its way out from under the dark glasses. "I feel I owe it to him. I was a size two when we married, can you believe it? I promised him I'd get back in shape again, and now, even though it's too late for Bradley"—she gave a loud sniff—"I feel I ought to do it."

"Of course." Gigi thought Barbara looked terrible—as

if she hadn't slept in days. Everything about her seemed to droop—her face, her posture.

"Do you think you can take me on? You're not too busy?"

"Of course not."

"Listen," Barbara pushed her sunglasses up on top of her head. "Do you know if they ever found my wrap?" She jerked her head in the direction of Declan's. "I lost it the night of Bradley's party. It must be at the restaurant somewhere. It's double-ply cashmere. Black on one side and cream on the other. Maybe when you cleaned up . . ." She shook her head. "Not that it matters now, of course. But Bradley bought it for me. We saw it in a store window, and he insisted on dashing into the shop to buy it for me." Another tear made its way down her cheek, and she brushed at it impatiently.

"I'm sorry, but as far as I know, we didn't find anything. You might check with Declan though. It may have turned up in the meantime."

Barbara nodded. "I suppose I will. And don't forget to call me." She tapped Gigi on the arm. "I'd like to get started right away."

Gigi assured Barbara she would call her later that afternoon, then walked down to the Sweet Kleen Laundry to collect her things.


"You certainly don't lack for suspects," Alice said as she poured a half gallon of milk into a blue-and-white flowered slow cooker.

"What are you making?" Gigi peered into the cooker. She had stopped by Alice's to return a drill she had borrowed earlier to hang some new pictures.

"I'm making homemade yogurt," Alice put the top on the cooker. She reached for a battered kettle on the stove and swung it toward Gigi. "Tea?"

"Sure." It was a gray day with a wind that had a bitter edge to it. Gigi's fingers were still cold, and some tea would be most welcome. She glanced at Reg, who had curled up underneath Alice's round oak kitchen table. Even he looked chilled, despite his heavy fur coat.

"I'll strain it afterward and turn it into Greek yogurt. I found the recipe online and had to try it." Alice turned the burner on under the water. "As I was saying, we've got ourselves plenty of suspects. Always assuming the police aren't wrong, and Declan really did do it."

Gigi slumped in her chair. "I'm positive Declan is innocent. Besides, why would he kill Bradley? He'd never met him before that night."

"You mentioned an argument," Alice said above the rattle of crockery as she set two teacups and saucers on the table.

"Yes, but it was about the tip for the waitresses. Declan would hardly have killed someone over that." Gigi ignored the little voice in her head reminding her that she was positive Declan had been lying.

"There were certainly enough other people wanting the nasty bugger dead." Alice poured boiling water into each of the cups.

Gigi dunked her tea bag in the hot water. "When I was at the Book Nook, this rather strange woman came in. Sienna said she used to work for Simpson and West but was fired for stealing money."

Alice nodded. "Yes. Janice Novak. Everyone knows about it. Do you think she—"

"Why not? Maybe she's harbored a grudge against Bradley all this time."

"True." Alice sank into the chair opposite Gigi. "And maybe she saw her moment to get revenge. She wanders around Woodstone at all times of the day and night in those strange getups of hers. She might have seen Bradley leaving Declan's and decided to seize the moment."

"But how would she have gotten hold of the ice pick?"

"Dunno. Perhaps she stole it earlier. She's like a magpie, collecting bits and pieces of trash here and there. I often see the back door to Declan's propped open when he's got a delivery. Easy enough for her to slip inside and pocket it while he's carting stuff down to the basement."

"I don't know . . ."

"On the other hand, there's the son, Hunter. One, from what you said, his father seems to be making his life a living hell, and two, he probably stands to inherit some decent cash." Alice ticked the reasons off on her fingers.

"He did leave the party early—right after that nasty remark his father made. I wonder if anyone knows where he went."

"The fiancée maybe? Isn't she one of your clients?"

"Yes. I suppose I could ask her a few questions," Gigi said reluctantly. She hated quizzing people. It didn't feel right. But if she didn't, Mertz would continue to blame Declan and Pia would have a meltdown . . .

And even though she knew Declan was lying about something, she also knew he wasn't a murderer.

When Gigi arrived with Madeline Stone's lunch later that morning, she was told that Madeline had gone home sick.

"Although she didn't look sick to me," said the rabbity looking girl behind the reception desk. She was wearing a cheap navy blue suit that puckered at the shoulders.

"Not sick?" Gigi said casually.

The girl shook her head, and her nondescript brown hair swung back and forth. "More like upset if you ask me."

"Did she say anything?

"To me?" The girl snorted. "No one talks to me. I just answer the phone. I'm like, you know, invisible."

Gigi knew what she meant. She remembered her early days in New York, trying to make her mark, suffering through one low-paying job after another.

Gigi waved her Gourmet De-Lite container at the girl. "I guess I'll deliver her lunch to her home address then."

"Do you think the police coming by had anything to do with it?" the girl asked as Gigi was turning away.

Gigi turned back to the desk and set down Madeline's lunch container. "The police?"

"Yes." The girl's face brightened. "This really hunky guy." She gestured with her hand. "Tall with really blue eyes."

*Mertz!* Gigi thought to herself.

"Kind of stiff though," the girl added.

*Definitely Mertz,* Gigi thought.

"And he spoke to Madeline?"

"Yup. And it was shortly after that that Madeline came rushing downstairs saying she didn't feel well and was going home."

"I guess I'd better deliver her lunch to her house then." Gigi brandished the container again.

"Do you need her address?" The girl jiggled the mouse next to her computer, and her screen came to life—it was filled with a picture of a beach in the background and, closer up, a fruity drink on an umbrella table.

"No, that's okay. I already have it."

Gigi's mind was whirling as she exited Simpson and West. Why had Mertz gone to Madeline and what had he said to upset her enough that she had left work early for the day?

Hopefully Madeline would be willing to tell her.

Gigi headed toward the address Madeline had given her. It was a small town house complex on the north end of Woodstone. The units were brick-fronted with slate gray shutters and glossy black doors. Gigi found number 25 and gently tapped the polished brass door knocker.

She was about to knock again when the door was yanked open. Madeline was wearing a scruffy pair of gray sweats with University of Connecticut barely visible on one leg of the drawstring pants. She'd obviously been crying and had a tissue balled up in her right hand.

"I'm sorry. I forgot all about my lunch. Can you imagine? Me, forgetting about food?" She made a halfhearted attempt at a smile.

"The receptionist said you were sick," Gigi said. "I hope I'm not disturbing you."

Madeline shook her head and held the door open wider. "Come on in."

The town house boasted a small foyer furnished with a narrow table and a brass lamp in need of polishing. The table was awash with letters, circulars and newspapers.

Madeline led Gigi into the living room, where an L-shaped sofa dominated the space. Madeline sat at one end and hugged a furry white pillow to her chest.

"I'm glad you're here. I needed someone to talk to. I hope you don't mind."

Gigi shook her head.

Madeline gave a loud sniff and dabbed at her nose with the crinkled tissue. "I had a policeman come by work today"—she gave a sob that ended in a hiccough—"asking me where Hunter went the night of our engagement party."

Gigi tilted her head and raised her eyebrows but didn't say anything for fear of staunching the flow of Madeline's conversation.

"The terrible thing is . . ."

"Yes?" Gigi leaned forward eagerly.

"I don't know where he went." Madeline wailed.

"Did you ask him?"

Madeline nodded, and her hair, which was pulled back into a haphazard ponytail, bobbed up and down. "I did. He said he went to the hospital. Said he'd had a call that there was an emergency. That's why he wouldn't drink anything alcoholic at the party—in case he got called in." She pulled her legs up close to her chest and wrapped her arms around them. "I went to the hospital and talked to Amanda. She's one of his colleagues. It was mortifying." She wailed again. "Amanda said she hadn't seen him at all on Saturday night. She assumed he was at the party." Madeline swiped the back of her hand across her nose. "I had to make up some story about why I was asking. She must have thought I was a fool."

She looked at Gigi with pleading eyes.

Gigi opened her mouth, but before she could say anything, Madeline was talking again.

"I know everyone thinks Hunter is marrying beneath

him. He could have any number of the lawyers at my firm, and goodness knows how many of his female colleagues are after him."

"But he chose you," Gigi reminded her.

"I know. It's just that sometimes I don't feel worthy, you know?"

Gigi didn't say anything. Playing amateur psychologist was not her role. Besides, she'd struggled with those very same issues while married to Ted. Starting and succeeding at her own business had given her the confidence she had lacked back then.

"I suppose the police were just asking routine questions. There's no need to be upset."

"I don't know." Madeline twirled a loose thread from her sweatshirt around and around her finger. "Hunter told them he was at the hospital just like he told me." She looked at Gigi and choked back a sob. "It won't be long before the police discover he was lying."

# Chapter 9

Poor Madeline. She must be quite worried about the possibility of Hunter having a role in his father's death. Gigi thought back to Saturday night and Bradley's obnoxious remarks. It was easy to understand how they might have inflamed Hunter. Still, she couldn't quite imagine him having anything to do with murder. The Hippocratic oath, after all, was about saving people, not killing them.

As Gigi drove back down High Street, she noticed a man in coveralls going into Bon Appétit. He had a stepladder slung over his shoulder. She supposed Evelyn was starting her renovations. Gigi glanced at the clock on her dashboard. Reg had been home alone for over an hour, and she still had to stop at Gibson's Hardware for a curtain rod. She'd have to give Reg an extra treat to make up for it.

She parked in the lot between Declan's and Gibson's. The lot was fairly full—Bradley's murder obviously hadn't had an impact on Declan's business. On the contrary, people were probably coming out of curiosity. Gigi shivered. She found that ghoulish. She didn't even like having to cross the parking lot, and she carefully skirted the area where Bradley's body had lain. There was no sign now of the violence that had occurred on Saturday night, but it still made the hair on the back of her neck stand up.

Gibson's smelled of mellow wood and the tang of metal. The floors squeaked as Gigi approached the clerk behind the desk. He had tied around his waist a dark blue apron with several pockets along the front.

"Help you?"

Gigi explained about needing a curtain rod.

"Will a thirty-six-inch do you?"

Fortunately Gigi had remembered to measure. She pulled a piece of scrap paper from her purse and glanced at it, then nodded at the salesman.

He told her to wait while he disappeared down one of the aisles. It was filled with things Gigi didn't recognize.

He returned promptly, rang up the sale and handed her the rod and a receipt.

"Sorry, but we don't have a bag that will fit that. Hope that's okay."

Gigi smiled. "No problem."

"Nice to have things get back to normal after, you know." He jerked his head toward the parking lot next door.

Gigi made some noncommittal noises. She thanked him and hurried out the door with her curtain rod.

She had parked in the back of the lot, perpendicular to the wooden fence that separated the lot from the one behind it. The slats were pointed at the top and a wire ran through them a foot from the top and a foot from the bottom. Gigi beeped open the doors of the MINI and was about to get in when something caught her eye. She left the car door ajar and walked closer to the fence.

Something was snagged on the pointed tip of one of the wooden slats. It looked like fabric or something knitted—a scarf maybe. Gigi went closer and saw that it looked like the edge of some sort of garment. The rest of it appeared to be hanging down behind the fence, on the side away from Declan's and Gibson's. Some innate sense of caution kept Gigi from touching it—instead, she stood on tiptoe and tried to see over the fence.

Drat—she was just a little too short. She looked around and noticed a discarded crate lying next to the Dumpster. She dragged it into place and carefully placed a foot on top. It creaked, and the wood gave slightly, but she was able to stand up long enough to see a piece of clothing hanging from the stake.

She couldn't tell what it was exactly, but it was white and definitely knit. She had a flashback to her conversation with Barbara Simpson. Her wrap had gone missing the night of the party, and it was white cashmere on one side and black on the other. It was highly unlikely that this was Barbara's missing stole, but Gigi didn't want to touch it and possibly destroy evidence.

She would have to go to the police.

Gigi walked the two blocks to the large, square brick building that housed the Woodstone Police Department. A former knitting factory, it was ugly and squat, and there was constant talk about tearing it down and rebuilding. Of course, no one wanted their taxes raised to pay for the construction, so the old building continued to do service. The Woodstone Women's Garden Club filled the planters out front with colorful flowers in the spring, and at Christmas the bushes were draped with lights.

Gigi hoped Mertz was in. She had the feeling that she might have uncovered a very important clue. She approached the receptionist with her fingers crossed. The woman was separated from the lobby of the police station by a thick piece of bulletproof glass. Gigi had to shout through the microphone embedded in the barrier.

The woman moved at a maddeningly slow pace as she picked up the phone and carefully punched in some numbers. She peered at Gigi over her Ben Franklins as she waited for the phone to be answered.

Four seconds, five seconds—Gigi held her breath as the phone continued to ring and ring. Finally, just as the woman was moving the receiver away from her ear, someone must have picked up. Gigi could see her lips moving, but couldn't hear what she was saying.

The woman leaned across her desk, closer to the microphone. "He's in his office. Said you were to come in. Said you knew where it was." She eyed Gigi suspiciously.

Gigi felt her face become suffused with color, but she tilted her chin up and nodded curtly. A buzzer sounded, and she was able to enter the inner sanctum of the Woodstone Police Department.

Mertz was at his desk, which was covered with stacks of meticulously aligned folders and papers. He was biting into a chocolate-covered candy bar as Gigi entered.

He waved it toward her sheepishly. "My lunch."

Gigi pretended to look at him sternly, and he laughed.

"I got called out again just as I was about to run out for a sandwich. This time someone swiped Mrs. VanZeldt's kissing Dutch couple from her front steps. I can't imagine what anyone is doing with all these lawn ornaments. As far as I'm concerned, it's a huge pain in the neck." He folded the now-empty candy wrapper neatly into thirds and carefully placed it in the wastebasket.

"This is a pleasant surprise." He smiled at Gigi and leaned back in his chair. He glanced at his watch. "I wish it were later. We could go for a drink at Declan's."

*Declan's is the last place I want to go,* Gigi thought. She wondered if Mertz had suggested it to prove he was no longer jealous.

"I think I've found something."

Mertz's chair sprang upright as he leaned forward. "Found something? What?"

"There's something hanging off one of the fence slats in the parking lot between Gibson's and Declan's. Where the . . . murder . . . took place. I couldn't see over the fence—"

Mertz grinned at her, and Gigi scowled back.

"Anyway, it looks like a sweater of some sort."

"It couldn't have been there on Saturday night. The scene-of-the-crime techs combed that parking lot for hours." He pursed his lips. "I guess I'd better have a look at it though. Just in case. Besides"—he grinned—"it will give me a chance to spend some more time with you."

Gigi could feel the eyes of the woman behind the reception desk following her as she and Mertz strolled out the front door. The wind had picked up, and dense gray clouds filled the sky.

"Looks like snow," Gigi said, running a little to keep up with Mertz's long stride.

Mertz glanced up at the sky. "Let's hope it holds off till we retrieve our evidence. If it is evidence."

Gigi pulled her collar up and yanked her hat down over her ears. Her hand brushed Mertz's as they walked, and she quickly stuffed them both in her pockets. The townspeople gossiped enough as it was. She didn't need to give them any ammunition.

Several more cars had pulled into the parking lot, Gigi noticed as they approached the back spaces and the wooden fence.

"Where exactly did you see this garment?" Mertz asked, stopping to scan the scene.

"Here." Gigi led him to the spot where the bit of knitted fabric was just visible.

Mertz stepped closer. "It's hooked over the slat." He stepped even closer and peered over the fence. "The rest of it is hanging down on the other side." He reached over and carefully touched the item with his gloved hand. "Looks like some kind of sweater or knitted shawl." He carefully unhooked it from its perch and pulled it over the fence.

It was a length of knitted material—black on one side and creamy white on the other.

And it was spattered with blood.

"I know it wasn't there the night of the murder or the crime scene guys would have caught it," Mertz said later that evening. Gigi had felt sorry for him as he'd had nothing but a chocolate bar for lunch, and she had invited him over for dinner. Okay, it wasn't only because she felt sorry for him— she'd looked forward to having his company.

He had arrived with a bottle of good red wine and had even hung his own coat up in the closet by the door. Reg greeted him like an old friend and rolled onto his back to have his stomach scratched. Gigi had managed to get a fire going in the fireplace, although how long it would last, she didn't know. She'd made a big pot of chili seasoned with a smoky chipotle pepper to serve over some brown rice and had set up tray tables in the living room in front of the fire. Mertz, dogged by Reg, followed her out to the kitchen, where she'd put out some cut-up raw vegetables and a bowl of herbed yogurt cheese.

"Delicious," Mertz mumbled around a bite of carrot and dip.

He uncorked the bottle of wine and poured them each a glass. Gigi perched on one of the stools that surrounded her kitchen island.

"Do you know anything more about that cashmere shawl we found? Was it blood?"

Mertz shook his head. "It looked like blood, but we won't know for certain until the lab gets through with it. My money is on its being blood though."

Gigi went to the stove and lifted the lid on the pot sitting on the front burner. She gave it a stir and reached for some bowls in the cabinet to her left. "It looked just like the shawl that Barbara Simpson described to me."

"But what was it doing there? It wasn't there when we searched the scene."

"True."

"So maybe the red stain *is* simply some barbecue sauce or tomato sauce that someone spilled on it, and they decided to throw it away. If Barbara Simpson bought it in that fancy shop on High Street—"

"Abigail's?"

"Yes, that one. Then it isn't beyond the realm of possibility that someone else had one just like it."

"True," Gigi admitted reluctantly. She filled the bowls with rice and steaming ladles of chili topped with shredded cheese and a dollop of sour cream. "If you carry the wine, I can handle these."

Mertz picked up both their glasses and the bottle and carried them into the living room, where he tucked into his meal immediately.

"Mmmm, so good," he said as he forked up a mouthful. "That candy bar was the only thing I've had to eat since this morning. Fortunately I'd ordered the farmer's breakfast at the Woodstone Diner."

Gigi had suspected as much. She waited while Mertz quickly polished off half the contents of his bowl.

"But don't you think it's strange that the exact same shawl, covered in what certainly looked like blood, wound up at that particular place?"

"I can't tell you how many strange things I've seen in my career. But I agree," he said, wiping some chili from his chin, "it is peculiar."

"I mean if I had a garment like that, and it had been ruined, I'd probably try to get the stain out first. Someone spent a lot of money on that thing."

"I agree. A good dry cleaner can work miracles these days."

A thought was swimming around in Gigi's brain, but she couldn't quite get hold of it. The harder she thought, the more it escaped her. She tried to relax. It came to her so suddenly, she almost knocked over her tray table.

"What if," she began excitedly, "that *is* blood on the stole, and it *does* belong to Barbara."

Mertz frowned. "If that's true, why didn't she take it home and dispose of it somewhere safe? Why bring it back to the scene of the crime after the fact?"

"She didn't," Gigi said triumphantly. "Someone else did. Barbara told me her wrap went missing the night of the party. I just saw her again, and she asked me if Declan had possibly found it."

"And?" Mertz prompted, his attention completely focused on Gigi now.

"What if her wrap wasn't lost? Someone actually took it—easy enough to do in the midst of the party. And they used it to cover their own clothes while they . . . they . . . murdered Bradley with the ice pick."

"Go on. I can tell there's more." Mertz's eyes had a twinkle in them.

"They took the wrap home with them thinking to destroy it. Throw it on the fire perhaps." She nodded toward the blaze that was quickly diminishing in her fireplace. "But then they had an even better idea. The bloodstained shawl was the perfect bit of evidence to incriminate Barbara Simpson. Who's always the first to be suspected in a murder case? The spouse, right?"

Mertz nodded.

"So they decided they wanted the wrap found, not destroyed. Eventually someone was bound to see it hanging from that fence and go to the police with it."

# Chapter 10

Gigi had barely gotten out of bed when the phone rang. She stared at it for a second, debating whether to answer. Whoever it was, she'd rather talk to them after she'd made her coffee. She snatched the receiver just as the phone rang for the fourth time. She'd never been good at letting a ringing phone go unanswered.

The caller was Barbara Simpson. She was hoping to start Gigi's diet plan that evening. Would that be possible? Gigi assured her it would. She'd need to make a stop at Bon Appétit for some ingredients but that was easily done. Besides, she wanted to see how Evelyn was coming with her renovations.

Gigi dressed quickly, poured her coffee into a travel mug and grabbed her coat and scarf from the closet. Reg sat right by the door, as if daring her to leave without him.

"Don't worry, buddy, you're going, too."

Reg wagged his tail so hard that his entire body squirmed with delight. He paced back and forth as he waited for Gigi to button her jacket and wind her scarf around her neck.

With Reg tucked safely into the passenger seat, Gigi backed down her drive and turned left. She was meeting with Barbara to discuss her meal plan and have her fill out some necessary papers. Barbara had given her directions to Arbor Ridge, the community where she lived, along with the code that would allow her entry through the ornate wrought-iron gates that protected the privacy of the inhabitants of the secluded estates.

Gigi pulled up to the gatehouse and carefully punched in the numbers. Nothing happened. Had she written them down wrong? She tried again. This time the massive gates parted, and she drove through quickly. Houses were set far back on either side of the road—Georgians, Southern Colonials, Victorians and a few modern-looking glass-and-wood structures. All were enormous and had more than an acre of land surrounding them. The street was completely quiet and not a thing was out of place—even the snow alongside the road was still pristinely white.

Gigi glanced at the piece of paper on the seat next to Reg. It seemed that the houses not only had numbers, they had names. Barbara Simpson's was The Laurels at number four Arbor Lane.

It came into view, and Gigi almost slammed on the brakes, she was so awed. The Laurels looked to be the size of the White House and was built in a similar style, with a conservatory on one side and a huge screened-in porch on the other. The driveway was brick and the front door was shiny black with a highly polished brass kick plate that echoed the pineapple-shaped brass door knocker.

Gigi assured Reg that she would be back shortly and headed toward the entrance to The Laurels. She expected a maid in uniform to come to the door, but Barbara Simpson opened it herself. She was wearing a black velour warm-up suit and a pair of large, dark sunglasses that she pushed to the top of her head when she saw it was Gigi. Her blue eyes were puffy and red-rimmed.

"Sorry," she said, as she pulled the door open wider. "I can't stop crying. It's been terrible." She sniffed and fished a tissue out of the sleeve of her zip-up jacket. "It's bad enough Bradley being gone." She paused and dabbed at her eyes. "I know what everyone thinks. And they're right. He was difficult to live with—demanding and stubborn. But he had a sweet, gentle side that people rarely saw."

Gigi tried and failed to picture Bradley Simpson with a gentle side.

"He had to be tough in his profession. Opponents would capitalize on any sign of weakness, he always said."

Gigi nodded and followed Barbara through the enormous foyer and a football field–size formal living room to the conservatory beyond. The glassed-in room was warm, with an almost tropical feel to it, and was filled with plants in every size and shape, including a few small trees.

Weak February sun slanted through the glass, throwing a beam of light across the slate floor. A tray with tea things stood atop a wrought-iron table in the middle of the room. Gigi sat opposite Barbara and watched as Barbara poured tea into delicate china cups. Her hand shook slightly, and the spout of the teapot knocked over the fragile, paper-thin cup.

"Oh, how clumsy of me. Bradley always said I was like a bull in a china shop."

She glanced up at Gigi with a look of consternation on her face. "That makes him sound so mean, which isn't fair. We used to get such a good laugh over it." She swiped at a tear that was wriggling its way across the bridge of her nose. "I kidded him, too—telling him he was color blind because of some of the ties and shirts he would put together." She righted the cup and poured out the tea. "He used to call me 'snookums.' I called him 'bear' because he was my big teddy bear." Barbara stifled another sob and turned her head away.

"How did the two of you meet?"

"At university." Barbara handed Gigi the tea and pushed the cream and sugar toward her. "I knew right away that he was going to go places. He was an A student and the highest scorer on the lacrosse team. I couldn't believe it when he asked me out. We got married while he was in law school." She stirred two spoons of sugar into her own cup.

"Have you always lived in Woodstone?"

Barbara shook her head. "No, we spent several years living in New York City. Bradley was working for a big firm on Wall Street, cutting his teeth, so to speak, but then decided he wanted to open his own place. He and the other partners worked long, hard hours to get Simpson and West off the ground, I can tell you. Bradley earned every penny he made and then some. Of course some people were jealous." She looked at Gigi carefully. "That's always the way, isn't it? They don't see all the hard work, they just see the rewards."

Gigi couldn't help wonder if Barbara was talking in

generalities, or was there someone specific who resented Bradley's success?

Gigi retrieved some papers from her purse and handed them to Barbara along with a pen. "If we're to get started right away, I need you to fill these out. It's nothing complicated," she added as Barbara looked alarmed, "just information about any allergies and your food likes and dislikes."

Barbara bent her head over the forms and began to fill them out. "It's been a nightmare." She looked up at Gigi and pressed a tissue to her nose. "The police have been here." Her mouth set in a thin, grim line. "It seems they found my wrap. It was covered in my Bradley's blood." She let out a sob. "Sorry."

Gigi had a sip of tea and waited while Barbara composed herself.

"I thought I lost it the night of the party. It was warm in the restaurant from all the people pressed together, so I folded it over the back of my chair and forgot about it." She looked at Gigi, her eyes round with horror. "It's bad enough that someone murdered my husband, but now the police seem to think I might have had something to do with it."

Gigi drove away from Barbara Simpson's feeling sad. Reg tilted his head at her as if asking *what's wrong?* The poor woman was mourning the loss of her husband and now she had the police to deal with. Gigi wished she could do something. Mertz had listened to her theory that the murderer was trying to cast blame on Barbara, but he had been noncommittal. There had to be some way to prove Barbara's innocence.

As Gigi drove down High Street, she passed the storefront where the new gourmet shop was supposedly going to be. So far there was no sign of construction—just a large banner announcing that the place would be opening shortly. Hopefully Evelyn would finish her renovations before it did.

Bon Appétit was empty when Gigi pushed open the door. Shelves had been moved away from the walls and draped in drop cloths. A man in coveralls was wielding a long-handled paint roller and transforming the formerly white walls into the sort of dark red that Gigi associated with Provence.

"Very nice," Gigi said as she approached the counter, where Evelyn was leaning over an open copy of the *Woodstone Times*.

"You like it?" Evelyn closed the paper, folded it and slid it under the counter.

"Very much." Gigi looked around. The rich, warm color was going to transform the shop.

"I've ordered some wreaths to hang on the walls—one is made from bay leaves and the other from dried chilies. I'm going for a sort of South of France feel."

They both watched as the painter dipped his roller in the paint tray and swiped a broad swath of red across the wall.

"I think it's just what the shop needed," Gigi said.

Evelyn sighed. "I don't know why I waited so long to redecorate. Complacency, I guess. I've been the only game in town for so long, I never expected competition to pop up on my own doorstep."

Gigi patted Evelyn's arm reassuringly. "With your new look and plan, you'll be attracting even more customers than usual."

"I hope so." Evelyn leaned her elbows on the counter. "What can I get for you?"

"I need another box of Arborio rice. I'm almost out, and I've picked up another client."

"Oh?"

Gigi nodded. "Barbara Simpson. I was just out to see her and discuss the plan with her."

"Rather strange that she wants to go on a diet now . . . under the circumstances. When my friend Rose lost her husband, the pounds just dropped off. She didn't have to do a thing."

"It seems she wants to do it for Bradley. She'd promised him she was going to get back in shape, and she wants to go through with it."

"Miracle she has any appetite at all. Although there are those who eat even more when under stress. Maybe she's one of them." Evelyn scratched her head. "I do remember when they first came to town. Quite a looker, she was. About this big"—Evelyn held up her little finger—"and cute as a button." She sighed. "But age creeps up on all of us, I guess. Quite the place she's got there, isn't it?"

"Yes." Gigi thought back to her first view of The Laurels.

"One of my customers said the police have been out there talking to her. Bound to happen, I suppose. Isn't the spouse always the chief suspect?" Evelyn snorted. "Although what I've seen of Bradley Simpson, you could hardly blame her."

"Barbara said he was very different in private. At least she seemed to really love him. You can see she's devastated."

Evelyn looked unconvinced. "Anyway, didn't she go home sick the night of the party?" She put air quotes around the word *sick*. "She was probably out cold when the murder occurred." Evelyn slipped the box of rice into a bag. "Anything else?"

"No, that's it for now."

"Had someone new come in earlier. She wanted to know if I had any instant dashi." Evelyn raised her eyebrows. "I don't even know what that is."

"I believe it's a kind of Japanese stock."

"Ah. The customer was Japanese. Very pretty and a lovely accent. The funny thing was"—Evelyn punched some numbers into the cash register—"Hunter Simpson was waiting for her outside. Isn't he the one the engagement party was for?" She tore off the receipt and handed it to Gigi along with her purchase.

"Hunter Simpson?" Gigi said in disbelief.

Evelyn nodded. "I'm not saying they were a couple or anything, don't get me wrong. But it did make me curious."

# Chapter 11

"Stacy still hasn't said anything," Alice said later that afternoon when Gigi dropped by the Book Nook between her deliveries. "Maybe it really was just a stomach bug."

Alice had stopped by to pick up some bedtime reading. She sat on the sofa in the coffee corner with a pile of dog-eared paperbacks in her lap.

Sienna juggled Camille in one hand and the handful of books she was trying to shelve in the other. "Most people wait till they're three months along. If she is pregnant, that's probably what she and Joe are doing."

"I hope you're right. I'd so love a little grandchild to fuss over." Alice glanced at Sienna. "Here, let me have the baby while you do that," she said, holding out her arms.

Sienna handed Camille over carefully, watching to see if she would cry. She didn't—just blew a large bubble and rubbed her cheek against Alice's sweater. Alice patted the top of Camille's head, a dreamy look on her face.

"Has there been any news about . . . you know." Sienna stopped as if she didn't want to say the words in front of the baby. She cocked her head in the vague direction of Declan's.

Gigi explained about finding Barbara's bloodstained wrap.

Sienna spun around. "Really? That seems quite conclusive. Have the police arrested her?"

"No. The wrap appeared after the murder. Mertz is positive the people searching the scene wouldn't have missed it. Personally, I think the real murderer is trying to frame Barbara."

"But are there any other suspects?" Sienna shoehorned a book into place on the shelf.

"The son, right?" Alice had stood up and was jiggling Camille on her hip. "Didn't you say he took off the night of the party?"

"Yes, and Evelyn from Bon Appétit said she saw him around town with some Japanese girl she didn't recognize. Although she couldn't say for sure they were a couple. And I don't know how that would relate to his father's murder."

"Phew." Sienna blew a lock of golden hair off her face. "Think we've got enough suspects?"

"There's more." Gigi helped herself to a cup of coffee. "Barbara Simpson's sister-in-law works at the studio where I went to record my radio commercial for Branston Foods. She all but admitted to having a motive for murder, too." Gigi was quiet for a moment. "Of course the police may have uncovered things I know nothing about."

Alice gave her a wicked smile. "Time for some pillow talk with Detective Mertz, perhaps?"


Gigi's face burned as she left the Book Nook. Did everyone think she and Mertz . . . ? She hit the gas pedal a little too hard, and the MINI lurched forward.

Well, there were some things she'd like to worm out of Mertz. Like whether or not he viewed Barbara as a serious suspect. She hoped not. The woman had endured enough already, and Gigi was convinced she was innocent. She just had to find a way to prove it.

The answer came to her as she was sitting at the light in front of the Silver Lining, a tony jewelry store that carried one-of-a-kind pieces that only the wealthier residents of Woodstone could afford. There was a white-bordered, navy blue sign in the window with *Protected by The Guardian* written in gold letters. Gigi remembered there had been one like it on a post alongside Barbara's driveway and another smaller one in her front window. A lot of the larger homes and estates sported similar signs.

Gigi had seen their commercials on television and had a vague idea of how their system worked. You turned the alarm on when you left the house, and when you returned, you had to enter a code to turn it off again. With all the computerization these days, perhaps the company would have a record of when Barbara returned home from the party?

Gigi chewed on a cuticle as she waited for the light to change. It had started to snow, and she flicked on her windshield wipers. The Guardian was unlikely to reveal any information to her. She would have to tell Mertz about it and persuade him to do the investigating.

Gigi turned around in a driveway just beyond the last shop on High Street and headed back toward the police station. The same woman was seated behind the desk when Gigi entered the building. The cold draft that followed Gigi sent a swirl of snow skittering across the smudged tile floor.

The woman gave her the same look as she had the last time Gigi was there. She dialed the phone, and they both waited for Mertz to pick up. Eventually, the woman replaced the receiver and leaned her mouth close to the microphone, jerking her head toward the door. "You know where to go."

Alice's words *pillow talk* rang in Gigi's ears as she walked down the corridor, and she knew her face was red as she entered Mertz's office.

He was working at his computer, sitting ramrod straight in his chair, notebook precisely aligned at his elbow. Gigi couldn't help but smile. If Mertz couldn't control the world, he was at least going to control his immediate vicinity.

He jumped up when he saw Gigi, and a smile spread across his face. "What a nice surprise."

"Yes," was all Gigi could think to say.

"I was going to call you." Mertz perched on the edge of his desk.

"Oh." When had she become so monosyllabic? Gigi wondered.

"I just read about this new restaurant that's opened not far from here." He grabbed a newspaper off his desk and scanned the page. "The Heritage Inn. And with Valentine's Day coming up . . ."

Gigi smiled. "I'd love to."

"Great." Mertz looked relieved. He carefully placed the newspaper back on the stack from which he'd retrieved it. "I understand they're known for their"—he grabbed the newspaper and scanned the column again—"innovative cuisine. Meaning you'll probably know what the dishes are, but you'll have to translate for me."

Gigi felt a warm glow. She knew that Mertz was more than content with the open-faced turkey sandwich they prepared at the Woodstone Diner, but he'd chosen this place because he thought she would like it.

"What brings you—"

"I stopped by because—"

They both laughed.

"You go first," Mertz said.

"Okay." Gigi took a deep breath. "I had an idea as to how we . . . I mean you . . . might prove that Barbara Simpson is innocent in Bradley's murder."

A bemused look settled on Mertz's face. Gigi knew what he was thinking. She should stick to cooking, and he'd do the detecting. She tried to keep her Irish temper under control. Hopefully the information she was about to impart would wipe the smug look off his face.

"You know that company the Guardian?"

"Certainly."

"The Simpsons have the system installed at their house. Surely their records will indicate what time Barbara turned the alarm off the night of Bradley's murder."

Mertz's brows rose as if pulled by a single string.

*Gotcha!* Gigi thought. She allowed herself to gloat for a moment.

"What's to stop her from going out again and just not setting the alarm?"

"It's possible, definitely, but not probable. Barbara went home sick from the party." Like Evelyn, Gigi put air quotes around the word *sick*.

"What does this"—Mertz copied her air quotes—"mean?"

Gigi stared at the carpet. "People are saying she was actually drunk. Everyone says she's been to rehab, but that she's been drinking again. I saw her the night of the party, and she was . . . unstable . . . to say the least. I can't swear she'd been drinking, but either way, my guess is she went home and collapsed into bed."

"I must say, that is some pretty good detective work."

Now he was patronizing her. Gigi felt a rush of irritation. "Are you going to check with the Guardian?" she said with more of an edge than she meant.

"Possibly."

"But don't you think—"

Mertz held up a hand. "I agree that it's a clever idea. It's just that some new evidence has come to light." He stared at his hands for a moment. "Have you heard of someone named Tiffany Morse? She's an associate at Simpson and West."

"Yes. According to Madeline, she's going to be the first female partner the firm has ever had."

Mertz nodded. "According to my sources, she was having an affair with Bradley Simpson."

"I know." Gigi crossed her arms over her chest and tried not to look too smug.

"But unbeknownst to Bradley, she was also seeing Declan McQuaid, the owner of Declan's Grille."

*I know who he is,* Gigi thought, clenching her fists at her sides.

"And?"

"And Bradley and Declan were heard arguing heatedly the night of the party."

"He said it was over the bill—the gratuity for the waitresses." Gigi's mouth had suddenly gone dry, and the words seemed to stick to her tongue.

Mertz gave her a sad look. "Much more likely it was because of Tiffany Morse. When the two men found out she was seeing both of them, they argued. Things got ugly and Declan stabbed Bradley with the ice pick."

# Chapter 12

Gigi barely remembered leaving the Woodstone Police Station. She knew she said good-bye to Mertz and even discussed their plans for Valentine's Day, but her mouth felt paralyzed, and there was a strange rushing sound in her ears. She didn't think Mertz had noticed anything awry. She hoped not. Although he did keep looking at her with an expression that combined wariness and concern.

Tiffany and Declan. The words rang in her ears as she walked to her car, her coat pulled closed against the icy February wind. As soon as she slid into the driver's seat of the MINI Reg jumped into her lap and began to lick her face, as if he sensed her distress.

What was she going to tell Pia? Or, more accurately, how was she going to persuade Pia to turn her affections elsewhere and move on to someone else? When Pia fell, she fell hard. And by all accounts, she'd fallen hard for Declan. They hadn't done more than have a few cozy chats together, but Gigi knew that to Pia, that was tantamount to declaring undying love. She remembered the first time her mother had taken the two of them swimming. Gigi couldn't remember where the pool was—probably at a friend's house. Pia had never been in the water before, but had jumped straight into the deep end with no hesitation. She was the same way when it came to romance.

Gigi thought about what Mertz had told her. She still didn't believe Declan had murdered Bradley. He might not have been telling Gigi the truth about their argument the night of the party, but she was certain he'd been telling the truth when he'd insisted he had had nothing to do with Bradley's death.

Gigi drove home slowly, her brain whirling furiously. She had to do something—bring Mertz some new evidence, a new fact—anything that would move the case in another direction.

"What are we going to do?" she said to Reg as she opened the front door. She stuck her hands in her coat pockets to retrieve the gloves she'd stuffed in them—she'd been too stunned to remember to wear them on the ride home. She pulled them out and put them on the top shelf of the hall closet. She was shutting the door when she noticed something on the floor wink in the light from the foyer.

Gigi bent down to see what it was. It was a tiny silver object—she was able to pick it up on the tip of her middle finger. She held it to the light. It was a sequin. Where on earth had that come from?

Then she remembered the night of Bradley's murder. She was crossing the parking lot when she saw something glinting in the splash of light from the lamp. A sequin. She'd mindlessly put it in her pocket and forgotten about it. It had stayed there until now when she pulled her glove out, bringing the sequin along with it.

The sequin had obviously come from a woman's garment. She remembered Tiffany Morse's dress the night of the party—short, tight and black with a row of sequins adorning the plunging neckline. Had Tiffany stolen Barbara's wrap, used it to cover her own dress and attacked Bradley with the ice pick?

Gigi felt stirrings of excitement. Maybe she was onto something. But why would Tiffany murder Bradley? He was her mentor and had nominated her for partner at Simpson and West. She had no reason to hate him. Unless there was something Gigi didn't know about? She would have to find out. Madeline might have some information, or maybe even Gigi's other client Penelope Lawson. Her husband worked at Simpson and West and must know Tiffany Morse as well.

Gigi would get her Gourmet De-Lite meals ready and she'd be sure to stop at Penelope's last so they would have time to chat. The woman had often tried to engage Gigi in conversation before, but Gigi had always been in a hurry to finish her deliveries. This time she would linger and find out what Penelope had to say.

Gigi passed the site of the new gourmet shop again as she drove through downtown Woodstone, but there was still no discernible activity. She could see Madison and her bright pink-streaked hair through the window of the Book Nook, and the clerk who had helped her pick out picture hooks was standing in front of Gibson's Hardware clearing some snow away from the front door. Gigi averted her head as she passed Declan's Grille. She didn't want to think about Declan right now.

She finished her deliveries in record time, cutting off anyone who wanted her to linger and chat, and was ringing the bell of Penelope Lawson's oversize center hall Colonial ahead of schedule.

Penelope opened the door and smiled when she saw Gigi. She shifted Hughie to her other hip and held her hand out for her Gourmet De-Lite container. Gigi hesitated on the doorstep. Normally Penelope tried to lure her into the foyer at least. Had Gigi made it too plain that she didn't have time for conversation?

Luckily, Penelope switched Hughie—his parents were convinced he was going to be a linebacker someday—back to her right side and motioned toward the entranceway. "Want to come in a minute? That wind has picked up something fierce, and I have a pot of tea brewing."

"Sure." Gigi stepped inside.

Penelope looked surprised. Normally Gigi was in too much of a hurry to stop and chat. She led the way down the center hall toward the kitchen at the back of the house.

The kitchen was huge, with a granite center island opening to a family room with an L-shaped slip-covered sofa that Gigi recognized from the cover of the Pottery Barn catalogue. A brick gas fireplace dominated one wall and a large, flat-screen television hung above it. The carpet was strewn with children's toys although the children were not in sight.

Penelope must have noticed Gigi's glance. "The au pair is giving Mason and Ava their baths so they'll be ready for bed when George gets home, and we can have a quiet moment together." She deposited the enormous Hughie in a combination bouncy seat/play station that was pulled close to the kitchen table. She put the Gourmet De-Lite container on the counter. "George is bringing home take-out for himself. Normally, I'd be tempted by what he chooses, but your food is so good that I don't even mind being on a diet." She smiled at Gigi.

Gigi smiled back.

Penelope got out two mugs and plopped a tea bag in each. "Earl Grey okay with you?"

"Sure."

Gigi glanced at Hughie, who was happily bouncing in his seat and pushing a button that made "Farmer in the Dell" play over and over again. She didn't know how Penelope could stand it, but she seemed oblivious to the racket.

Penelope poured boiling water into their mugs and replaced the kettle on the very expensive Viking stove that dominated one wall and that, based on various things Penelope had said, was rarely used for doing much more than heating water. She plunked a bowl of sugar and a pitcher of milk on the table and slid into the seat opposite Gigi.

"I was so sorry to have missed Bradley Simpson's party," she said, idly dunking her tea bag into her mug of hot water. "We found some spots on Mason's stomach, and George was afraid he was coming down with chicken pox. He had the vaccine, of course, but apparently it's not foolproof." She took a sip of her tea. "Of course, it didn't really matter since I didn't have a thing to wear. Nothing fits yet, although I'm getting there." She smiled reassuringly at Gigi. "Having a baby really does wreak havoc on your figure. I've told George, no more. He's made an appointment at the doctor's for a . . . you know." She hid her face in her mug of tea.

Gigi nodded reassuringly.

"Anyway," Penelope continued on, much like a locomotive after a brief stop at a railroad crossing, "I was sorry to miss the party. Although not what happened afterward." She gave an exaggerated shiver. "I haven't seen much of anything in the papers lately. Do they know what happened? Who did it?"

"No, we don't know anything yet. The police are still investigating."

Penelope leaned forward and wiped a blob of drool from Hughie's chin with her napkin.

"I assume that Tiffany Morse was at the party?"

"Yes," Gigi managed to slip the word in before Penelope was off and running again.

Penelope made a face. "I can't stand that woman. She made a big play for George at one point. Of course I was out to here with Ava." She indicated the distance with her arms in front of her stomach. "I felt unattractive enough as it was. It was the firm's big Christmas party and Tiffany was dressed in something all slinky red and cut to here." Penelope pointed to a spot on her chest. "I could barely squeeze into this heinous black velvet tent I'd found in the maternity department. Besides, my feet were so swollen I had to wear a pair of flip-flops even though it was the dead of winter! Of course George had just bought me this divine diamond and pearl necklace to wear, so that kind of helped." Penelope paused momentarily to sip her tea. "She only went after George because it was his turn."

"What?"

Hughie let out a cry, and Penelope put her foot on his bouncy chair, setting it in motion and aborting the full wail that he was clearly contemplating.

"Tiffany made her way through all the men in the firm.

She wanted to become the first female partner of Simpson and West."

"I've heard that," Gigi said as Penelope took a breath.

"They've only recently begun hiring women associates. Old man West is a misogynistic so-and-so, and he held out as long as possible. But Tiffany was determined to crack the glass ceiling, even if it meant seducing every man in the firm. Probably even old man West." Penelope laughed. "That desiccated old fossil."

"I understand that she and Bradley . . ."

"Yes." Penelope nodded. "Bradley fell for her act. Everyone knew, George said. They'd come back from a three-hour lunch, and Tiffany always made sure her hair was just that little bit mussed up and her clothes a teensy bit rumpled so everyone would know." Penelope snorted. "All that work, and it didn't do her a bit of good."

Gigi sat up straighter. "Why? What do you mean, it didn't do her any good?"

"She didn't make partner. Bradley told her right before his big party. George said they had a terrific fight about it. Everyone in the office could hear them. She even threatened to kill Bradley, George said."

Gigi was so excited by the news from Penelope that she had to concentrate extra hard on her drive home. Her hands shook on the wheel, and more than once, she found herself inching a little too close to the curb. So Tiffany wasn't making partner after all. She'd put her whole life into gaining that position—including romancing Bradley Simpson and, if Penelope were to be believed, every man in power at

Simpson and West short of old man West himself. She must have been absolutely furious when she found out. Gigi thought back to the day she'd delivered Madeline's lunch and Tiffany had come stomping through the lobby. Had that been when Bradley told her?

And her big show at the engagement party, flirting with all the young men while Bradley was forced to look on. Payback time?

But it hadn't been enough. She wanted real revenge for not getting what she wanted. She could have stolen the ice pick as easily as anyone and then waited until Bradley stepped outside. Barbara had already gone home. Tiffany knew he would be alone, and the other guests would have all departed. It was the perfect setup.

The sequin Gigi found in the parking lot must have come from Tiffany's outfit. She would have to take it to Mertz tomorrow. He would be able to obtain a warrant, or whatever was necessary, to pick up Tiffany's dress and see if it matched. Gigi's car slid slightly on the ice, and she forced her attention back to the road and her driving. She was relieved to pull into her own driveway, but her heart sank when she saw Pia's VW van pulled up to the garage. She had forgotten all about her.

How was she going to break it to her that Declan was seeing someone else?

Gigi sighed and pushed open the back door. She closed her eyes in dismay. Wet, slushy footprints led from the mud-room to the kitchen table, the sink was piled with dishes and crumbs were scattered across the counter. Gigi felt her fists clench. She was going to have to have a word with Pia soon. Either Pia got her own place, or she learned to keep Gigi's the way Gigi wanted it.

Pia's coat was draped over a kitchen chair, and her scarf trailed off the end of one of the stools that surrounded the island. Had Pia gone to bed early? Gigi noticed the lights were on in the living room. Most likely Pia was in there.

Gigi's sister was in front of the fireplace, poking at some embers that were giving off more smoke than fire. She whirled around when she heard Gigi.

"Hey. I'm just getting a fire going. It was awfully cold in here."

Gigi bit her lip. "Yes, I can see that. Did you open the damper?"

Pia gave her a questioning look.

Gigi reached into the fireplace and pushed the damper open. "That opens up the chimney to let the smoke out. And when it's closed, it keeps cold air from coming into the room."

"No wonder it got so smoky in here." Pia waved her hand in front of her face.

She had a mug of cocoa on the coffee table. Gigi unobtrusively slid a coaster under it.

Pia looked at her sister. "You know, I think you work too hard. You need to take it easy and enjoy life more."

Gigi snorted. "I'd love to, but there's this little thing called money."

Pia curled up on the sofa, her legs crossed in the lotus position. She was wearing black leggings and a red-and-white-striped sweater. "Didn't you make a bundle selling your stuff to that outfit? What's its name?"

"Branston Foods? No, I didn't make a bundle unfortunately. Enough though, and I'm really grateful. It allowed me to buy my cottage, but there's nothing left over, so I need to keep working."

Pia made a sad face. "At least you need to get out more. Doesn't your cop boyfriend ever take you anywhere?"

"He's taking me out for Valentine's Day."

"Good." Pia picked up her mug and stirred the contents with her index finger. "I wonder if Declan will ask me out for Valentine's Day."

"Has he asked you out at all?" Gigi poked at the ashes in the fireplace.

"Not really. But we've had some lovely times at his restaurant. He likes me to keep him company while he works behind the bar."

Didn't Pia see that that meant nothing? Gigi had kept Declan company on more than one occasion herself.

Gigi sat on the edge of the sofa and put a hand on her sister's arm. "Pia, I have something to tell you. I'm afraid, it's probably not the sort of thing you want to hear."

Pia jerked as if scalded. "What? Has something happened? Is something wrong? You want me to leave, don't you?"

Gigi was already shaking her head. "No, no, it's nothing like that. Honest." She held up her hand as if taking an oath. She bit her lip and looked down at her lap. "I don't know how to tell you this, but Declan—"

"What about Declan?" Pia jumped to her feet.

"Declan is, well, Declan has . . . I don't know any other way to say it. Declan is seeing someone."

"That's not true." Pia paced back and forth in front of the fireplace, her fists clenched at her sides. "He's going to ask me out. I know it." She was silent for a moment, then whirled on Gigi. "Who is it?"

Gigi sighed. "Tiffany Morse. She's an attorney at Simpson and West."

"Is she attractive?"

"Very." *If you liked the type,* Gigi thought.

"It's not true," Pia spat. "You're just making it up because you fancy him yourself."

She stomped from the room. Gigi followed her into the kitchen, where Pia grabbed her scarf from the stool and began winding it around her neck. She pulled on her jacket, and her arm got caught in the sleeve. Gigi could see the tears springing into her eyes.

"Pia, I'm really sorry. But you'll meet someone else. It's not as if you've been dating Declan or anything." She grabbed Pia's hand.

"You just don't understand." Pia yanked her arm away and pulled open the kitchen door. A wintry blast swirled through the room, and Gigi shivered.

"It's late. Where are you going?"

"I don't know." And Pia slammed the door shut behind her.

Gigi slumped at the kitchen counter. That hadn't gone well at all. Pia had always had hair-trigger reactions to things, ever since she was a baby. Gigi suspected she could use a few sessions with a good therapist, but that was unlikely to happen.

Gigi went back to the living room and curled up on the couch, Reg snuggled at her feet. The fire had gone out completely, and the room was chilly. Gigi pulled up the woven throw she kept over the arm of the sofa and didn't fight it when her eyes began to close.

# Chapter 13

"A sequin?" Mertz tucked into his Denver omelet and forked up a huge bite.

Gigi had gone to the Woodstone Police Station the next morning with her find as soon as she'd delivered her Gourmet De-Lite containers. The same woman had been at the reception desk, and she'd given Gigi the same knowing look when she asked for Detective Mertz. Mertz, however, was not in his office but instead catching a late breakfast at the Woodstone Diner.

Gigi watched in amazement. How could he eat such calorie-laden dishes and not gain weight? She pulled the tissue from her purse, opened it and placed it between her and Mertz. The silver sequin glinted in the overhead light.

"I found it the night of the murder."

"You took this sequin from the murder scene?" Mertz scowled at her over a forkful of hash browns.

"I didn't know there'd been a murder. Yet," Gigi said defensively. "I was leaving Declan's." She felt her face become suffused with color as she remembered how late it had been. Hopefully Mertz had forgotten. "I was walking toward my car when I saw something sparkle in the light from the lamp. I picked it up and saw it was a sequin." She gestured toward the silvery decoration. "I put it in my pocket and forgot about it. It was only when I was pulling out my gloves that I found it again."

"Unfortunately, I doubt it means much of anything," Mertz said around a mouthful of bacon. "Who knows how many people walked through that parking lot that night . . . and other nights. It could have fallen there at any time." He gestured at the sequin. "Women seem to like these things."

"But it could indicate that the murderer was a woman. Tiffany Morse perhaps."

"Tiffany Morse and Bradley were lovers. Why would she kill him?"

"Perhaps because Tiffany Morse wanted to become a partner at Simpson and West, and she thought Bradley would be able to secure the position for her. She was only seeing him to get what she wanted."

"All the more reason not to kill him, it would seem to me." Mertz poured a stream of sugar into his coffee and stirred.

"Yes, but Bradley was unsuccessful in getting her the partnership. West wasn't having it, and Bradley was forced to go along. Tiffany was furious."

Gigi was gratified to see that Mertz was now sitting at attention. "Really?" He stopped with his coffee cup halfway to his mouth.

Gigi nodded. "They argued violently right before the

party, when Bradley gave her the bad news. She'd been expecting to learn that her dream had come true when it was the exact opposite. She'd wasted all that time and energy at Simpson and West, and it was now obvious that she would never achieve her goal."

"I don't suppose you've managed to find out whether or not she has an alibi?" Mertz asked with a smile.

Gigi made a face at him. "No, I haven't. That's your job, I'm afraid."

"Nice to know you do recognize that I have a job to do."

Gigi made another face, and he laughed.

Mertz put down his cup and put his hand over Gigi's. "Seriously. You're not just trying to take the focus off of Declan?"

Gigi jumped. "No. Not at all."

"I need to know." Mertz's tone was serious. "I really care about you, Gigi." He squeezed her hand. "If you prefer this other guy, I need to know."

"No," Gigi said again. "No, I don't." She was doing it for Pia, but decided not to tell Mertz that. She didn't want it coloring his judgment.

Mertz's face split into a huge grin, and he quickly ducked his head. "I never thought I'd meet someone like you," he said, more to his eggs and bacon than to Gigi. "You're beautiful and smart, and . . . and . . . easy to be with. You know what I mean?" He risked a glance at Gigi's face. "You're not demanding or fussy or . . ."

"High-maintenance?" Gigi suggested.

Mertz snapped his fingers. "Yes, that's it. You're not high-maintenance." He stared at his hash brown potatoes. "I dated this girl once. Everything had to be a certain way. We had to go to the most highly rated restaurant, have the best seats at the theater, order the most expensive wine. Nothing was ever enough."

Gigi made a noise to indicate she was listening.

"And I love that you make dinner for me. It's so nice spending time at your place. It feels like home."

Good heavens! Gigi thought. Was Mertz about to propose? She hoped not. She wasn't ready. It was too soon. She looked around wildly for the waitress, hoping she would stop by and refill their coffees or bring fresh water or something to derail Mertz from the track he was on.

But he just forked up another mouthful of his omelet and continued eating.

Gigi was relieved. But just a teensy, tiny bit disappointed, too.

Gigi tossed and turned all night thinking about both Bradley's murder and what Mertz had said at the restaurant. Mertz had promised to look into the origins of the sequin. She had no idea if he was going to approach Tiffany Morse or not, but she had to trust that he knew how to do his job.

She turned on her left side and pulled the covers higher. Reg, who was curled up by her knees, gave a grunt of disapproval at being disturbed. Mertz's declaration had come as a surprise to Gigi. She knew he cared for her, but it was unlike him to verbalize it. She loved being with him, but did she love him? With Ted it had been infatuation at first sight. He had charmed her from the get-go and had slowly taken control of her life until she had become convinced she was head-over-heels in love with him.

Her mother had been wary, even taking Gigi aside on her

wedding day and assuring her she didn't have to go through with it if she didn't want to. Gigi had laughed. Of course she was in love with Ted! She couldn't imagine it any other way. They'd purchased a small, spare but elegant co-op in a fashionable neighborhood on the Upper East Side. Ted was a huge fan of mid-century modern, and Gigi went along with his decorating scheme even though the cottage she was now living in was far more to her than the place she'd shared with Ted had ever been. In the time since their divorce had become final, she'd realized she'd sublimated a lot of her own wishes and desires to Ted's.

Mertz, on the other hand, didn't appear to want to change Gigi in any way—her clothes, her hair, her style of decorating—it all seemed fine to him. But was she ready to commit to another serious relationship? Gigi heaved herself onto her other side, causing Reg to give another grunt of disapproval as the movement of the bed unsettled him from his peaceful slumber. How she longed to have a conversation with her mother!

Gigi's mother had devoted her life to raising Gigi and her sister after their father died fighting a terrible fire on Boston's north side. But with the girls grown and on their own, she had reclaimed her life and fallen in love with an executive who had swapped the corporate grind for life aboard a sailboat. They'd taken off on a yearlong cruise and, as far as Gigi knew, should be rounding the Cape of Good Hope within the next few weeks. Communication was scarce, short and filled with static.

She would have to talk to Sienna instead.

As soon as she got up, Gigi peeked into Pia's room. The bed was empty, the quilt bundled on the floor in the same position it had been the last time Gigi had looked. Gigi supposed Pia was staying at her studio. Gigi would have to give her time to calm down. Pia's meltdowns could last for days, but they always came to an end. Still, Gigi was slightly worried, and thoughts of Pia weren't far from her mind.

She packed up her Gourmet De-Lite breakfasts, made her deliveries, and then turned her MINI toward the carriage house Sienna and her husband Oliver had renovated. It had been part of a larger estate, and the original house was still there, a quarter of a mile down the road—an enormous Southern Colonial–style mansion. Sienna's front door was painted a cheerful red and had a heart-shaped wreath made of twigs hanging from it.

Gigi knocked softly on the door. She didn't want to wake Camille if she had gone down for her nap.

Sienna opened the door with the baby on her hip. She looked concerned when she saw Gigi standing on her doorstep.

"Is everything okay?"

"Yes. Of course." All of a sudden, Gigi wasn't sure she wanted to talk about Mertz and their conversation yesterday. She'd probably read way too much into it anyway.

Sienna didn't think so.

"It sounds like he's serious," she said as she kneaded bread dough. Camille was sleeping peacefully in a bassinet that Sienna had rolled into the kitchen. "Like he's ready to propose." The dough snapped and crackled beneath her hands as she pushed it away from her and then pulled it back again.

Gigi grunted. "You think so?"

Sienna nodded, her breathing slightly labored from her

exertions. "What will you say? Are you ready to settle down again?"

"I'm not sure."

"I imagine after Ted, it's hard to believe in love again, but if I were you, I'd make sure Mertz didn't get away. He's a keeper."

She wasn't very good at keeping men, Gigi thought—look at Ted.

"Did I tell you about Stacy?" Sienna formed the dough into a ball, rubbed oil on it and placed it in a bowl.

"No."

"I saw her at the mall yesterday. And she was peering into the window of A Bun in the Oven."

"Really?"

"Unless it's just wishful thinking, it looks like Alice may be right, and she is pregnant."

"Have you told Alice?"

"No. I don't want to spoil the surprise if that's what Stacy is planning."

Gigi felt better after leaving Sienna's. She wouldn't worry about things or rush them or allow herself to feel rushed by them. If a relationship with Mertz was meant to be, it would unfold in its own time and at its own pace.

Gigi was headed down High Street when she noticed a group of people gathered on the sidewalk, which was quite unusual for Woodstone. Occasionally a gaggle of teenaged boys or girls might go strolling through downtown, but the sidewalks were rarely crowded. She slowed as she approached the group. They were gathered outside the police station and several of the people were carrying placards. They began to chant, but Gigi couldn't distinguish the words. She pulled into the parking lot between Gibson's and Declan's, parked the MINI, and walked back toward where the crowd was standing.

As she got closer, the voices became clearer, and one of the group, a tall fellow with a navy blue knit hat pulled down low over his forehead turned toward her, and she was able to make out the words on his sign. It read *Keep Woodstone Safe*. A youngish woman turned toward Gigi as well. She had one hand on a stroller and the other holding a sign that read *Catch the Woodstone Thief*.

*What on earth?* Gigi hurried toward the group. An older woman in a red-and-green-plaid car coat was standing on the fringes. Gigi approached her.

"Do you know what's going on?"

The woman whirled around. She had vivid blue eyes set in a nest of puckered skin. "It's about the thefts." She gestured toward one of the posters.

"Thefts?"

She nodded and fixed Gigi with a stern gaze. "The lawn ornaments. Don't know why the paper hasn't been onto it yet. But someone is going around taking people's lawn ornaments. They got my Bambi, and my neighbor Sybil's birdbath. The police aren't doing a thing about it. We want this person caught."

Gigi groaned inwardly. Poor Mertz! He was doing his best to catch the sneak thief—even giving up lunch on more than one occasion—but so far he had been unsuccessful.

A woman on the edge of the crowd sidled toward Gigi. Gigi recognized her as Janice Novak, the woman she'd seen in the Book Nook who Sienna said used to work for Simpson and West. Gigi was startled when she pulled an iPhone from her pocket. Where on earth had she gotten the money for that?

She was dressed in her usual thrift shop–type getup—a pilled and frayed red wool jacket, baggy pants with worn spots at the knees and a pair of loafers with duct tape holding the right one together. And yet she was carrying around a telephone worth hundreds of dollars. Had she dug that out of a Dumpster, too? If so, it had probably been thrown away by accident and someone was searching for it at this very moment.

Just then the chanting grew louder, and a rough-looking man in a pair of Carhartt overalls and jacket jumped up onto the steps leading to the police station. He raised his fist in the air, and slowly the crowd quieted.

"And when are the police going to find the murderer who is roaming our streets?" He pointed in the direction of the parking lot where Gigi had left her car. "A man was killed in cold blood, and what are the police doing about it? Nothing! The streets of Woodstone are no longer safe for women and children."

"Hear, hear," a number of the people assembled on the sidewalk shouted.

Soon the chant was taken up by the entire crowd. "Catch the killer, catch the killer," they cried in unison.

Gigi felt her stomach plummet. She wondered if Mertz could hear them from his office. She knew he was doing his best to solve the case, but that clearly didn't mean much to this mob.

Janice Novak had moved closer, Gigi noticed, and she was fiddling with that expensive phone again. It seemed apparent that she had no idea how to use it. Gigi hesitated, then decided to approach her.

"Nice phone. Where did you get it?" Gigi tried to keep her tone light and non-accusatory.

Janice clutched the phone to her chest. "I found it. Someone tossed it in the Dumpster behind Gibson's Hardware. No harm in that is there?" Her hair hung in greasy strands on either side of her thin face.

"No, of course not." Gigi inched closer to Janice and tried to peer over her shoulder.

Janice pushed some random buttons on the phone, and the screen saver came to life. It was a picture of a house—one that looked very much like Bradley Simpson's The Laurels.

"That's a nice picture," Gigi said, trying to keep her tone bland although her heart was hammering with excitement. If the phone was, indeed, Bradley's, maybe it would hold some sort of clue to Bradley's death. A text, a message or a call?

Janice clutched it to her more tightly and backed away. "You can't take it. It's mine. I found it fair and square."

Gigi inched closer, but Janice just took another step backward. Gigi stepped forward, and this time Janice turned her back on Gigi.

"Can I just see it?"

Janice began to walk away, her steps brisk and businesslike. She glanced over her shoulder at Gigi. Gigi hesitated, then began to follow her. She had to get a look at that phone.

Janice increased her pace, and Gigi increased hers. They covered the block between the Woodstone Police Station and the parking lot next to Gibson's in no time. Janice was amazingly spry, and it wasn't long before Gigi was panting. She vowed to start jogging, or at least taking longer walks with Reg, immediately. Janice darted glances over her shoulder, the phone still clutched tightly to her chest.

"Please. I don't want to take your phone. I just want to look at it." Gigi pleaded. Janice had broken into a slow jog, and Gigi followed suit. Passersby on the sidewalk gave them a strange look, and some even stopped in their tracks to watch as Janice, with Gigi in hot pursuit, rounded the corner.

Despite the frigid temperatures, Gigi broke into a sweat. She undid the buttons on her coat as she continued to pursue Janice. Gigi was closing the gap when she tripped on an uneven patch of sidewalk and went down on one knee. She put her hand down to save herself and winced as the rough concrete scratched her palm. But even worse, by the time she had struggled to her feet, Janice was gone. She'd disappeared.

Gigi paused to catch her breath and look around. The woman couldn't have gotten far.

They were on the backside of Woodstone's business district now. The rear doors of Abigail's and Folio faced Gigi. Had Janice ducked into one of those shops? Gigi opened the door to Abigail's and peered inside. The narrow corridor that led to the store proper was empty and stacked with empty boxes waiting to be recycled. She peeked into the shop, but there was no sign of Janice.

Gigi closed the door and opened the one that led to Folio. A young girl and her mother were looking through the wedding invitation books while the clerk hovered solicitously, but again, there was no sign of Janice. Gigi backed out of the shop and stood on the pavement scratching her head. Where had the woman gotten to?

A movement and a flash of red near the Dumpster behind the Woodstone Diner caught Gigi's eye. She headed in that direction, trying to look and act as if she had given up the pursuit. She actually strolled past the rear of the diner before abruptly turning on her heel and doubling back. She had nearly reached the Dumpster when Janice darted out the other side and took off running, the sole of her mended loafer making a slapping sound with each step.

Gigi followed, vowing again as she ran to find the time to work out more. Walks with Reg, who stopped every five seconds to take in the smells, had done little for her cardiovascular conditioning. Her breath tore at her throat and her heart hammered a steady rat-a-tat-tat with barely any time between beats.

"Is something wrong, miss?"

"What?" Gigi stopped short, startled by the sudden voice. She turned around to see a uniformed Woodstone patrolman approaching her. He was breathing heavily.

"Is something wrong?" He panted slightly.

"Oh, no." Gigi gave him what she hoped was her most reassuring smile.

"I saw you running like all the furies of hell were on your tail, and I wondered if something was wrong."

Gigi felt her face turn crimson. "No. I'm fine. Perfectly fine." She stuck her leg behind her and eased into a runner's stretch. "Just getting a little exercise is all."

The patrolman looked at her doubtfully, but tipped his hat. "If you're sure?" He turned around hesitantly.

"Oh, absolutely." Gigi gave him another big smile and sighed with relief as he walked away.

Janice was now nowhere in sight. Gigi stamped her foot in frustration. She started to walk back the way she had come, toward the parking lot by Declan's and her car. She unbuttoned her coat to the chill February air. She knew her face was red from her Olympic sprint through Woodstone.

She was just passing Gibson's when someone grabbed her arm. Gigi whirled around and found herself face-to-face with Janice Novak.

She held the iPhone up to Gigi. "Do you think someone might have thrown it away by accident, and maybe there's a reward?"

"Yes," Gigi said emphatically, wishing she had thought of that herself. "Definitely there might be a reward." Hopefully Janice wouldn't zero in on the ambiguity of that statement.

"Like money?" Janice licked her lips.

"Yes," Gigi nodded. Janice ought to see the wisdom in trading a phone she didn't know how to use for some cash.

"You really think so?" Janice picked at the frayed edge of sweater that stuck out beneath the too-short sleeve of her coat.

"I'm sure."

"How do I get it?"

"We need to contact the owner of the phone." Gigi held out her hand.

"How do we know who that is?" Janice ignored Gigi's outstretched palm.

"The person's name is probably in the phone's memory somewhere."

Janice hesitated and then reluctantly handed over the cell.

Gigi glanced at it quickly. The battery was low, and it was going to run out at any minute. She thumbed through the texts. The last one was sent late the night Bradley Simpson was murdered. It read: *Tiffany, good news, they've changed their minds. Come back to Declan's, and meet me in the parking lot.*

# Chapter 14

Gigi ended up giving Janice fifty dollars she could ill afford in order to get her to part with the iPhone. She was about to explain that it could be important evidence in a murder case when she stopped short. What if Janice was the one responsible for Bradley's death? She had every reason to hate him according to the stories Gigi had heard. Gigi had had to promise Janice she would contact the owner of the phone about a reward for its safe return. Gigi didn't tell her the owner was dead. Janice had pulled her frayed sleeves down over her hands, a doubtful look on her face. But she had skulked off, leaving Gigi in possession of the cell.

Gigi tucked the phone into her purse and walked back toward her car. The crowd was still gathered in front of the police station. She hesitated, thinking she ought to take the phone straight to Mertz, but she didn't want to brave the group that was continuing to chant outside. Besides, she wasn't sure if Mertz would be working. Policemen didn't keep to a regular schedule, and his seemed to change weekly depending on the caseload.

Gigi hoped that she would see Pia's van in the driveway when she got home, but it wasn't there. Reg greeted her with his usual enthusiasm, and she quickly clipped on his leash and took him for a stroll around the block. She was itching to check out Bradley's phone further, but she knew Reg had been waiting long enough.

The kitchen was as clean as Gigi had left it, so obviously Pia had not been by in Gigi's absence. Gigi's worry notched up a level. Had Pia decided to head to California? Her things were still in Gigi's guest room, but her possessions were so meager, perhaps she had decided to leave them behind rather than confront Gigi again?

Gigi sighed, fixed herself a cup of Earl Grey tea and sat down at the kitchen island. She pulled Bradley's iPhone from her purse and put it beside her. Based on evidence from the cell, Bradley had texted Tiffany asking her to meet him at Declan's. He had alluded to good news, but perhaps that had been a pretext? Had he been hoping to convince her to make up and keep the affair going? Had Tiffany fallen for the lie and then been disappointed? So disappointed that she had stabbed Bradley to death?

Hopefully Mertz would be able to sort it all out.

Bradley's cell phone squatted on Gigi's kitchen counter all day like an unwelcome toad. She glanced at it as she chopped, minced and sautéed her way through her next Gourmet De-Lite meal. Finally, she could no longer stand it and she picked up the telephone and dialed the Woodstone Police Station.

She wondered if the receptionist recognized her voice, but it didn't matter. Mertz wasn't in. In fact, he wouldn't be in all weekend. He had been assigned to some training course in Hartford.

Gigi sighed. She would have to wait till Monday morning to see him. She planned to be at the station bright and early.

Pia still hadn't returned by the time Gigi was ready for bed. Gigi had peeled back the curtains and looked out the kitchen window at least a dozen times hoping to see Pia's wreck of a van pulling into the driveway. Her sister was probably fine. It was completely in character for her to disappear for days without saying a word. Nonetheless, Gigi couldn't help worrying, and she went to bed with a heavy heart.

Gigi's legs felt stiff as she crawled under the covers. Her sprint through downtown Woodstone had taken its toll. She thought about doing a few stretches, but it was so warm and cozy under the comforter that she couldn't be bothered. She just hoped no one she knew had seen her desperate dash after Janice and the cell phone. What on earth would they think of her! The pedestrians on the sidewalk had gone by in a blur. She had an inkling that there had been at least one slightly familiar face among them, but she couldn't put her finger on who it was. Probably no one.

She punched her pillow and turned onto her other side. Reg grunted and moved down toward Gigi's feet. It wasn't long before they were both asleep.

Gigi woke with a pounding heart two hours later. Had she heard a noise? She glanced at Reg, who was still curled up at the foot of the bed, one ear twitching in the stream of his breath. Gigi collapsed against the pillows. If Reg wasn't responding, the sound must have been in her dreams.

She was drifting off again when Reg suddenly stirred. He lifted his head and tilted it this way and that, as if attempting to pick up a faint radio signal. Gigi sat up, too, and listened hard. Had Pia returned? She hoped so. She reached for the bathrobe at the foot of her bed and slipped into it.

Reg jumped off the bed and stood at attention, his low, deep growls soon turning to real barks.

It couldn't be Pia, Gigi realized, because Reg would definitely not be barking that way. Gigi's heart beat cranked up a notch. Was there an animal lurking outside? A coyote, a possum or a stray cat or dog?

Gigi turned on the bedside light and fished her slippers out from under the bed. The rosy glow from the lamp mocked her fears. It was probably nothing, but Reg wouldn't settle down until they'd had a good look around.

She shuffled out to the living room first. The room was dimly lit by the faint glow of the streetlight outside. Gigi could make out the silhouettes of the sofa and chairs and the small gate-leg table pushed up against the wall. The faint odor of smoke clung to the room. Gigi wished she hadn't been so hard on Pia about the fireplace damper.

The kitchen was just as she left it. Gigi peered out the back window, but there was no sign of Pia's van. She sighed in disappointment and headed back to the bedroom. Reg gave a final, disappointed growl and joined her on the bed.

Seconds later, Gigi could hear Reg's faint snore as he settled into slumber. Her eyes refused to stay shut. She switched from her right side to her left, from her front to her back, but still, sleep eluded her. Her heart had finally stopped trying to pound its way out of her chest, but every little noise made her jump.

She was finally relaxing when the unmistakable sound of breaking glass came from the kitchen. Reg immediately bolted upright and began to bark furiously, his fur standing out around his strong, stout body. He started to leap off the bed, but Gigi grabbed him by his collar.

"No, boy, don't go out there. We've got to call the police."

Gigi had left her cell on the nightstand, and she quickly punched in 9-1-1. Reg struggled to get free, but she maintained her grip on his collar, urging him to hush. His sharp barks turned to deep growls low in his throat, but he finally stopped fighting and sat down next to Gigi on the bed, his back stiff and his ears alert.

Even above the pounding of her heart, Gigi could hear someone moving about in the darkened kitchen. What on earth were they after? She had little of great value. Her few pieces of jewelry were tucked underneath her lingerie in her bureau.

Keeping her voice to a whisper, she explained the situation to the 9-1-1 operator, who promised that a patrol car was on its way.

Gigi listened hard, but there were no approaching footsteps. So far the thief seemed to be most interested in whatever was in her kitchen. Suddenly she heard the back door slam. Reg began a fresh round of barking, and this time Gigi let go of his collar. He shot off the bed and made a beeline down the hall with Gigi right behind him. She heard a car starting up and the ping of gravel as it shot out of her driveway. It was then that Gigi finally heard the faint sounds of a police siren in the distance.

A Woodstone police car screeched to a halt in Gigi's driveway. The strong beam of a flashlight flickered through the windows as a policeman made his way toward the back door. Gigi flicked on the lights and gasped. Broken glass was scattered across the kitchen floor, and she could hear the patrolman's footsteps crunching on the pieces that had fallen outside.

She was reaching for the doorknob when he thumped the back door briskly.

"Come on in." Gigi held the door wide. Reg stood at her side, eyeing the newcomer warily. Gigi turned to him. "It's okay, boy. It's a policeman."

Reg cocked his head, but stayed close to Gigi's side.

The patrolman looked around the room. He was tall and thin with bluish bags under his eyes that made him look like a bloodhound.

"You okay, ma'am?"

"I'm fine."

"Looks like you've had a break-in," he said eyeing the broken glass and the missing pane from the window in Gigi's back door. "Any idea what they were after?"

Gigi shook her head.

"Anything missing?"

Gigi was about to shake her head again when her glance fell on the counter where Bradley Simpson's cell phone should have been . . . but wasn't.

"Yes," she said, her voice trembling for the first time. "A cell phone."

She explained the situation to the policeman, who immediately called headquarters and was patched through to Detective Mertz.

The patrolman hung up. It looked as if Mertz would be missing his second day of training in Hartford because he was already on his way over to Gigi's.

The patrolman waited with Gigi until Mertz arrived. She made them both a cup of tea and then sat at the island with her hands around the warm mug. She'd turned the heat down before going to bed, and the kitchen was chilly. Reg was curled up on the rug by the door, occasionally opening one eye as if he were solely responsible for keeping things under control.

It wasn't until Mertz opened the back door and strode into the room that Gigi began to shake. She felt as if she'd suddenly been afflicted with St. Vitus' dance—her hand jerked so badly she spilled hot tea down the front of her bathrobe.

Mertz gave a brief glance to the patrolman and then took Gigi in his arms. She felt the cold on his coat and the roughness of the fabric under her fingers. He enveloped her in a strong hug, his chin tucked on top of her head. They stood like that for several seconds before the patrolman cleared his throat loudly.

"If that will be all . . ."

"Thank you, yes," Mertz said without taking his arms from around Gigi.

Slowly the shivering stopped, and she looked up at Mertz. "I'm sorry. I don't know what happened. I was fine . . ."

"It's a normal reaction." Mertz reassured her. He glanced at Gigi's abandoned cup on the counter. "Any chance of a cup of tea? It's freezing out there."

"Of course." Gigi suspected that Mertz wanted to keep her busy to get her mind off of what had just happened, and she was grateful. She brewed them each a fresh cup of Earl Grey, and they settled on the stools around the kitchen island with their mugs.

"Why don't you tell me what happened first, and then I'll have a look around. Is anything missing that you know of?"

Gigi felt her face flush red, and it wasn't from the hot tea. She explained to Mertz about Bradley's cell phone and how she had secured it from Janice Novak.

"I'm really sorry I missed that. It must have been quite a sight."

Gigi made a face at him. "I called the station, but they said you were away on a training course. I was going to bring the cell phone in first thing Monday morning."

"But now it's gone. Someone wanted it back pretty badly." Mertz glanced at the broken glass that still surrounded Gigi's back door.

Gigi nodded.

"Any idea as to why?" Mertz tried to hide a smile but wasn't entirely successful.

Gigi felt the heat in her face intensify. "I did glance at it. Just to see if there were any texts or calls that might explain what happened."

"Clues?"

Gigi glanced at Mertz, but his expression was bland.

"Yes, I guess you could call them clues."

"And did you find any?"

"Yes. Bradley texted Tiffany Morse shortly after leaving Declan's. I think it went through around 11:58 P.M."

"And what did it say?" Mertz was at attention now.

"It said to meet him in the parking lot at Declan's. He had good news for her."

Mertz whistled. "So if she did as he asked, that puts her at the scene of the murder."

"And she had a motive. Bradley had promised her a partnership, but then he snatched it away."

"But you said he alluded to good news?"

Gigi twirled her mug around and around between her hands. "I think that was meant to lure her there. He was probably hoping to convince her to continue their affair."

"But when she found out—"

"Exactly. She killed him."

Mertz shifted off the stool. "Monday I'll send someone around to collect the dress she wore the night of Bradley's murder. We'll see if that sequin matches—not that that would be conclusive—but we can also check for traces of blood."

"You probably won't find any blood. I think she stole Barbara Simpson's wrap and wore it while she killed Barbara's husband."

"You might be right, but the forensic boys can find even the minutest trace of blood." Mertz stretched and yawned. "Meanwhile, I'd better have a look around."

He pulled his coat back on, and Gigi went into the living room and curled up on the sofa, the throw pulled up to her chin. She was feeling cold again and was grateful when Reg curled up at her feet. Before she knew it, her eyes were closing.

She awoke to find that Mertz had come back inside and was kissing her forehead.

She struggled to sit up. "Did you find anything?"

He shook his head. "Your gravel driveway doesn't allow for tire marks. I found a large rock right outside your back door. I'm pretty certain the thief used it to break the window. But since they were either wearing gloves or had wrapped something around their hand to protect it, I'm certain we won't be finding any prints. Even assuming the perp's prints are on file. If it was Tiffany Morse, then I doubt she'll have a record. I can't see Simpson and West hiring her in that case."

"That's true," Gigi murmured drowsily.

"I took a couple of pieces of cardboard from your recycling bin and taped them over the hole in the window. You can call Campbell's Glass in the morning to replace the broken panes."

"Okay," Gigi said, only vaguely aware of what Mertz was talking about.

Mertz shed his coat and draped it over the chair in front of Gigi's fireplace.

"You look cold," he said, as he slipped onto the sofa beside her.


Gigi woke up late on Sunday morning barely remembering the events of the night before. She'd dreamt that she was running through the streets of Woodstone again in pursuit of Janice and the cell phone. The faces of the pedestrians had gone by in a blur, just as they had in reality, but one face stood out in her dream—Tiffany Morse. She was wearing the red coat Gigi had seen her in before with a silk scarf around her neck. Gigi sat up on bed.

"Oh!"

Reg looked at her strangely, and she put her hand on his head to reassure him.

She'd thought she'd seen a familiar face in the crowd the day she was chasing Janice, and the dream had brought it all back. It had been Tiffany Morse.

Gigi wandered into the kitchen in her bathrobe and slippers and stopped short when she saw the piece of cardboard taped over the broken glass in the window in her back door. It brought back her terror at hearing someone prowling around her kitchen, her relief at Mertz's arrival, and the warmth and coziness of the time they'd spent snuggling on her sofa.

She filled the coffeepot with water and her favorite brew and pushed the on button, leaning on the counter as she waited for the coffee to trickle into the pot. She ached all over—probably from the tension of the night before. But when she remembered Mertz taking her in his arms to still her shivering, she smiled and suddenly felt considerably better.

Reg wandered out from the bedroom, yawning broadly. He, too, was tired from their middle-of-the night escapades. He flopped down on the rug in front of the back door and promptly went back to sleep.

Gigi filled her mug, popped some bread into the toaster and sat down at the kitchen table. She thought she heard a noise similar to the sound Pia's old van made, and she braced herself for the back door to suddenly be flung open and for Pia to burst into the room. Seconds ticked by, then minutes, but there was no sign of Pia. Gigi's shoulders slumped. She was really getting worried about her sister. She'd never stayed away this long before. Surely she couldn't be sleeping in her studio. She'd said it was so cold she had to wear fingerless gloves while she worked, and the bathroom—a toilet and small sink—was down at the end of the hall. If nothing else, Pia would be craving a hot bath or shower by now.

If only Pia had given Gigi the address of her studio. Gigi thought about mentioning it to Mertz—perhaps he would be able to locate it—but she knew that would make Pia furious. Better to just wait for her sister to come to her senses.

Gigi spent the day relaxing—napping off and on—and finishing the paperback she'd picked up at the Book Nook at Sienna's suggestion. Mertz had called to check on her, and just the thought made Gigi smile. She'd told him about seeing Tiffany in the crowd the day she'd wrested Bradley's cell phone from Janice Novak. He told her that the police would soon be paying a visit to Miss Morse.

Victor Branston called before Gigi had even finished preparing her clients' breakfasts on Monday morning. He wanted her to record another radio commercial, which they would start running immediately.

Gigi was a little less nervous this time, but she still wasn't exactly looking forward to it.

The good thing about recording for radio, she thought as she stared into the depths of her closet, was that it didn't matter what you looked like. That was fortunate since she needed to do laundry, and her wardrobe these days mainly consisted of jeans and various tops—short-sleeved in summer, long-sleeved in winter. She'd given away many of the clothes she'd worn in her New York City life to make room in her tiny closet.

Gigi grabbed the pair of jeans she'd taken off last night and left on the bathroom floor and added a dark green wool turtleneck she'd ordered from a catalogue sale. It set off the red tones in her hair and the green of her eyes. And made up for the fact that her jeans probably smelled like last night's dinner.

"Sorry, bud, but you'll have to stay home this time," she said to a disconsolate Reg. She'd given him an extra-long walk to make up for her desertion—allowing him plenty of time to sniff the bases of the trees and climb the snowbanks—but he didn't seem impressed.

Gigi hopped in the MINI, made her deliveries and then headed toward Keith's Recording Studio. A dark blue late-model sedan was already parked under the dented metal sign that read *For Keith's customers only. All others will be towed*. It looked as if Alec Pricely had already arrived.

Cheryl was behind the reception desk when Gigi entered the studio. She was wearing a skirt that was way too short for someone her age, and the slim-fitting shirt she'd tucked into the waistband emphasized her sagging midriff. She had the telephone clamped between her shoulder and her ear and was chewing the cuticle on her thumbnail energetically.

Gigi hovered at the desk for a second, but she needed to use the restroom so she pointed wordlessly in that direction. Cheryl nodded but didn't suspend her animated conversation.

Gigi exited the bathroom stall and washed her hands. The paper towel dispenser was empty so she rubbed her wet palms up and down her jeans. When she pushed open the swinging door from the ladies' room, Cheryl was still on the phone. Her words brought Gigi up short.

"I don't know how we're going to pay it back," she said to the person on the other end of the line.

Gigi backed up until she was leaning against the door to

the ladies' room. Hopefully Cheryl couldn't see her from the reception desk.

"We're up to our eyeballs in debt as it is," Cheryl continued her conversation. "We got a shut-off notice from the electric company last week, and it was all I could do to scrape together enough to satisfy them. Jimmy just doesn't understand. He's always so optimistic. Something good will happen soon, he always says."

Cheryl listened for a moment, then shook her head vigorously.

"It didn't do us any good," she said into the telephone. She listened some more. "I know what I told you, but I was wrong. Barbara expects us to pay the money back anyway."

Cheryl swiveled her chair around and Gigi pressed herself as far into the recess of the ladies' room door as she could. She looked up and down the corridor, but all the doors were closed, and there was no one to see her skulking out of sight. Cheryl swiveled her chair back toward her desk, and Gigi leaned forward slightly, straining to hear the rest of Cheryl's conversation.

"I know! I mean after all Jimmy went through, risking everything like that . . ." Cheryl's voice trailed off.

Gigi stood rooted to the spot. Was Cheryl hinting that Jimmy had . . . ? Her mind refused to complete the thought. Before she could hear any more, Pricely stuck his head out of the recording area, and beckoned Gigi to enter.

Gigi fumbled her way through another recording. Her mind was reeling after overhearing Cheryl's telephone conversation. She could tell Pricely was getting impatient with her, but she couldn't help it. Cheryl's one-sided conversation kept running through her mind, and she would blurt out the wrong words even though the ones she was supposed to record were clearly written on the piece of paper in front of her. She spent a brief moment thanking the heavens that she had remembered to put on deodorant that morning because her armpits were becoming sticky with perspiration.

Finally Pricely stuck his head in the recording room and told her it was a wrap. Gigi grabbed her coat and scarf and practically ran for the front door. Cheryl looked startled as Gigi bolted past the reception desk in her haste to leave.

She beeped open the MINI and sat for a minute in the driver's seat, her head resting on the steering wheel. She was utterly confused. The murderer had to be Tiffany Morse. She must have misunderstood Cheryl's conversation. She'd only heard the one side so it was a distinct possibility. All the evidence pointed to Tiffany. What reason would Cheryl have for breaking into Gigi's cottage and stealing Bradley's cell phone? Gigi had barely scanned the call log, so struck had she been by Bradley's text summoning Tiffany back to Declan's the night of the murder. Was there some other damning voice mail or text that she'd missed? One that pointed to Cheryl's husband as the murderer? She debated phoning Mertz and telling him what she'd heard but decided against it. She had no real evidence—just a one-sided conversation that might have been about something else altogether.

# Chapter 15

Gigi's head was spinning as she put the car in gear and slowly drove out of the parking lot of the recording studio. There were too many people who might have wished Bradley Simpson dead—Declan, if the reports were true about him and Tiffany. Barbara Simpson was the typical neglected wife, and Tiffany was the mistress who wasn't going to get what she was after—not marriage in this case, but a partnership in Bradley's law firm. And then there was Janice, whose reputation had been tainted forever by her dismissal from Simpson and West. Gigi was convinced that neither Declan nor Barbara Simpson was guilty. But that still left Tiffany and Janice. Personally, she was putting her money on Tiffany. She had struck Gigi as a cold, unfeeling woman who would do anything to get what she wanted.

Gigi couldn't wait to get home. She caught the red light at the corner of High Street and Elmwood and sat staring out the window waiting for it to change. The house across from her had a metal sculpture of a frog playing the violin on its front lawn. Gigi had briefly taken up the violin in sixth grade, but had quickly learned she had little musical talent. Fortunately the violin had been rented, and Gigi wasn't at all sad when her mother took it back to the store.

The sculpture was a whimsical piece, different from the usual sorts of lawn ornaments. Gigi turned to look at it again and it was . . . gone. She rubbed her eyes, but they weren't deceiving her. The violin-playing frog was gone. She heard the thud of someone running and caught a brief glimpse of a bright yellow jacket as a person rounded the corner.

It was the lawn ornament thief Mertz had been trying to catch! Gigi thought of the crowd protesting in front of the Woodstone Police Station. If she could catch him, the Woodstone Police would be redeemed. The light changed, and Gigi flipped on her left blinker. The car behind her honked impatiently at her sudden change of heart. Gigi ignored them, and as soon as there was a break in oncoming traffic, she turned the corner onto Elmwood.

She thought she saw a speck of yellow ahead in the distance. She squinted, but she couldn't be sure. As she got closer, it resolved itself into someone's recycling bin left at the curb for pickup. Gigi slowed to a crawl and tried to peer between the houses. The thief couldn't have gotten far. The frog ornament was fairly large and cumbersome, and running with it had to be slowing him or her down.

Gigi decided her best bet was to follow on foot. She pulled the MINI over to the curb, got out and beeped the doors locked. Fortunately she was wearing flats. She was almost always wearing flats—her heels were gathering dust in the back of her closet. She scanned the front yards of the houses along the road for any sign of movement. She thought she saw a flicker of something toward the end of the block, near an ornately painted Victorian, and took off in that direction.

Gigi jogged along, her eyes peeled for movement of any sort. A young girl came toward her with two greyhounds on leashes.

"Excuse me," Gigi said somewhat breathlessly, "did you happen to see anyone go by carrying a . . . a . . . lawn ornament?"

The girl gave Gigi a strange look, shook her head and pulled on the dog's leashes to urge them forward.

*So much for that.* Gigi debated going back to her car but perhaps she'd try one more block. She turned the corner and stopped for a moment with her hands on her knees, her chest heaving. When she'd finally caught her breath, she continued on—walking this time.

In the distance she thought she saw someone trying to squeeze through the boxwood hedge surrounding a small white Cape Cod. She imagined she could discern dark hair and something yellow—a jacket maybe. She hurried forward, but by the time she got there, the person, if it had even been a person, was gone.

Gigi returned to her car, panting slightly. The thief had certainly been fast. Faster than Gigi, at any rate. She really was going to have to check out the fees at the local fitness center. She used to jog when she lived in New York City. It was one of the things she and Ted did together—laps around Central Park followed by bagels smeared with salmon cream cheese from the deli down the street. She hadn't had to worry much about calories back then.

She beeped open the MINI and got behind the wheel. Five minutes later she was pulling into the empty driveway of her cottage. Her shoulders slumped. She had so hoped to see Pia's pathetic van parked in its usual spot behind the garage.

After an excited greeting, and a biscuit that Gigi saw him hide under the edge of the kitchen rug, Reg sought out his favorite spot—directly in the middle of the sunbeam coming through the back window. Gigi glanced at the door where Mertz had taped the piece of cardboard over the broken pane of glass. She would have to call Campbell's Glass as soon as she delivered her meals.

Gigi was chopping carrots, celery and onions—a combination the French called mirepoix and the Italians *soffritto*—as a base for soup when the telephone rang.

Maybe it was Pia?

"Hello?" Gigi said hopefully.

It wasn't Pia—it was Tiffany Morse. Gigi was so surprised she almost dropped the phone into her simmering pot of Tuscan bean soup.

Tiffany's honeyed tones came over the line, and all Gigi could imagine was the image of her standing over Bradley Simpson with Declan's ice pick.

"Madeline, here at the firm, has told me about your wonderful diet plan."

Gigi held the phone in the crook of her shoulder and added a handful of chopped, fresh parsley to the concoction on the stove. Tiffany had a splendid figure—why on earth would she need Gigi's diet plan?

"I've put on a few odd pounds"—Tiffany's melodic laugh tinkled over the phone wires—"and I'm desperate to get rid of them. I have a big event coming up, and I positively have to fit into my new Donna Karan. I'm afraid it's completely unforgiving, so this weight has got to go. Do you think your plan will work for me?"

"It should. The calories are carefully calculated. Always assuming you don't cheat." Gigi thought back to some of her clients who had complained that her diet didn't work— but then they were supplementing the food Gigi brought them with cookies, ice cream and other goodies.

Tiffany's voice took on a steel-like tone. "Don't worry. I won't cheat. I've been told I have iron willpower."

Gigi shivered. She could easily imagine that. "I can stop by your office after delivering my meals, and we can go over the paperwork, and I can explain the plan to you in detail. Would that work?"

"Perfectly, but I'm working from home today. Do you mind coming here?" She gave Gigi the address.

Gigi whistled as she hung up the phone and gave the soup another stir. Not only did she have another new client, she had the golden opportunity to talk to Tiffany. With any luck, she might let something slip that would reveal her involvement in Bradley's murder or in the theft of his cell phone from Gigi's kitchen.

Tiffany lived in a set of very exclusive condominiums designed to look like Georgian townhomes. Each was three stories and built of red brick with glossy black shutters, shiny brass hardware and multipaned bay windows. The street was lined with mature trees and old-fashioned streetlamps. It was obviously a very expensive enclave.

Gigi found Tiffany's condo easily enough. Her flame red Mustang was parked in the driveway. Gigi gathered up the file she had started on Tiffany—she created one for each client where she kept their paperwork, the contract and notes about their likes, dislikes and allergies. She sat for a moment contemplating the front of Tiffany's building. She had to play this just right. She didn't dare arouse Tiffany's suspicions by asking too many obvious questions. If Tiffany was the murderer . . . Gigi shivered. She didn't want to think about what might happen.

The walkway to Tiffany's front door was paved with cobblestones. They were slick with ice, and Gigi slipped halfway to the front door, turning her ankle slightly. She stopped for a moment to rub it.

She held the railing tightly as she climbed the three front steps. Two empty terra-cotta pots sat on either side of the slightly recessed door. Gigi could imagine them overflowing with flowers in the spring and summer.

She pressed the doorbell and waited, her heart hammering lightly in her chest.

There was no response.

Maybe it was broken?

She grabbed the brass, pineapple-shaped door knocker and went to tap it when she realized the door was already an inch or two ajar. She put a hand against it and pushed it open further.

"Tiffany?" Gigi called tentatively as she stepped into the foyer.

A small table was pushed against the wall. A brass lamp stood on top and a woven basket held several pieces of mail. There wasn't a speck of dust on the highly polished surface.

An Oriental rug shimmered like a jewel on the dark wood floor. Gigi took another tentative step forward. A small but elegant living room opened off the foyer to the left with a formal dining room on the right. Sunlight came through the bay window and glanced off the crystal chandelier that hung over the antique dining table.

Gigi called out again, but there was still no answer. Perhaps she ought to come back at another time. Tiffany must have been called out or had managed to forget about their appointment.

But why, then, was the front door open? And Tiffany's car was parked in the driveway. Unless someone had picked her up, she had to be around somewhere.

Gigi called again, louder this time. She followed the hallway back toward a spacious kitchen outfitted with high-end appliances and richly veined granite countertops. The double-door stainless-steel refrigerator hummed softly in the background.

The kitchen opened to a sunroom with windows on three sides. A small table was pulled up in front of a sofa slipcovered in a textured cream-colored fabric and brightened with several patterned throw pillows. The table was set with two teacups, two dessert plates and forks, a small teapot and a platter with an iced cake missing two pieces.

Tiffany was on the sofa dressed in black slacks, a sapphire blue cashmere sweater and black, patent leather-tipped flats. Diamond studs glittered in her ears. She was slumped sideways and her long, blond hair cascaded over the arm of the couch.

Gigi stopped short. Had Tiffany fallen asleep? She cleared her throat loudly, but there was no response from the woman on the sofa.

Gigi had a bad feeling. There was something unnaturally

still about Tiffany's body. She watched for several seconds but could not discern any rise and fall to her chest. Gigi reluctantly went closer and reached out a hand to Tiffany's neck. She could not find a pulse.

Tiffany was dead.

She had to call 9-1-1. Gigi dumped the contents of her purse on the counter and dug through the mess until she found her phone. She pressed the numbers with shaking fingers. After a brief chat with the 9-1-1 operator, she ended the call and immediately hit speed dial for Mertz.

Within minutes, a patrolman pulled into the driveway, and what seemed like only a moment later to Gigi, Tiffany's elegant town house was crawling with police. Gigi stood by the front door, peering through the glass panes alongside, hoping to see Mertz's car pull up front.

She had turned away momentarily when the door opened and Mertz stepped in. Once again, he enveloped Gigi in his arms. She let her head drop against his chest, and they stood like that for several minutes. Finally, she looked up.

"Do you want to tell me what happened?" Mertz asked gently. He steered Gigi toward the living room, where they both perched on the sofa.

"Tiffany called me. Said she wanted to start my diet plan—she'd gained a few pounds and needed to get rid of them."

Mertz jerked to attention. "She called you?"

"Yes. We agreed to meet at her house, but when I arrived"—Gigi's chin wobbled dangerously—"she didn't answer the bell. Then I noticed the front door was slightly open."

Mertz swore softly. "Didn't it occur to you that you might have been walking into something dangerous?" He shook his head. "I mean, we'd just talked about the possibility of Tiffany being the murderer as well as the person who broke into your kitchen last night. What if she had lured you here to—" He couldn't finish the sentence.

"I just didn't think, I guess. I was so startled to find the door open." She squeezed her eyes shut. "And then I found Tiffany."

"Can you come here a minute?" One of the policeman beckoned to Mertz.

Mertz squeezed Gigi's hand. "Just stay here. I'll be right back. And try to touch as little as possible, okay?"

Gigi nodded, her arms crossed over her chest. Suddenly she was very cold.

She heard noises coming from the other room and shuddered. The front door opened, and two men came in pushing a gurney. Gigi looked away quickly.

Finally, Mertz returned.

"What happened? Do you know?"

Mertz shook his head. "We won't know much until the autopsy is done and the toxicology tests come back. Whoever . . . or whatever . . . killed her isn't obvious. I would like to know who her guest was. Someone cut two pieces of cake, but there isn't a bite out of either of them."

"I noticed that. The table was set for two, so Tiffany was obviously expecting someone."

Mertz put an arm around Gigi's shoulders. "Unfortunately, unless two murderers are loose in Woodstone, and that seems highly unlikely, Tiffany Morse didn't kill Bradley Simpson. We're back to square one."

# Chapter 16

Mertz had to remain at the scene. They were dusting for prints everywhere although he wasn't particularly hopeful of finding anything useful. Gigi's story had been officially taken down, and there was no reason for her to stay.

The adrenaline from the shock had worn off, leaving her limp and exhausted. She would be glad to get back to her warm, cozy cottage.

For once Gigi wasn't thinking about Pia when she pulled into the driveway, so she was startled to see Pia's rattletrap van parked in its usual spot. Unfortunately, at this particular moment she would have preferred to be alone, but she braced herself and pushed open the back door.

Pia was sitting at the island eating macaroni and cheese out of a microwaveable container. She spun around when she heard Gigi enter.

"Where have you been?" Gigi didn't mean it to come out

sounding so harsh, but she'd been worried and now, after the day she'd had, her patience was down to a fine thread.

"That's a fine how-do-you-do." Pia sniffed. "I've been working." She forked up a mouthful of cheesy pasta. "And, okay, I thought it would be best if I got out of your hair for a bit. I could tell I was bugging you."

Gigi opened her mouth, then closed it again. What was the use in protesting? Pia *had* been getting on her nerves.

"Besides, I needed some time to get over that news about Declan." She shook her head. "I sure do know how to pick them, don't I?"

Gigi had forgotten all about that. Should she tell Pia that Tiffany was dead? Perhaps it would be best to wait until the news became public. Or at least until Mertz had given her the go-ahead.

"If you don't mind, I'm going to go soak in the tub." Gigi had her clients' dinner cooking in the slow cooker so she could afford to take an hour or two for herself.

"Doesn't matter to me." Pia's face was half hidden by her container of macaroni and cheese.

Gigi was leaving the kitchen when she noticed Pia's jacket draped over the kitchen chair. It was bright yellow.

The same color the garden ornament thief had been wearing. Surely that was a coincidence?

Gigi filled the bath with hot water, poured in a good dose of lavender bubble bath and sank into its warm, scented depths. She put a rolled-up towel behind her head and stretched out as far as she could, resting her feet on the top of the faucet.

The warm water did the trick. She felt her muscles relaxing and she was nearly dozing off when she thought about Pia's jacket again. Was it possible that Pia was going around Wood-stone stealing garden ornaments? Gigi worried her bottom lip with her teeth. The thefts had started shortly after Pia's arrival. But what on earth would she *do* with them? As a child, Pia had been something of a magpie, hoarding strange items like paper clips, hair ties and stray buttons. It would seem that her recent nomadic lifestyle would have cured her of that. She'd arrived with just a backpack and a small suitcase—not enough room to carry much of anything around.

Gigi pushed the thought from her mind and let the warm water soothe her. Finally it grew tepid, and she stepped out of the tub and wrapped herself up in an old terrycloth bathrobe.

She was heading down the hall toward her bedroom when she heard voices coming from the kitchen. Was Pia on the phone or did she have company? Curious, Gigi tiptoed closer and peered around the corner.

Mertz was sitting at the kitchen island, companionably chatting with Pia.

They both swiveled around when they sensed her presence.

"I've finally met your detective," Pia said.

Gigi pulled her robe around her more tightly. "I can see that." She smiled at Mertz, who looked exceptionally weary. "If you'll give me a minute, I'll go put some clothes on."

Gigi hastily donned some clean jeans and a turtleneck sweater. When she returned to the kitchen, she noticed Pia and Mertz were drinking cups of tea.

"Would you like one?" Pia gestured toward her cup.

"No, thanks."

"Guess I'll take mine into the living room and leave you

two alone." Pia picked up her mug. "Nice to meet you." She called over her shoulder at Mertz.

He smiled in Pia's direction. "Your sister is quite a character. I'm glad I've finally had the chance to meet her."

"She keeps rather strange hours, or you would have probably met her sooner."

"I stopped at the station on my way back from the scene. The chief was nearly apoplectic when I told him what happened." Mertz rubbed a hand across the back of his neck. "I guess the mayor has been busting his chops about the murder and the thefts around town. And now this. I'm afraid I'll be wearing a uniform and patrolling a mall somewhere if I don't get these murders solved, stat."

Gigi's heart ached for him. She could understand the pressure he was under.

"Did anything else turn up at the scene?"

Mertz shook his head. "Not really. We found fingerprints, of course, but they're unlikely to lead to anything. We did find one of those fancy cushions she had on the sofa in the sunroom—"

"Throw pillows?"

"Is that what you call them? Anyway, one was on the floor next to the sofa. It's possible someone used it to smother her. There were traces of blue around her lips. But we won't know for sure until the ME gets through with his examination."

"You'll figure it out. I know you will."

"I hope so."


News of Tiffany Morse's murder made the headlines of the *Woodstone Times* the next day. The story was short and relatively factual and included a quote from the mayor that the police of Woodstone would not rest until the murderer was caught.

Another small crowd had gathered outside the Woodstone Police Station, Gigi noticed, as she drove past on her way to Bon Appétit. She felt terribly sorry for Mertz.

She passed the location of the new cookery store again and quickly glanced at the storefront as she went by. As far as she could tell it was still empty, and there were no signs of construction. Perhaps the owners had changed their minds? That would certainly be a relief to Evelyn.

Evelyn looked considerably more chipper than she had the last time Gigi had seen her, and the renovations to Bon Appétit were much further along. Gigi admired the new paint and wall décor.

Evelyn leaned her elbows on the counter, her gray bob swinging forward to touch her cheeks. "It's all thanks to you. I was stuck in a rut and not seeing things as they were. At least now I've got a fighting chance."

"I went past the storefront where the new place is supposed to be. They don't seem to have done a thing yet. Maybe they've changed their minds?"

Evelyn frowned. "I doubt it. They'll probably bring in a huge crew and get it all banged out in a couple of days. Like they do on those home shows on television." She clenched her fists and raised them in the air. "Bring 'em on. I'm ready for them." She glanced around her newly decorated shop. "There are still a few more things I want to do. I'm waiting on some antique dressers I ordered—the kind you put in the kitchen for your dishes, not the kind that holds clothes. I'm going to use them for display to give the place more ambiance."

"That's a great idea." Gigi looked around. The dressers would be far more attractive than the wire shelving units Evelyn was using now.

"And I'm going to stock some kitchen accessories—linen dishtowels, fancy aprons, hors d'oeuvres plates. Things like that." She sighed. "It's taken me this long to get with the times. I hope it's not too late."

"I'm sure it's not."

"I've always carried French and Italian gourmet items, but I'm branching out there, too. I've gotten in a whole batch of Asian seasonings and ingredients as well. Even the stuff that Japanese woman was asking for—dashi, I think it's called." She was quiet for a moment, then pointed at the newspaper folded up next to the register. "Read about that second murder in this morning's paper. What is Woodstone coming to?"

Gigi shook her head. "I don't know.

"We'll all be murdered in our beds before we know it."

"I don't think we have to worry. This murder was . . . personal."

Evelyn shook her head. "Well, here I've been nattering away when you've obviously come in for something. What can I get you?"

Gigi read off her list, and Evelyn scurried among the shelves, bringing various items to the counter.

Gigi went through her list one more time. "That's it," she said.

Evelyn began ringing up Gigi's purchases. She looked up suddenly and whipped off her reading glasses, leaving them to dangle from the chain around her neck. She pointed toward the window. "There she is."

Gigi spun around. "Who?"

"The Japanese woman I saw with Hunter Simpson the other day. You don't think he's playing around, do you? Doesn't seem the type. Not like his father." Evelyn snickered.

"You're right, he doesn't seem the type." Gigi watched as the woman strolled past the window. She was slim, elegant and very pretty.

Gigi decided to follow her.

"Thanks," she threw over her shoulder to Evelyn as she grabbed her bag and moved quickly out of the store.

The sidewalk wasn't crowded, and Gigi easily spotted the woman up ahead. She stayed a discreet distance behind her, stopping when she stopped and moving on when she did. She was wondering whether she might have a second career as a private investigator when the woman disappeared from view.

Darn! Gigi scanned the heads in front of her. A couple walked ahead of her, holding hands. They parted briefly, and Gigi caught a glimpse of the woman's long, shiny, dark hair. Yes! She gave a very discreet fist pump and quickened her pace.

Gigi followed her all the way through downtown Woodstone. The wind had picked up, and Gigi's hands were numb. She pulled her collar up around her neck and stuck her hands in her pockets.

The woman had left downtown behind and was now walking along tree-lined streets. She turned into the small park where Gigi sometimes took Reg to romp, and took the path that traversed the green from north to south. Gigi couldn't imagine where she was headed.

Few people were out in the park, and Gigi was worried the woman would spot her, but she never turned around—just continued her purposeful walk. They crossed the park and came out on the other side facing Woodstone Hospital. Was she meeting Hunter, Gigi wondered?

The woman walked up the circular drive and disappeared through the hospital's front door. Gigi waited a second or two, then whooshed through the revolving door and into the hospital lobby. It felt blessedly warm inside.

Men and women in scrubs rushed back and forth, charts tucked under their arms, stethoscopes draped around their necks. The woman Gigi had been following hovered near the information desk. Gigi lingered behind a fake hibiscus tree and watched.

Hunter Simpson came rushing across the lobby toward the woman. He smiled and shook her hand briskly.

Gigi looked on, puzzled. If this was a romance, wouldn't Hunter have been a bit more . . . romantic . . . in his greeting? A discreet touch on her arm, her hand lingering in his . . . nothing that would arouse suspicion, of course.

Gigi watched as they left the lobby together. The woman had taken off her coat and was carrying it over her arm. Gigi could see a hospital badge pinned to the lapel of her suit. Was she simply another employee?

She would have to see if she could get any information out of Madeline.

Gigi went about delivering her diet lunches. She'd been as quiet as possible so as not to wake Pia while she prepared them, but she suspected that it didn't matter—her sister could sleep through anything. She seemed to be catching up on z's after being away for so long and, according to her, working like the devil.

Gigi rang Barbara Simpson's bell, and a uniformed maid answered, accepting the container and assuring Gigi she would bring it to Barbara immediately. Gigi headed toward Simpson and West with Madeline's lunch, figuratively crossing her fingers that Madeline would be feeling chatty.

She pulled into the law firm's lot and carefully parked the MINI in one of the spaces marked *Visitor*.

As Gigi entered, the girl behind the reception desk looked up, a bored expression on her face.

"Hi," Gigi said as she approached the girl. "I'm here with a delivery for Madeline Stone." She brandished the Gourmet De-Lite container.

The girl's mouth settled into discontented lines. "Not here. Said to give it to me." She held out her hand and wiggled her fingers impatiently.

"Oh," Gigi said. "You'll be sure she gets it? It's her lunch."

The girl heaved an enormous sigh. "I know," she said and waggled her fingers again at Gigi.

Gigi bit back her disappointment and placed the container on the highly polished reception desk.

"Be sure she gets it," she said, tapping Madeline's lunch and turning to go.

The girl gave a grin that was more of a smirk than a smile. Gigi had no recourse but to leave the Cobb salad and low-fat vinaigrette in the girl's hands and hope it got to Madeline in time for her lunch.

Gigi slumped behind the wheel of her MINI. She had so hoped to have a chance to chat with Madeline and possibly glean some information about Hunter. She started the car and backed out of the space.

She was waiting to turn left out of the parking lot when

her cell phone rang. She was definitely not a fan of talking and driving—or worse, texting and driving—but since she was stuck waiting for traffic to clear, she decided to answer the call.

It was Alec Pricely, the marketing manager for Branston Foods. They wanted Gigi to rerecord a tiny bit of the commercial she had done for them the other day. Something about background noise intruding onto the tape.

Gigi groaned. She absolutely hated, hated, *hated* having to make these commercials. Hearing them on the radio was even worse. She thought she sounded as if she were holding her nose the entire time. Did anyone like the sound of their own voice?

She switched her blinker from left to right, and when the traffic cleared, she pulled out onto High Street and headed toward Keith's Recording Studio.

Pricely's car was already in the parking lot when Gigi got there. Gigi pulled in next to it and got out. She tried to console herself with the thought that she might learn something new from Cheryl, but she sincerely doubted it.

"Hey," Cheryl said as Gigi pushed open the front door. She snapped her gum loudly, and spun her chair around so she was facing Gigi. "How's it going?"

"Oh, fine." Gigi fiddled with the ends of her scarf, trying to think of a way to introduce Hunter Simpson into the conversation.

Unfortunately, Pricely called her into the recording studio before she was visited by any flashes of inspiration.

This time the recording session went more smoothly. Pricely gave Gigi an oily smile and a thumbs-up as she exited the recording room. He flashed his oversize gold watch.

"Great job. Gotta run. Have a meeting with the big guy in fifteen minutes." He graced Gigi with another toothy smile, slipped on his coat and bolted for the door.

Cheryl rolled her eyes as she watched Pricely through the window heading toward his car. She shuddered. "Can't stand that guy. The first time he was here he tried coming on to me. Honestly, if Jimmy ever found out . . ." Cheryl let her comment trail off.

"He is kind of creepy, isn't he?" Gigi agreed.

"You can say that again." Cheryl giggled.

Gigi felt as if the two of them had established at least some sort of rapport. She decided to put a toe into the water. "Jimmy's Hunter's uncle, right?"

Cheryl nodded.

"How is Hunter taking things? I feel so sorry for him. Losing his father like that . . ."

"Poor Hunter is so conflicted!" Cheryl swiveled her chair to face Gigi. "He does feel just terrible about his father. After all, Bradley was his dad, and that alone puts him in a special category. But he was so *mean* to Hunter sometimes. My girlfriend, she sees one of them psychologists once a week, said that that would make it even harder for Hunter to grieve."

Gigi nodded her understanding. She began to open her mouth, but Cheryl was already off and running.

"I mean, you heard what Bradley said at Hunter's engagement party. Bambi, that's my girlfriend, said that would cause Hunter to be conflicted. On the one hand, he loves and respects his father, but then his father goes and does something flat-out mean like that. What is Hunter supposed to think?" She paused to chew on the side of her thumb. "Then when Hunter brings him this invention of his and asks for money and Bradley laughs in his face . . ."

"What?" Gigi stood up a little straighter.

Cheryl nodded briskly. "Believe me, I have no idea how the thing is supposed to work, or what on earth it's supposed to do, but according to Hunter, his invention would replace something he called the LVAD. Said it worked way better and cost less. And it would save people's lives. I mean, who wouldn't want to save someone's life?"

"So Bradley refused to invest in Hunter's invention?"

Cheryl nodded and swiveled her chair back and forth. She had one leg on the ground and the other tucked up underneath her.

"Does Hunter inherit money now that his father is dead? Maybe he can go ahead with his plans."

"Could be. I don't know. Bradley might have left the whole pot to Barbara." Cheryl rolled her eyes. "Although goodness knows, there's more than enough to go around. We'd been kind of hoping . . . well, never mind about that."

What had Cheryl been about to say, Gigi wondered? Was she going to admit that Barbara expected repayment of the money that had been loaned to them?

But, more importantly, how desperate was Hunter to see his invention launched? If he really did have something that would replace the LVAD, a device that kept heart patients alive while they waited for a transplant, then his career would be assured and his name would go down in history.

Was that something worth killing for?

# Chapter 17

Gigi thought about going home, but she needed to talk to someone. She pulled up to the curb in front of the Book Nook, locked the MINI, got out and pushed open the door to Sienna's store.

Madison was behind the counter. She gave Gigi a brief nod. Gigi noticed that her pink streak had undergone a color change and was now green. Gigi couldn't decide which she liked better—or perhaps which one she disliked the least would be more accurate.

Sienna was in the back room going through several boxes of books that had just been dropped off. She picked up a volume and blew the dust off. She held it toward Gigi.

"Why would anyone think I'd want a mildewed copy of *Vanity Fair*?" She flipped through the pages of the book. "Look at that! The edges of the cover are all bent, the pages are foxed . . ." She tossed the book into a box on the floor.

"Where's Camille?" Gigi looked around, but the baby's bassinet was not in sight.

"I didn't want her back here while I was going through all these dusty old volumes. Alice is taking her for a walk in that absurd pram Oliver's mother insisted on buying us. A Silver Cross! It cost more than that old beater car I had in college. The good thing is that it does keep Camille well protected from the cold and wind."

Sienna wiped her hands on the smock she'd put on over her clothes. "So what have you been up to?"

"Well—" Gigi began.

Sienna linked her arm through Gigi's. "Come on. Let's get a cup of coffee or tea. I've been on my feet for hours, and you probably have, too."

They were settling into the coffee corner when the front door opened and Alice arrived with Camille. She parked the unwieldy carriage by the front door and carried the baby over to where Gigi and Sienna were sitting.

"Let me get her bouncy chair." Sienna disappeared, returning almost immediately with a bright red-yellow-and-blue-covered baby seat. She eased Camille into it. The baby's cheeks were flushed pink from her walk outdoors, and her eyes were already closing, her long lashes casting dark shadows on her cheeks.

"She is just so precious," Alice cooed. Her face puckered in concern. "I do so hope Stacy is expecting, but she still hasn't said a word."

"Give her time. If she is expecting, I suspect you'll be the first to know." Sienna smiled.

"You're right." Alice worried the ends of her scarf.

"Gigi was just about to tell me what she's been up to."

Gigi recounted everything that had happened recently—from finding Tiffany Morse dead in her own home to her conversation with Cheryl about Hunter and his invention.

Alice clapped a hand to her chest. "What on earth is the world coming to! Such goings-on in Woodstone. It used to be such a quiet town! When Tom and I moved here, may he rest in peace, there were only a handful of shops on High Street. And none of this highfalutin stuff, either—we had practical stores like the hardware store, the five-and-dime, the butcher and the fishmonger." Alice's cheeks flushed red. "Now it's all these fancy places where I can't even afford to breathe the air."

"Well, I don't think we have anything to worry about," Sienna said dryly.

"No," Gigi concluded. "Someone hated Bradley enough, or was mad enough at him, to kill him. I suspect Tiffany somehow got in the killer's way. These murders weren't random."

"You mentioned Hunter." Sienna put her foot on Camille's bouncy chair and gently rocked it. The baby cooed softly and turned her head to the side. "Maybe Tiffany overheard him arguing with his father about that invention and put two and two together."

"Are you thinking blackmail?" Alice asked.

"She has expensive tastes," Gigi said.

"I'll say," Alice snorted. "I've seen that red Mustang of hers blazing up and down High Street more than once. Woe betide any pedestrian who gets in the way of Miss Tiffany 'La-di-da' Morse. I'm surprised she hasn't racked up enough speeding tickets to wallpaper her living room."

"Every Friday I see her coming out of Abigail's with a couple of shopping bags," Sienna added. "Spending half her paycheck, I should imagine."

"Keeping up appearances." Alice nodded sagely.

"Her condo is very nice," Gigi said, trying to think about the décor without visualizing Tiffany's body on the sofa in the sunroom. "Pretty expensive, I'd say." Her thoughts drifted to her own furniture—the pieces she'd split with Ted but had jettisoned because they didn't suit her sweet, little cottage. The hand-me-downs from family, the pieces picked up at yard sales and secondhand stores. She lifted her chin a little higher. Everything had come together rather well, in her opinion, and she was very comfortable. It might not be fancy, but it suited her perfectly.

"On the other hand"—Sienna stroked Camille's cheek softly—"maybe this Cheryl is lying about Hunter and the invention to take the heat off of her husband."

Gigi delivered her dinners in a haze. She was thinking about what Sienna had said about Cheryl possibly lying to distract attention from her husband. Gigi thought about her conversation with Cheryl. Gigi certainly didn't fancy herself as being particularly good at judging whether someone was telling the truth or not. Ted used to tease her about believing everything everyone told her—from the well-dressed fellow on the street claiming to have been robbed and asking for money for a train ticket home to Washington to the sales girl insisting that the dress Gigi was trying on was absolutely *made for her*. She supposed she was a bit naïve when it came to things like that—the commandment *thou shalt not lie* had been drilled into her by the nuns in school.

Pia was on her way out when Gigi arrived back home. She tried not to stare at Pia's bright yellow jacket. Pia had an egg roll in one hand and a fountain drink in the other. She waved the plastic cup at Gigi.

"I'm heading out. I ran into Declan at the Shop and Save, and he said to stop by sometime, so I think I'll head over there first and see if he's free to chat. I realize he's on the rebound, what with his girlfriend having been killed, but I really do fancy him." She shrugged.

Gigi's spirits sank. So Pia hadn't gotten over her crush on Declan. At least he was no longer police suspect number one. Pia might still get her heart broken, but at least she wouldn't be visiting him in jail.

As soon as the door closed behind Pia, Gigi collapsed at the kitchen table. She was exhausted. She knew she ought to eat something but she was too tired to be hungry. She was contemplating a good soak in a hot, lavender-scented tub when the telephone rang.

It was Mertz.

"I've been meaning to call you. Tomorrow is Valentine's Day, you know."

Gigi glanced at the calendar by the stove. February 14 was circled in red.

"I'm afraid I have bad news." Mertz cleared his throat nervously. "The Heritage Inn was completely booked. Apparently people call weeks in advance for these holidays." Mertz's sigh came over the line. "I imagine even the Woodstone Diner will be full." He gave a hollow sounding laugh.

"That's all right," Gigi said, trying to keep the disappointment out of her voice.

"But I had an idea." Mertz's tone lightened. "How about if you come over here for dinner? I'm not much of a cook, but there are a few things I can manage. I know it's disappointing, but frankly I've found restaurants to be so overcrowded on Valentine's Day, and half the time the food isn't up to their regular standard."

Gigi forced the thought of Mertz taking other women to dinner on Valentine's Day out of her mind. "That sounds lovely. I could bring something."

"No need. I've got it all planned." He gave a self-deprecating laugh. "It won't exactly be fancy, but you won't starve. I'll get a nice bottle of wine, and we can relax and enjoy each other's company."

"I'd like that very much."

They settled on seven o'clock, and Mertz insisted that he would pick Gigi up so she wouldn't have to worry about driving at night.

Gigi felt considerably peppier when she hung up the phone. Her stomach grumbled, and she went to dig in the refrigerator for the leftover chicken in red wine sauce that had been her clients' dinner for the evening.

Gigi woke up on Wednesday morning with an excited feeling in the pit of her stomach. She was going to Mertz's for dinner. It was definitely going to be an experience. She hadn't been to his place yet and was curious to see it. Would it be the typical bachelor pad with beat-up leather sofas and a giant-screen television holding pride of place?

Gigi had really hoped to talk to Madeline and perhaps learn more about Hunter and his invention, but Madeline had called to say that she would be in Hartford for a conference all day and wouldn't be needing Gigi's meals.

The day started out excruciatingly slowly—the way it

always does when you're looking forward to something in the evening—but eventually things picked up, and suddenly Gigi was getting ready to go to Mertz's.

Once again, she bemoaned the state of her wardrobe. Reg seemed to concur, turning his nose up at everything she pulled out of her closet. She finally unearthed a relic from her New York days—a pair of black pants she'd scored at a Carolina Herrera sample sale and a turquoise silk blouse. The pants were long enough for her to wear her high-heeled suede booties, and the charming whisk pin Mertz had given her would complete the outfit.

As Gigi had suspected, Mertz was smack-dab on time— three minutes early, actually. She was a punctual person herself and really appreciated it when others followed suit.

She already had her coat on and opened the door quickly.

Mertz kissed her on the cheek. It was snowing again, and his lips were cold.

"Sorry, Reg, but you're going to have to stay here."

"Why not bring him? He can play with Whiskers."

Mertz had rescued Whiskers from a tree last fall. Gigi could still remember the pride she felt as she watched Mertz easily pull himself up into the old oak, and the applause that rang out from the crowd on the sidewalk when he jumped back down, the kitten tucked safely into his shirt pocket.

"Do you think they'll get along?"

"Why not? Reg is a friendly fellow, and Whiskers loves to play."

It was barely a five-minute drive to Mertz's condo. Reg was a little huffy about being relegated to the backseat instead of his usual spot in the front, but he soon got over it and eagerly pressed his nose to the window.

"Here we are." Mertz pulled up to a small group of condos—not quite as fancy as where Tiffany had lived—but well maintained and attractive. He stopped outside an end unit with a cheerful red door and a light shining through the front window.

Mertz parked in front of the attached garage and went around to open Gigi's door. Reg bounded into the front seat and out the door, right at Gigi's heels. Mertz opened the door to his condo, and Reg dashed inside. Whiskers was waiting by the entrance, and Reg's sudden appearance startled her, sending her to the top of the foyer table where mail was neatly stacked alongside the day's rolled-up newspaper. She switched her long, fluffy tail back and forth, voicing her displeasure at Reg's overly aggressive greeting.

Reg ignored her and darted around the condo getting acquainted with the smells. Gigi looked around while Mertz hung up their coats. As she had suspected, his place was very tidy, with a few pieces of plain but comfortable-looking furniture. There was a framed photograph of an older couple on one of the end tables—his parents?—and one of those collage-type frames filled with pictures of school-aged children. She knew Mertz came from a big family—they were probably his nieces and nephews.

On the wall across from the sofa was a large photograph of a young man at the beach holding a life preserver and leaning casually against the lifeguard stand. His blue eyes stood out strongly in his tanned face. She moved closer to get a better look.

"I was head lifeguard for the Connecticut State Parks when I was in school. That was taken right after I'd rescued this little kid from a riptide." A faraway look crossed his face. "It was one of the proudest moments of my life. I'll never forget his parents' gratitude. And it made me realize I wanted to help people, which is why I went into police work." He made a face. "Of course I didn't realize I'd be spending half my time trying to track down a lawn ornament thief."

Gigi gave a last look at the picture—she imagined Mertz had caught more than one girl's eye on the beach—and followed him out to the kitchen, which, like the rest of the condo, was clean and tidy. The counters were bare save for a coffeemaker and a toaster. Gigi thought about her own kitchen and the tangle of utensils and spread of appliances she couldn't live without.

A platter sat on the counter with two prime-looking New York strips on it.

"I thought I'd throw some steaks on the grill." Mertz motioned toward a sliding glass door leading to a small deck. "I've shoveled the deck off so I can use the gas grill all winter long."

"Sounds great. It feels like ages since I've had anything barbecued."

Gigi noticed that his kitchen table was set with placemats, flowered china, and fancy folded linen napkins. She stared at it, trying to figure out how to bring up the topic of Bradley and Tiffany's murders.

Mertz must have noticed her glance. "I turned the dining room into an office for myself. Didn't think I'd have much use for it otherwise." He uncorked a bottle of malbec that was sitting on the counter and poured some into two glasses. He handed one to Gigi and raised the other in a toast.

"Here's to my not overcooking the steak or burning the green beans."

Gigi laughed, and they clinked glasses.

Mertz grabbed a pepper mill from one of the cabinets and began to grind pepper over the steaks. He gestured toward the table with his shoulder. "The china belonged to my grandmother. I had to blow the dust off it, it's been so long since I used it."

Gigi followed him to the open door to the deck where he slid the two steaks onto the preheated grill. They spit and sizzled briefly, and in moments a delicious smell wafted toward her.

Mertz rubbed his hands together. "I've got baked potatoes and green bean casserole to go with them." He glanced at his watch. "Better check on those green beans. I was only joking about burning them."

He pulled open the oven door and peered inside. "Phew, everything looks fine. Five more minutes should do it."

Gigi practically had to sit on her hands. She wanted to check the steaks, look at the green beans, monitor the potatoes, but she knew she had to let Mertz do this himself. Instead, she had another sip of her wine and tried to stay out of his way.

Fortunately, he pulled it off to perfection. The steak, when Gigi cut into it, was seasoned to perfection and medium rare; the baked potatoes were delicious with butter, sour cream and fresh chives, and the green bean casserole was . . . a green bean casserole. Gigi debated whether or not she ought to offer Mertz a recipe for a fresh casserole that did not include a can of soup, but she decided it was probably best to let it rest.

They were halfway through the meal when Mertz again mentioned the lawn ornaments that had gone missing. Gigi cringed, thinking of Pia's yellow jacket and the person she had glimpsed so very briefly. She wracked her brain for something to change the subject. Unfortunately the only thing on her mind seemed to be the murders of Bradley and Tiffany.

Gigi took a big gulp of her wine. How to bring up the subject? She didn't want Mertz to think she was poking her nose in where it didn't belong. She knew from experience that that made him unhappy. To put it mildly.

"I recorded another commercial the other day," Gigi began, spearing a slightly overcooked green bean. "Actually rerecorded because of some technical issues."

Mertz nodded, his mouth full of baked potato and sour cream.

"Cheryl, the woman who works at the recording studio, is the sister-in-law of Barbara Simpson."

Mertz looked up, his mouth still full, but his eyebrows raised as if in concern.

"She told me that Bradley Simpson's son Hunter wanted to borrow money from him to launch some medical device he'd invented, but that his father had turned him down."

Mertz was chewing furiously as if he were desperate to interject something. Gigi decided to overlook that fact.

"So it seems quite possible that Hunter killed his father to get money for his invention. Apparently, it's quite revolutionary and could propel him into the annals of medical history."

Mertz swallowed quickly, and judging by the look on his face, it was slightly painful.

"Really," he finally managed to say.

Gigi decided to take that as encouragement to continue. "And . . ." She paused dramatically and pointed her fork at

Mertz. The green bean speared on the end drooped sadly. "Cheryl and her husband had their own reasons for wanting Bradley out of the way." Gigi put down her fork and rubbed her index finger and thumb together. "Money, of course. With Bradley out of the way, they were convinced that Barbara wouldn't demand repayment of the loan she'd made them."

A muscle was now jumping in Mertz's jaw, but Gigi again decided to ignore the warning sign.

"But it looks as if it backfired. I overheard Cheryl say something about it to a friend on the telephone. She said 'after all Jimmy went through.' Now doesn't that sound suspicious?" Gigi popped the green bean into her mouth.

Mertz sighed loudly. "Words taken out of context are just that—words. It could mean anything."

"But don't you think it's worth investigating?"

Mertz pushed his plate away and got up. "I've got ice cream sundaes for dessert. Rather unsophisticated, I'm afraid, but it was all I could manage."

"Sounds delicious to me."

Mertz opened the refrigerator and began pulling out small bowls of toppings and a can of whipped cream. "Unfortunately, we can't go around bothering innocent people just because they've been overheard saying something, which, *taken out of context*," the way he said the words clearly underlined them in Gigi's mind, "sounds suspicious. We'd be chasing our tails all day long."

He lined the toppings up on the counter, retrieved the ice cream from the freezer and a scoop from the drawer. He filled two etched glass bowls with vanilla ice cream.

"Help yourself. I've got cherries, chopped nuts, chocolate sauce and whipped cream."

"Looks great." Gigi served herself ice cream, then squirted on a swirl of whipped cream.

They took their dessert back to the table. "So does this mean you're not going to look into my theories?"

"If I find something more solid to go on . . . maybe." Mertz dug into his sundae. "Right now we have no reason to believe anyone besides Declan McQuaid is responsible." Mertz put down his spoon, and counted on his fingers. "One, the murder weapon was his ice pick. Two, his are the only prints on the weapon. Three, he was heard arguing violently with the victim, and four, Tiffany Morse was cheating on the victim with him."

"But then why kill Tiffany?" The ice cream was forming a frozen ball in the pit of Gigi's stomach.

Mertz shrugged. "Because she was cheating on him? Whoever killed her had been expected. Remember the tea things all set out? We don't have the reports back yet, but it looks as if someone drugged her and then smothered her with one of those . . . what did you call them?"

"Throw pillows," Gigi said glumly.

"And the most likely person is Declan."

# Chapter 18

They finished their ice cream sundaes in near silence, Gigi's head whirling with the information Mertz had just revealed. And here she had thought Declan was off the hook. She was going to have to come up with some information that would lead Mertz in a different direction. But how?

Mertz's reasoning was sound. Declan had a motive in both murders. But so did Hunter. Tiffany might have learned or overheard something that made her a liability to the murderer so Cheryl and her husband were still suspects in Gigi's book.

Mertz poured them each a nightcap—a snifter of Baileys Irish Cream—something Gigi could never resist. They sat together on the sofa, and it wasn't long before Mertz was kissing her.

He swore when his cell phone rang. He glanced at the number. "Sorry, I've got to take this."

His side of the conversation was short and terse. He punched the end call button and frowned. "Another lawn ornament has gone missing. The Fosters came home from a trip to Europe to discover someone had nicked a metal frog from their front lawn." Mertz laughed. "Apparently, the frog was playing the violin." He shook his head. "What will they come up with next?"

Gigi was bending down to pick up her purse when she stopped short. She was about to tell Mertz that she'd seen the actual theft when she remembered the flash of yellow, and Pia's yellow jacket. Somehow she couldn't bring herself to mention it. She was going to locate Pia's studio somehow and find out once and for all if Pia was involved. Then she would let Mertz deal with it.

"I'm sorry our evening has to be cut short." Mertz got Gigi's coat from the closet and held it out for her. "Just when it was getting good." He gestured toward the sofa.

Gigi felt her face heat up. She had enjoyed kissing Mertz. And she appreciated the fact that he wasn't rushing her into something she wasn't ready for.

Mertz put on his own coat and slipped his hand into the pocket. He pulled out a white envelope and handed it to Gigi. This time his face reddened. "I hope you like it. I think I read every card in the store before I chose that one."

Gigi ripped open the flap on the envelope and pulled out the card. The design was simple and pleasing, the prose equally simple but poignant. The message was clear.

Mertz gathered Gigi into his arms. "Happy Valentine's Day," he said, his lips hovering over hers.

As they drove through the darkened streets back to Gigi's

house, Gigi glanced at Metz's profile in the flickering light from the streetlamps. She felt a rush of warmth and thankfulness. There had been a few other men who had caught her attention since her move to Woodstone, but Mertz had stayed the course. She had made the right choice.

The house was dark when they pulled into Gigi's driveway. Reg gave a giant yawn and stretched before jumping out of the backseat. He made straight for one of the rose bushes and lifted his leg.

Mertz waited until Gigi got inside and turned on the light. She waved from the back door and watched as he backed down the driveway. She turned away as his taillights disappeared down the street. She was putting the kettle on for a cup of tea when she noticed a white envelope sitting out on the counter. It was addressed to her.

At first she thought Pia had gotten her a Valentine's Day card, but it was a business-size envelope and didn't look at all like a card. Was it a good-bye note? Had Pia finally taken off for California? Gigi hoped not. She was enjoying having family around and hoped that Pia might settle down—in her own place, to be sure—but at least close to Woodstone.

Gigi slit open the envelope and pulled out the piece of paper inside. It looked like some sort of certificate. She read it through. It was a gift certificate for a manicure and pedicure at the new nail salon that had opened behind Abigail's. Stuck to it was a sticky note with *thanks for everything and happy Valentine's day, love Pia* scrawled across it.

*How terribly sweet,* Gigi thought. She hadn't treated herself to a manicure or pedicure in ages. It would be fun and relaxing. Maybe she'd go tomorrow.

Meanwhile, it was off to bed for her. "Come on, Reg."

They padded down the hall to the bedroom where they were both soon fast asleep.

Pia was still sound asleep when Gigi left to make her deliveries the next morning. Gigi wanted to thank her for the gift certificate so she penned a quick note and left it in the bathroom where Pia was sure to see it.

Her plans were to deliver her breakfast Gourmet De-Lite meals and then head to the Perfect Ten Nail Salon to use her gift certificate. Reg was quite put out that he wasn't able to go along as she dropped off her meals, which was their norm, but she suspected that the sunbeam coming through the kitchen window would be calling his name in no time.

A drooping plastic banner with *Grand Opening* on it hung from the front of the Perfect Ten Nail Salon. Gigi pushed open the front door. The girl at the reception desk was simultaneously talking on the telephone and shaking a bottle of bright red nail polish.

She moved the receiver away from her mouth. "Manicure or pedicure?"

"Both."

Gigi glanced around. A row of manicure tables were lined up at the front of the shop and behind those were half a dozen pedicure stations. A middle-aged blond woman was getting a set of acrylics applied, and Gigi could see the back of another woman, with her pants rolled up to her knees, who was about to climb onto one of the pedicure platforms. Other than that, the shop was empty.

The décor was simple and streamlined, with a Zen-like

feel to it. Everything was in black and white except for an acrylic wall of shelves where bottles of nail polish provided a splash of every color imaginable, from dark purple to bubblegum pink.

A young girl came rushing out of the back toward Gigi. She wore slim-fitting cropped black pants and a white blouse with a mandarin collar. She smiled and motioned toward the wall behind her. "Please, pick your color."

Gigi went over to examine her choices. They were endless, it seemed. She settled on a neutral sort of mauve shade for her nails and a bright red for her toes. Even though no one would see them, she would enjoy the pop of color when she took her shoes off.

The girl summoned her to the pedicure area. The other woman was now seated, and Gigi got a better look at her.

"Mrs. Simpson," she exclaimed.

Barbara looked up from the magazine she was reading. "Gigi! Please do call me Barbara. Why don't you sit here," she motioned to the station next to her, "and we can chat."

Gigi was glad to see that Barbara was getting out, although there were still dark circles under her eyes and an air of sadness about her. Her shoulders drooped, and she looked as if she might start to cry at any moment.

Gigi slipped out of her shoes and socks, cringing at the sight of her toes—it had been at least a year since she'd last had a professional pedicure—and slid her feet into the basin of warm, bubbling water. A sigh escaped her lips as she settled back into the chair.

"I've been enjoying your food so much," Barbara said, putting down her magazine. "I've only lost a pound so far, but I know I have to be patient. I just wish Bradley were here to . . ." She wiped at a tear that had collected in the corner of her eye. "But I mustn't dwell on that. Tell me how you're doing."

"Oh . . . just fine I guess."

"I was horrified when I heard about Tiffany Morse," Barbara confided in a near whisper. "She was a very ambitious young woman. Bradley was quite taken with her and was acting as her mentor. It was just unfortunate that that old geezer West was so old-fashioned about allowing women into the partnership." Barbara watched as the nail technician painted a wide swath of hot pink polish down the middle of her big toe. "I learned quite a bit about self-actualization in the . . . the . . . well, in all the magazine articles and self-help books I've read." She gave a self-deprecating laugh. "Bradley used to tease me about it." Her expression turned serious. "But a woman needs to do whatever necessary to reach her full potential."

"Yes." Gigi agreed, sighing again as the salon technician rubbed a citrusy-smelling scrub over her feet and lower legs. This was heaven. She should have done it sooner.

"I'm just afraid," Barbara stopped abruptly.

"Yes?" Gigi tried not to look too eager.

"It's about Hunter." Barbara's voice was still barely above a whisper. "Well, not Hunter exactly, but his fiancée. I adore Madeline, but she's rather . . . ambitious . . . for Hunter."

Gigi's ears perked up. That was a surprise. Madeline had certainly never struck her that way.

"Hunter has created this medical device, you see." Barbara winced as the nail technician briskly rubbed a pumice stone up and down the bottom of her foot. "And he needs funds to get it off the ground. He didn't want to ask his father, because he wanted to do it all on his own."

*Was it that, or was he afraid to ask his father?* Gigi wondered.

"But Madeline kept pushing him to do it. Finally, she said she was going to take matters into her own hands and speak to Bradley herself." Barbara's lower lip quivered. "I'm just afraid that she might have . . . gone too far." Barbara turned her wedding ring around and around. "Hunter thinks the world of Madeline. If anything happened to her . . ."

Gigi reached over and patted Barbara's hand. "I'm sure everything is going to be okay," she said with a lot more conviction than she felt.

Gigi had to sit for what felt like hours as her nails dried. She thought about what Barbara had said, but she couldn't reconcile an ambitious Madeline with the Madeline she knew. *But she did decide to lose weight in order to better fit the culture at Simpson and West,* a small voice whispered inside Gigi's head. Was it possible that Madeline had become ambitious enough to kill? Logistically it was possible. It would have been easy enough for her to slip into the kitchen at some point and take Declan's ice pick. Hunter had stormed off, leaving her alone. No one knew exactly how she got home that night. Or when.

Gigi shook her head. Not Madeline. It just wasn't possible.

She almost put her gloves on as she was leaving Perfect Ten but remembered just in time that her nails still weren't completely dry. She paused for a moment by the door, admiring the pretty mauve color she'd selected.

Gigi was leaving the nail salon just as Alice was coming down the street. Alice saw her and waved furiously, rushing along to catch up with Gigi.

"Gigi," Alice said, panting slightly. "Do you have time for a cup of tea?" She gestured toward the Woodstone Diner. "I've got some news."

Gigi glanced at her watch quickly. "Sure. A quick one. Then I need to get back home."

"I am just so excited!" Alice declared as they walked toward the diner.

Gigi could easily guess what Alice's news was, but she decided to let her play it out her way.

They settled themselves in a booth, and the waitress immediately appeared at their table with two glasses of ice water. She pulled her pad from the pocket of her apron.

"What can I get you?"

"Just two cups of tea." Alice looked at Gigi for confirmation, and Gigi nodded her head.

The waitress headed toward the kitchen, and Alice could contain herself no longer.

"It's true!" she exclaimed. "My Stacy is pregnant. I'm going to be a grandmother!"

"That's wonderful," Gigi said, taking Alice's hand in her own and giving it a squeeze. "When is the baby due?"

"The end of June. A perfect time to have a baby," Alice said as the waitress slipped cups of tea in front of them. "She'll deliver before the weather gets too hot." Alice ran a finger around the neck of her sweater as if imagining the summer temperatures. "I was nine months pregnant with Stacy in August, and it was nearly unbearable."

"How is she feeling?"

"Much better. She's back at work. It's those first three months that are so hard. She said she could barely stand the smell of food. Not the best thing when you work in a restaurant!"

Gigi finished the rest of her tea and checked her watch. She needed to be getting back home. The waitress had just slid their check across the table when the front door opened, letting in a blast of cold air. Gigi glanced up briefly, then did a double take. It was Hunter Simpson and the Japanese woman Gigi had seen him with before.

Alice was about to get up, but Gigi motioned for her to stay. Alice plunked down in her seat, a puzzled look on her face.

Hunter looked around, then headed toward the booth in back of Gigi and Alice. Gigi couldn't believe her luck.

"What?" Alice whispered, pushing her teacup to the side and leaning across the table toward Gigi.

"It's Hunter Simpson. With that Japanese woman he's been seen around town with."

Alice's eyebrows shot up.

The waitress walked past their table, looked questioningly at the check abandoned next to Gigi's saucer and continued on to Hunter's booth.

Gigi leaned back in her seat and listened. Hunter ordered coffee with cream, but she couldn't hear what the woman said.

Alice started to open her mouth, but Gigi put a finger to her lips and shushed her.

Hunter's words were not as distinct or easy to hear as his order to the waitress had been. Gigi picked up a few words here and there—*finance, interest, ownership*. She was desperately trying to make sense of them when Hunter's next words came through loud and clear.

"Looks like we have a deal. If you have the paperwork drawn up, Simpson LLC and Gaishi Enterprises will join forces to develop and market the . . ."

"I didn't hear the last of it," Gigi whispered to Alice, "but it sounds like she represents a company that is going into partnership with Hunter to market his invention."

Gigi motioned toward the waitress, who quickly picked up the check and the dollar bills Gigi and Alice had put out on the table. As they left the diner, Gigi gave one last backward glance at Hunter and his partner.

"I didn't think Hunter was playing around," Gigi said as they stood on the sidewalk. "He just didn't seem the type. It looks like it's all business."

"So Hunter is innocent in Bradley's murder."

"Not necessarily. Just because he's found a backer for his invention doesn't mean he didn't go to his father for money first. And if Bradley had turned him down, that might have made Hunter mad enough to kill."

# Chapter 19

Gigi took a slight detour on her way home, taking some of Woodstone's back streets that led her past several industrial parks. She hoped she would see Pia's wreck of a VW bus parked somewhere, but no such luck.

It also wasn't in the driveway of her cottage when Gigi pulled in. Perhaps Pia was at Declan's, keeping him company and having a bite to eat?

She finished the preparations for the lunches she was bringing to her clients and filled her Gourmet De-Lite containers. Reg hovered around hoping for a treat, but Gigi had noticed that he was putting on a bit of weight, and she was determined not to give in to his pleading looks. It wasn't easy—he had a way of tilting his head and making his eyes look extra large and bright that pierced her heart every time.

Finally, Gigi had everything ready and was heading out the door again, this time with Reg. He was content to sit in the car while she dropped off the meals, even if she occasionally spent a few minutes chatting with her clients at their front doors.

Reg jumped into the car eagerly and settled himself into the passenger seat. Gigi headed toward town and made the left turn onto High Street. She slowed as she reached Declan's Grille and quickly scanned the parking lot. As far as she could tell, Pia's VW bus wasn't there. Of course it might have been there earlier, and she could now be on her way to the mysterious studio she'd rented.

Gigi pulled into the tiny lot adjacent to Simpson and West.

"I'll just be a minute," she said to Reg, who was already curled up on the seat. He opened one eye and glanced at Gigi briefly before giving a deep sigh and heading into dreamland.

Gigi went around toward the front door of the law firm. She had her hand on the doorknob when someone went by on the other side of the street. The movement caught Gigi's eye, and she turned to look. It was Janice Novak, dressed in her usual strange conglomeration of clothes that were either too big or too small. The hems of her pants were dragging along the sidewalk, and even from where she was standing Gigi could see that the constant friction was wearing them out. Her buttercup-colored corduroy coat was open despite the frigid temperatures, revealing a silver sequined top underneath. It was hardly the sort of thing most people chose to wear during the day, but Janice didn't seem to care what others thought.

Gigi suddenly remembered Tiffany's cell phone and the fact that she had promised Janice a reward, but Janice went on past, seemingly not even recognizing Gigi. Gigi breathed a sigh of relief and pulled open the door to Simpson and West.

The usual hush hung over the elegant lobby. Gigi always felt underdressed when she arrived with Madeline's meals. Madeline wasn't waiting downstairs as she sometimes was, so Gigi pushed the button for the elevator. It opened with a melodic ping, and closed behind her with a silent whoosh.

Madeline was in her cubicle, bent over a stack of papers, when Gigi arrived on the third floor. She jumped when Gigi, standing in the doorway, cleared her throat.

"Oh, my, lunchtime already?" Madeline smiled at Gigi.

Gigi thought Madeline looked tired. There were bags under her eyes, and her complexion was paler than usual.

"Busy?"

Madeline nodded. "That's for sure. We've got several big cases going at once." She rubbed her temples with her fingers. "Listen, do you have a minute?" Her voice dropped to a near whisper.

"Sure." Gigi slid into the chair in front of Madeline's desk.

Madeline gestured toward the door to her cubicle. "You'd better shut that."

Gigi reached out and eased the door shut. She couldn't imagine what Madeline was about to tell her.

"With Tiffany . . . gone . . . her office needed to be cleaned out. Mr. West asked me to do it." She gestured toward the stacks of papers on her desk. "I haven't had much time, what with everything else I've got to do."

Madeline's lip quivered, and for a moment Gigi thought she was going to cry.

"I came in early this morning, and thought I might get a slight start on it." Madeline stopped and rubbed her temples with her fingers again. "At least assess the situation and see how long it was going to take. Papers and files all have to be put back in the appropriate places so it's not just a matter of boxing up the pictures on her desk or the handful of personal items in her drawers. Her secretary could do that."

Gigi nodded, wondering what Madeline was getting at.

"Her door has been shut since . . . since it happened. The police looked through everything right after the murder, but I guess they didn't find anything significant because they said we could do what we wanted with the office. I saw the place after the police were finished searching. They were very neat, and it was hard to tell they'd even been in the room."

*That sounded like Mertz,* Gigi thought.

"Tiffany's office is on the second floor. With a window," Madeline added, looking around her own crowded space. "She had a special antique desk brought in and hung real art on the walls. That's what made it even more shocking."

"What was shocking?" Gigi was thoroughly confused.

"I used the key Mr. West gave me to open the door. We've kept it locked ever since . . . well, ever since. So no one else has been in there. But the office has been ransacked. Papers everywhere, drawers open." She looked up at Gigi, her eyes wide. "Someone was in there desperately searching for something."

"Have you called the police?"

Madeline shook her head. "No. What if it was someone from the firm simply needing to find something and not caring if they made a mess? Mr. West would be furious with me for calling in the authorities."

"But you said you had the key. How did they get in?"

"Her secretary had a key, too. She kept it in her top desk drawer. Anyone could have taken it."

*So much for security,* Gigi thought.

"So you think someone from the firm might have been looking for something?"

"What else could it be?"

"It might have been the murderer. Maybe Tiffany knew something or had something that put them in danger." Gigi ran her hands through her hair. "Do you have any idea what cases she was working on?"

Madeline shrugged. "No, not really."

Gigi was thinking fast. They had to get into Tiffany's office. Would she be able to convince Madeline of that?

"If we could look around, we might find something. An answer to this whole mess. I'm sure that would be a huge relief for you and Hunter."

"You mean you want to . . . snoop around Tiffany's office?" Madeline began to push her chair back as if by doing so she could distance herself from the idea. "We couldn't do that. If Mr. West found out, he'd be furious. I might be fired."

"Don't you want to find out what happened to your future father-in-law?"

"Yes, but—"

Gigi closed her eyes and crossed her fingers behind her back. "I really don't want to have to tell you this," she bit her lip as if she couldn't go on.

Peg Cochran

"What?" Madeline asked, the alarm sounding in her voice.

"The police are zeroing in on . . . on Hunter as a possible suspect."

"No!" Madeline's hand flew to her mouth.

"They think he was after his father's money. For some invention of his." Gigi crossed her fingers. She felt terrible lying to Madeline like this, but it was the only way. "He did leave the party early. I'm sure you remember that. And you told me that he'd lied about where he went that night."

Madeline's face had become alarmingly pale. For a minute, Gigi was afraid she might faint.

"But that's not true. Hunter wouldn't . . ."

Gigi remained silent.

Madeline looked at her pleadingly. "You've got to help us. We've got to do something."

"You still have the key to Tiffany's office?"

Madeline nodded eagerly.

"We need to get into her office. How late do people usually work?"

Madeline shrugged. "It depends. Sometimes all night. But I don't think that will be a problem. If someone is staying late, they generally have their head down and don't notice what's going on."

"What would be a good time?"

"Ten o'clock maybe? Just about everyone will have left by then unless they're under a huge deadline."

"Where should I meet you?" Gigi was relieved to see that Madeline was going along with her scheme.

"It's probably best if you don't park in our lot. It would

be better to park where you won't be noticed—Declan's maybe. I'll be by the door, and I'll keep an eye out for you."

Gigi was about to leave when Madeline grabbed her arm. "Do you think we'll find something? We have to." She gulped down a sob. "Hunter didn't do anything, I know it. He'd never hurt his father."

Gigi squeezed her hands into fists. She'd lied to Madeline and now Madeline was all upset. It wasn't fair. But she had to get to the bottom of this. She just had to.

"Don't worry. I'm sure everything will turn out okay." She gave Madeline a quick hug. "I'll see you at ten o'clock by the front door."

By the time Gigi got back to her car and Reg's exuberant greeting, she had nearly managed to convince herself that lying to Madeline had been for Madeline's own good. In reality, she was hoping to prove to Mertz that Declan was not responsible for Bradley's murder. Because if he was, her sister's heart was going to be broken again. Never mind that she and Declan had never even had a proper date. In Pia's mind they were practically engaged and just a walk down the aisle away from eternal romantic bliss.

Gigi drove home through the back streets again, but there was still no sign of Pia's VW bus anywhere. Ralph's pizza truck was at her curb when she got home, however, and Pia's VW was at the head of the driveway. Gigi pulled in behind it and got out. Reg began tugging her toward the street so Gigi thought she would give him a walk now rather than later.

Reg pulled her past the neighbors' house—an elderly couple who had lived there for more than fifty years. Their front door opened, and Mrs. Prescott wobbled down the steps and tottered toward the mailbox at the end of their driveway. She held her coat closed with one hand and had a kerchief covering her permed gray curls.

"Good afternoon, Hermione," Gigi called loudly, knowing that her neighbor was hard of hearing.

"Eh? Good afternoon you say?" Hermione pulled a stack of mail from her box and waited as Gigi and Reg caught up with her. She gestured toward the pizza delivery truck outside of Gigi's house. "Aren't you running that diet business no more? I seen that truck there a couple of times this week already." She pointed a bony finger in the direction of Gigi's house. "I wouldn't think pizza would be something you'd be eating real regular."

"It's not me; it's my sister." Reg gave a tug, and Gigi let the leash out slightly.

"That girl with the short hair?" Hermione made a twirling motion above her head.

Gigi nodded.

Hermione stared at Gigi, her watery blue eyes wide open. "Don't you cook for her? You cook for all those strangers— you can't even do that much for your own sister?"

Gigi wished she could close her eyes and just disappear. Were other people thinking the same thing?

She smiled at Hermione. "My sister likes pizza unfortunately."

"Of course she does," Hermione said illogically. "Everyone likes pizza. Can't say I blame her, can you?"

"No, no, I can't." Gigi gave Reg a discreet tug in the direction of home. "Nice seeing you, Hermione." Gigi waved good-bye.

By the time she'd dragged Reg to the back door, she was fuming. Pia had to stop ordering pizza. Better yet, Pia had to find somewhere else to live. Gigi couldn't take it anymore.

When Gigi entered the kitchen, Pia was seated at the island, pizza box flipped open and a piece in her hand. She waved the slice toward the box when she saw Gigi.

"Want some?" she mumbled indistinctly around a mouthful.

Gigi shook her head curtly.

"What's the matter?" Pia ran a hand through her short hair, making it even spikier than usual.

"Nothing." Gigi tried to smile, but the movement felt forced and she abandoned the attempt.

"Look, I'm sorry if I'm in your way." Pia closed the pizza box and began to gather up the crumpled paper napkins that littered the island.

Gigi let her shoulders drop. "No, don't be silly, it's fine. I'm just a little tense, that's all." Thinking about the night ahead and rummaging through Tiffany's office was making her more nervous than she wanted to admit. She could only imagine how Madeline must feel.

"I'll make you some tea," Pia offered.

"No, that's okay." Gigi just really wanted to be alone to think.

Fortunately, Pia threw the remains of her pizza crust in the box and stood up. "There's more if you want some." She pulled her jacket from the hook by the back door and struggled into it. Her arm caught on the lining and she swore briefly. "I'm heading to the studio. See you later."

"Don't you think you're working too—" But before Gigi

could finish the sentence, the door slammed in back of Pia, nearly dislodging the framed poster of sage, or *Salvia officinalis*, that hung on Gigi's kitchen wall.

Gigi left the cottage with plenty of time to spare. She left Reg lying on the rug in the front hall, his head on his front paws and a disappointed look on his face. She had no idea how long she would be and couldn't risk leaving him in the car, even though he was making it clear he disagreed with her decision.

The streets of Woodstone were quiet, and there were only a few cars in the lot next to Declan's. Gigi parked in the back, hoping her MINI would escape notice. For once she wished she had purchased a slightly less recognizable car—a Taurus or Focus wouldn't have caught anyone's attention.

She sat for a moment behind the wheel of the darkened car. She was early and didn't want to have to hang around in front of Simpson and West waiting for Madeline to open the front door.

Finally, at one minute to ten, she got out, locked the MINI and began walking in the direction of the law firm. The wind whistled down the street, shaking the bare trees and making Gigi shiver. She was glad when she finally reached the front doors of Simpson and West. She heard Madeline turn the latch as she approached, and the door was pushed open.

Gigi quickly ducked inside. The lobby was dimly lit, the reception desk tidied for the night. She noticed the retreating back of a night watchman as he disappeared through one of the doors, and her breath caught in her throat. She gestured toward him mutely.

"Don't worry about him," Madeline reassured her. "It's

fine as long as you're with me. Besides, he's more interested in taking a nip out of the bottle he keeps in the housekeeping closet than catching intruders."

Madeline swiped her employee badge in the slot next to the elevator, and the doors whooshed open. Neither woman spoke as they watched the indicator sweep toward the second floor and stop, with a final quiver, just as the doors opened.

"Her office is down here," Madeline said in hushed tones as she fished a key from the pocket of her suit jacket.

The hallway was dimly lit at this time of night, but Gigi noticed that a pool of light spilled out of an office further down the hall. She gestured toward it. "Someone's here."

"Probably just working late. Don't worry about it."

Suddenly a man came out of the office. His suit jacket was off, his shirtsleeves rolled up and his tie loosened. He had a sheaf of papers in his hand and barely looked up as he swept past Gigi and Madeline, who had flattened themselves against the wall.

Gigi felt sweat breaking out under her arms, but Madeline seemed unperturbed as she inserted the key in the lock and pushed open the door. A cloud of stale air seeped out. Madeline felt along the wall for the light switch. They both started and blinked furiously as the overhead fixture blazed on. Madeline strode toward the desk and clicked on a small brass reading lamp, motioning to Gigi to turn the other light off.

The lamp trained a bright circle of light on top of the desk, leaving the corners of the office dark with shadows. Gigi looked around. File drawers gaped open like giant tongues sticking out, and papers and folders were spewed across the top of the desk as if scattered by a strong breeze. Someone had indeed been looking for something. But what?

"Where should we start?"

Madeline shrugged her shoulders. "I have no idea. The desk probably. That's where she'd keep whatever she was working on most recently."

Gigi certainly had no idea what to look for as she flipped through a stack of folders, and Madeline looked through a second pile. All the folders were carefully labeled and appeared to pertain to various tax cases Simpson and West was handling for their clients. She was beginning to think this hadn't been a very good idea. What did she think she was going to find? A note with the murderer's name written on it?

She tossed the last of the folders on the desk, ready to admit defeat.

"Anything?" she asked as Madeline put down the last of her files.

"No. These are all tax cases. I can't imagine they have anything to do with the murders." She chewed on the side of her index finger. "Maybe the intruder found what they were looking for and took it away."

"That's possible. But judging by the mess they made, it wasn't easy to find. No, I suspect that whatever it is, it's still here somewhere."

The sound of something squeaking came from the corridor, and they both froze. Madeline peeked around the edge of the door.

"It's just the cleaning lady with her cart."

Gigi let out her breath. "I'm sorry. I don't think this was such a great idea. I don't know what I expected to find."

"That's okay. I know you're trying to help me and Hunter." Madeline sniffed and dabbed at her eyes.

"I guess we'd better go."

"What do we do next?" Madeline looked at Gigi, her nose reddening and her eyes brimming with tears.

"I don't know. But I'll think of something."

Gigi could have kicked herself as soon as the words were out of her mouth. She had no idea what that something was going to be.

Gigi turned on the overhead light, and once again the sudden glare had them blinking furiously. Madeline switched off the lamp on the desk and was walking toward the door when the heel of her black suede booties caught on the edge of the oriental throw rug Tiffany had placed between her desk and the door.

"Oh," Madeline gave a little cry as her ankle twisted, and she began to fall.

Gigi rushed to her side. "Are you okay?"

"Fine." Madeline rubbed her ankle. "I don't think it's sprained or anything."

Gigi held out her hand and pulled Madeline to her feet. Madeline tested her foot gingerly and gave a crooked smile. "It's fine."

They both looked down and noticed that the edge of the rug, which had caught on the heel of Madeline's boot, had been peeled back. And peeking out from underneath it was a manila file folder.

"What the . . ." Gigi said as she bent to retrieve it.

She picked up the folder and several photographs spilled out. Gigi picked them up and glanced through them quickly.

They appeared to be snapshots of cars heading through downtown Woodstone.

"What are these do you suppose?" Gigi held one up for Madeline to see.

Madeline took it by the corners and studied it. "Looks like these were taken by that camera they installed at the intersection of High Street and Elmwood to catch people running the light. See?" She pointed at the picture. "The camera is situated so that it gets a good shot of the car's license plate. The police use these to send out tickets."

Gigi looked at the photo again. Madeline was right. It was the back end of a Mercedes with the vanity plate *SNKMS*. "What would she be doing with these, I wonder?"

"I have no idea. Traffic violations are hardly the sort of thing we handle. And Tiffany's specialty was tax law." Madeline picked up the folder the photo had been in. "Strange. There's nothing written on here." She turned the manila folder over and looked at the back. She waved it toward Gigi. "No label, no paperwork, nothing."

"Are all the pictures the same?"

Madeline spilled the rest of them out onto the desk. "No." She pointed at one photo of the tail end of red pickup truck and another that was clearly the back of a Land Rover.

"What on earth was it doing under the rug?" Gigi pointed at the folder in Madeline's hands.

"I can't even begin to imagine. It looks like she was hiding it."

"Do you think you can find out what she was working on? Maybe that will give us some idea of what to look for. You could ask her secretary?"

A horrified look crossed Madeline's face.

"After all, if the police think Hunter . . ." Gigi let the words hang. She didn't have to wait long.

Madeline nodded her head briskly. "I'll ask Betty if she knows anything." She bundled the pictures back into the folder and held it out. "What should we do with it?"

"I would put it back under the rug. Just in case it has anything to do with Tiffany's murder."

The very words sent a chill through Gigi, and she shivered violently.

They turned out the light and slipped from Tiffany's office into the corridor. Gigi was relieved to see it was empty. The fewer people who saw her sneaking around the halls of Simpson and West, the better.

After all, one of them might very well be a killer.

# Chapter 20

Gigi once again took a circuitous route home through the back roads of Woodstone where several industrial parks were located, along with Moe's Towing and Storage, the bus depot, an electrical plant, and the building where the *Woodstone Times* was printed. The sidewalks were cracked and buckled, and the few scrawny trees were sickly looking.

It was eerily quiet as Gigi drove along the shadowy street. A few of the streetlamps were out, making it even darker. She couldn't imagine Pia wanting to come here late at night, by herself, but where else would she find a cheap place to use as a studio?

Gigi's head swiveled left and right, looking for any sign of Pia's VW bus. She was coming up to a long, low building on her right that had multiple doors along the front. All the dirt-encrusted windows were dark, save one where a faint glow of light was visible through the grime.

And right outside was Pia's van.

Gigi slammed on her brakes and pulled into the parking lot. The macadam was split and pitted, and she shuddered as the left wheel of the MINI sank into a deep pothole. She pulled up next to Pia's van and got out.

An icy wind immediately grabbed her scarf and tossed it over her face. Gigi clawed it away frantically. The whole place was giving her the creeps, and she felt the hairs on the back of her neck stand up.

She stood outside the door that was directly in front of Pia's van. She hesitated. Would knocking scare Pia? Gigi knew it would certainly scare *her* if she were alone in a place like this. She decided she would use her cell and call Pia instead. She debated getting back in her car, but it didn't seem worth the effort. She huddled in the lee of the door and scrabbled through her purse for her phone. The cold made her fingers stiff and awkward, but she finally found it. She pulled off her gloves and hit the speed dial number for Pia.

Pia sounded startled when she answered. "What's wrong? Is something wrong?"

"No," Gigi reassured her. "But I'm right outside your door."

"My door? What do you mean? You're here at the studio?"

"Yes, and I'm freezing, so I'd be really grateful if you'd let me in."

Gigi waited while Pia dealt with the lock on the door. She was terrified of what she was going to find. Was Pia stockpiling lawn ornaments in this place? Was she the Woodstone thief the police were desperate to catch? Gigi remembered some pieces Pia had made a long time ago—an assortment of all sorts of things—hubcaps, a deflated soccer ball, a handful of tools—arranged into a sort of collage. Some of the items had been partially melted with a welding iron so that they drooped like the objects in a Salvador Dali painting. Pia had called it *found art*, probably because she had found all the elements while roaming the streets and picking through junkyards. There had been a certain appeal to the arrangement, although Gigi couldn't imagine anyone hanging it on their wall. Was Pia doing something like that on a bigger scale? Using parts of lawn ornaments belonging to the citizens of Woodstone?

Pia finally unlocked the door. It was dented and warped and stuck slightly so that she had to tug to get it open.

"How did you find me?" Pia asked as soon as Gigi entered the studio.

"Your van. It's parked right outside."

Pia bit her lower lip. "I knew I should have pulled it around back, but it was cold, and I didn't feel like walking around to the front of the building."

The room itself was frigid, and Pia had on a paint-stained men's shirt with the buttons missing over a thick wool sweater and was wearing fingerless gloves. She moved aside, and Gigi was able to look around. The room was quite large, and Pia had used several halogen work lights on tripods to light the space. A scarred wooden table, with a stack of books propping up a broken leg, was littered with tubes of paint, a handful of brushes and several sticks of charcoal.

An enormous piece of paper was tacked to one wall and was covered with a sketch that mirrored the huge canvas leaning against the other wall. The painting was a scene of the French countryside with lavender in the foreground and a field of sunflowers in the background. It was very beautiful.

Gigi approached it in awe. "This is fabulous. I feel like I can almost smell the flowers."

Pia ducked her head. "Thanks. I'm quite pleased with it myself."

Gigi glanced around quickly but there was no sign of the missing lawn ornaments. She felt relief wash over her. "Why didn't you tell me about this?"

Pia shrugged. "Dunno, really. I never like showing my stuff until it's done."

"Are you going to sell it?"

"It's a commission actually. For that new gourmet shop that's opening in town."

"Oh." Gigi's spirits plummeted. The place was going to look incredible with this fabulous piece on the wall. Evelyn had nothing like it for Bon Appétit. How would she compete?

"Why were you so determined to find my studio?" Pia squeezed a blob of bright blue paint onto her palette and dabbed at the right corner of the canvas where a brilliant sky lit the fields below.

"Oh. No particular reason. Just curious." Gigi felt her face getting red.

"Would you like some tea? I've got an electric teakettle." Pia gestured toward the far wall where a kettle was plugged into an outlet. Next to it were two of Gigi's mugs.

"No, thanks. I should be going home."

"Satisfied now?" Pia paused with her brush hovering over the palette.

"Yes." Gigi pointed at the painting. "It really is beautiful."

She left Pia's studio feeling very small. Very small indeed. Of course her sister wasn't responsible for the theft of the lawn ornaments. How could she have thought such a thing? Instead, Pia was working on one of her best works so far, and working hard under less-than-ideal circumstances. Gigi shivered again as she thought of being alone in this desolate place.

She beeped open the MINI and got behind the wheel. She couldn't wait to get home to her comfortable cottage and curl up in her warm bed with Reg at her feet.

Gigi hit the snooze button twice the next morning. Her late-night sleuthing had worn her out. She dressed, put on some coffee, threw on her jacket and headed to the end of the driveway to collect her newspaper. Reg followed behind her. He lifted his leg on several bushes and nearly disappeared into one. Gigi heard a lot of rustling before Reg backed out slowly. He was probably after some small woodland creature, Gigi thought, which had eluded his capture.

Pia's van was missing from the driveway. Her sister must still be at the studio. Gigi felt a pang of guilt. Pia really was working awfully hard.

By the time Gigi got back inside, her coffee was ready. She poured a cup, climbed onto one of the stools around the island and opened up the *Woodstone Times*. The paper was cold to the touch, and Gigi wrapped her hands around her mug to warm them. Once again, there were several letters to the editor demanding to know what the police were doing to solve the two recent murders and to catch the lawn ornament thief. Gigi winced as she read them. She imagined

Mertz would be hearing from his boss, and it wouldn't be good.

Gigi sighed and folded up the paper. She had to get moving and get her clients' breakfasts prepared and delivered. She had prepared the dish the day before—baked oatmeal with bananas and blueberries that only needed to be warmed in the microwave. She was packing everything in her Gourmet De-Lite containers when she had a thought. Perhaps Pia would like something to eat. She microwaved one portion and also filled a thermos with the remains of the hot coffee. It would certainly be a more nourishing breakfast than Pia's usual toaster pastries or powdered sugar doughnuts.

Gigi delivered her clients' breakfasts quickly. Her route took her past the Woodstone Police Station, where a small crowd was again gathered outside. Gigi was able to read one of the placards that demanded an immediate arrest of the criminals responsible for both the murders and the thefts. She passed the site of the new gourmet shop, but it was obvious, even from the street, that nothing had been done inside yet. Finally, she headed toward the far side of town and Pia's studio. It occurred to her that Pia might already be on her way back to Gigi's cottage, so she was relieved to see Pia's van parked in the same spot as the previous evening. What she didn't expect to see was another car parked right next to it—a late-model Land Rover that made Pia's vehicle look like even more of a wreck.

Gigi pulled in next to the two cars and hesitated. Maybe she ought to leave well enough alone? She glanced at the container of food and the thermos on the seat next to her. She squared her shoulders and got out.

Pia looked slightly startled when she opened the door. She was wearing the same sweater and fingerless gloves as the night before, but had taken off the paint-stained workshirt. Her pixieish hair was even more disheveled than usual, and she was clutching a Styrofoam container of coffee.

She opened the door just wide enough to see who it was.

"I've brought you some breakfast." Gigi handed her the Gourmet De-Lite container. "Although I see you already have some coffee. I don't want to disturb you . . ."

"Thanks." Pia gave a tired smile. "That's very nice of you. I'm about ready to wrap it up here." She gave a big yawn.

"Yes . . . well . . . I'll get going then."

Pia began to shut the door but not before Gigi caught a glimpse of a man standing in the far corner of the studio.

A man who looked an awful lot like Declan McQuaid.

Gigi drove away in a rush, her tires kicking up bits of loose gravel as she pulled out onto Broad Street. So Pia and Declan were . . . Her mind didn't want to finish the sentence. It was now more important than ever that she prove Declan wasn't responsible for the two murders. It would kill Pia if he were arrested.

Gigi was so distracted by her thoughts that she missed the turn onto Elmwood Street that would take her back to High Street and the center of town. She pulled into the nearest driveway to turn around. When she looked to her right, she noticed a large metal sign with one corner missing announcing that she had arrived at Manny's Junkyard. Underneath, in smaller letters, it read—*We take scrap metal, car parts and all sorts of junk. When in doubt, bring it in.*

Gigi was about to back out onto Broad Street when she

saw something that made her change her mind. She put the MINI in drive and cruised into the parking lot of Manny's Junkyard.

The front gate was open. Pieces of metal, car parts and all sorts of junk were piled as high as Gigi could see. She hoped there wasn't a junkyard dog. She looked around cautiously, thinking back to an experience she'd had at Moe's Towing and Storage.

"Can I help you?" A man called, coming down an aisle that had been created through several mounds of twisted metal. He was bald with a gray beard and was wearing a blue shirt with *Manny* embroidered above the pocket.

"Manny?"

"One and the same," he said, pointing to his name on the sign. "What can I do for you?" He pulled a rag from his back pocket and wiped his hands.

"I was curious about this piece over here." He followed Gigi to the front of the lot. "I wondered if you remembered who brought it in."

Gigi gestured to a lawn ornament that was slightly bent and twisted, but was clearly a frog playing a violin. The very same piece she'd seen someone swipe from that front yard on Elmwood Street.

Manny scratched the side of his head with one hand and stroked his beard with the other. He gestured toward the piles of junk behind him. "You see all this stuff here?"

Gigi nodded.

"Yeah, well, there's a lot of it, isn't there?"

Gigi nodded again. She had a sinking feeling that Manny wasn't going to be able to help her.

"There's no way I could remember every single person

who comes here with an old radiator, some copper wire or a piece of sheet metal, is there?"

Gigi shook her head.

"But!" Manny paused dramatically. "I do happen to remember that piece. It was only a couple of days ago. Fellow by the name of Jimmy brought it in. The metal isn't worth all that much, but what's not much to me might be a king's ransom to someone else. You know what I mean?"

Gigi certainly did.

"Jimmy's brought me a couple of pieces like this. He's a nice guy."

"Do you know where he got them?"

"Don't know, don't ask and don't tell, that's my motto."

"Haven't you seen the stories in the *Woodstone Times*?"

Manny shrugged. "I'm not much for reading papers. Get all the news I need from the television."

*Which wouldn't include a local story like missing lawn ornaments.*

"Someone has been swiping lawn ornaments from front yards all over Woodstone. Ornaments just like that one there."

Manny's look turned hostile. "Hey, lady, I'm not dealing in stolen goods, all right? Like I told you, I don't know where Jimmy got the stuff, and it's not my business to ask or my problem. You have a problem with it, I suggest you talk to the police." He turned his back on her and began to walk away. "And I suggest you leave now," he tossed over his shoulder.

Gigi didn't need to be told twice. She was back in her car in a nanosecond and sped out of the driveway before another minute had gone by.

# Chapter 21

Gigi headed straight to Mertz's office. She racked her brain frantically as she drove—she needed to explain to Mertz why she didn't immediately report the theft of the lawn ornament to him. It would be too embarrassing to admit that she thought her own sister was responsible. What would he think of Pia? Worse, what would he think of her?

By the time Gigi arrived at the Woodstone Police Station, she had decided that her best line of defense was to say nothing. No need to report having seen the piece stolen. She would just say that she noticed it at the junkyard and wondered if had been one of the pieces that had gone missing from a Woodstone resident's lawn.

The receptionist barely hesitated to wave Gigi on through. She didn't even bother to ask if Gigi knew the way.

Mertz was at his desk munching on a granola bar when Gigi arrived. He jumped to his feet immediately.

"What a nice surprise." He hugged her and gave her a brief kiss.

"Please, sit." He pulled an empty chair closer to his desk.

Gigi perched on the edge and wet her lips.

Mertz frowned. "You look terribly serious."

Gigi fiddled with the fringe on her scarf. "I think I might have a clue in the missing lawn ornaments case."

"Really?" Mertz sat up straighter and pulled a yellow pad toward him. He plucked a pen from a holder on top of his desk. "Shoot."

Gigi explained about turning around in Manny's parking lot. "This one piece caught my eye so I stopped and went in. It was a metal sculpture of a frog playing a violin. It stood out against all the twisted metal and car parts."

Mertz was quickly jotting down notes. "I'll head over there right away." He picked up the phone, barked some orders and began to reach for his coat.

Gigi hesitated. Should she tell him about Jimmy?

"What's the matter?" Mertz paused with one arm in the sleeve of his coat. "There's something you're not telling me, isn't there?"

Gigi drew a circle on the carpet with her right foot. "Well, I did ask Manny, the junkyard owner, if he knew who brought the piece in. He said it was some guy named Jimmy."

Mertz sighed. "There are a lot of Jimmys out there. I'm not sure how helpful that's going to be."

"Manny said he's brought stuff in before. All lawn ornaments."

"But no last name, I gather?"

Gigi shook her head. "No. But I wonder . . ."

Mertz smiled. "You wonder what? Have you been snooping again?"

"Oh, no." Gigi crossed her fingers behind her back. Well, she hadn't been snooping exactly. More like overhearing and certainly that didn't count, did it?

"Bradley Simpson has a brother-in-law named Jimmy. His wife works at the recording studio where I went to make the commercials for Branston Foods. I heard her on the phone talking to someone about their financial troubles. Manny said the metal from the lawn ornaments doesn't bring in much, but for someone who's desperate . . ."

Mertz sighed, louder this time. "Unfortunately, I can't use that as a basis for arresting the guy." He stopped with his hat halfway to his head. "But maybe we could set up a sting . . ." He leaned over and pecked Gigi on the cheek. "I've got to get going. You know the way out?"

Mertz turned right down the corridor, and Gigi turned left. She was pushing open the front door when her cell phone rang. By the time she located it at the bottom of her purse, the ringing had stopped. She checked the number and saw the name *Simpson and West* on the call log. The only person who would call her from there was Madeline.

Gigi hit redial as she walked toward her car. Madeline picked up on the second ring. Her voice was low—practically a whisper.

"Gigi? Listen, I've got some news. I can't talk over the phone. Can you meet me for a quick cup of coffee at the Woodstone Diner?"

Gigi glanced at her watch. Lunch for her clients was going to be a healthy veggie wrap that wouldn't take long to prepare. "Sure."

"Great. I'll see you there in five."

Gigi clicked off the call and spun on her heel, turning in the other direction, toward the Woodstone Diner.

Two of the booths were occupied when she got there. There were four women in one having a late breakfast. Gigi imagined they were headed to the mall afterward for some shopping. A single man sat in the other booth, nursing a cup of coffee and scrolling through the texts on his phone. Gigi thought he was probably a salesman looking for a place to get in from the cold and check his messages.

She grabbed a booth way in the back and had barely sat down when the door opened and Madeline came in.

"Hey," she said as she unbuttoned her camel hair coat, folded it carefully and placed it on the seat beside her.

The waitress immediately glided up and slapped menus down on the table. She started to walk away, but Gigi called out to her.

"Just a coffee for me, please."

"I'll have a cup of tea." Madeline pushed the menus toward the edge of the table.

The waitress nodded, her mouth set in a grim line. Gigi could understand—cups of tea and coffee didn't bring much of a tip.

Madeline rubbed her hands together. They were red from the cold. She was quiet as they waited for the waitress to return with their order. As soon as the woman was safely back behind the counter, Madeline began to talk, keeping her voice low so that Gigi had to lean closer to hear.

"I talked to Betty, Tiffany's secretary."

Gigi nodded encouragingly. "Yes?" She pulled a napkin from the dispenser and put it under her cup to soak up the coffee that had sloshed over the edge.

Madeline shook her head. "Unfortunately, she didn't know much of anything." She rolled her eyes. "Tiffany was working on a case that Mr. Flanagan himself had asked her to handle. He's a partner in the firm, although his name isn't on the actual masthead." Madeline took a sip of her tea and grimaced. She reached for a packet of artificial sweetener, tore it open and dumped the contents into her cup. "She didn't know what the actual case was. Just that it was somehow related to Mr. Flanagan."

"And?" Gigi prompted.

"That's all. That's all I've been able to find out. It was supersecret, and Betty herself never even saw the files. Apparently all the paperwork went to Mr. Flanagan's secretary. She's been with the firm for forty-five years, and rumor has it, she knows more than all of the partners put together."

Frustration washed over Gigi like a tidal wave. She felt like she was taking one step forward and two back. There had to be some other way to discover what it was that Tiffany had been working on. Why else would someone have searched her office? It didn't make any sense.

"I'm sorry I wasn't able to find out anything more," Madeline said as she sipped her tea. "But I do have some good news." A brief smile crossed her face.

"Yes?" Gigi was too disappointed to be more than mildly enthusiastic.

"I talked to Hunter. You know he wouldn't tell me where he went the night his father was . . . was . . . murdered." Madeline looked down at her cup. "I finally got him to talk about it. Apparently after that speech his father gave, he decided not to approach him for the money for his invention. He'd hoped to keep it in the family, but Bradley had made it obvious that he had no interest in what Hunter was doing. Hunter had already been approached by a representative from a Japanese firm. They were very interested in providing him with the needed capital."

Gigi tried to look surprised although Madeline wasn't telling her anything she didn't already know.

"Hunter had been resisting the idea, but after bolting from Declan's, he called the woman who was here from the investment company and asked to meet up with her. He'd decided to accept their offer."

"So he was with her when his father was killed?

Madeline nodded. "Yes."

Gigi was disappointed—another lead that hadn't panned out. But she was happy for Madeline. If that woman could verify that Hunter was with her when Bradley was killed, Hunter was no longer a suspect. Unfortunately, that made one less person standing between Declan McQuaid, Pia's current love of a lifetime, and an arrest for murder.

Gigi and Madeline finished their drinks just as the waitress slid their tab across the table.

Gigi fished a couple of dollars from her wallet. "Let me take care of this."

"Thanks." Madeline retrieved her coat and buttoned it up. "I'm sorry I couldn't be more helpful. Betty really had no idea what Tiffany was up to." She frowned as she tightened her belt around her waist. "It's very unusual. Whatever Tiffany was working on must have been top secret."

Pia was home and asleep when Gigi arrived back at her cottage. She was relieved. She didn't want to hear about

Declan's visit to Pia's studio. She was terrified that Pia's heart was going to be broken.

Gigi went about preparing her clients' lunches and dinners. She was dropping them both off at once this time since the weather forecast for later in the day was quite dire. High winds and whiteout conditions. Gigi thought about what Tiffany had said as she washed lettuce for a salad. What case could be so top secret that Tiffany's secretary wasn't even allowed to see the papers, and did it have anything to do with her murder or with Bradley Simpson's?

Gigi glanced out the window, where snowflakes had already begun to fall and a strong wind was shaking the trees like an invisible hand. She shivered. It would be so nice to stay inside and curl up with a book. She gave herself a little shake. She really had it easy. She thought back to her days in New York, slogging through all kinds of weather, struggling to get on crowded buses and subways, walking for blocks in the frigid temperatures. Now all she had to do was deliver these meals to her clients, and then she'd be able to spend the rest of the day warm and snug in her cottage.

Reg was waiting by the door as Gigi slipped into her coat.

"Sorry, not this time, buddy. You stay here and keep Pia company, okay?"

He tilted his head this way and that, his ears twitching, as if to say, *okay, I understand. I'll guard the fort, don't worry.*

Gigi ran the scraper over the MINI's windows as quickly as possible. The wind blew snow in her face, and it felt like icy pinpricks against her bare skin. She threw the scraper in the backseat and slid behind the wheel.

Barbara Simpson's car was parked at the far end of

the circular driveway, facing Gigi, but it was still the maid who opened the door to Gigi's ring and accepted the Gourmet De-Lite containers. Gigi wondered how Barbara was doing. Was her grief slowly lessening or was it too soon for that?

Gigi dashed into Simpson and West with Madeline's containers, leaving them in the hands of the receptionist. The snow was coming down more heavily, and the wheels of the MINI lost traction on the icy road several times.

Penelope Lawson was Gigi's last stop. She dashed up the front steps of the Lawsons' brick Colonial. A woven grapevine heart wreath hung from the front door, nearly obscured by clumps of newly fallen snow. Gigi shivered as she waited for Penelope to answer the door.

"Gigi!" Penelope flung open the door. "You must be freezing. Come in and have something warm to drink. I've just made some cocoa."

Gigi was about to politely refuse when she noticed a shattered vase on the floor of Penelope's foyer, a little pile of shards of glass right next to it.

Penelope noticed her glance. "Oh, that. The kids have kept me running, and I haven't had a chance to deal with it. I got it swept into a pile, and that's as far as I've been able to get. George was in a bit of a temper this morning and knocked it over on his way out." Penelope sighed. "Sometimes I wish he'd quit that firm. Oliver—you know Sienna's husband—wants George to join up with him in his practice, but George is worried about the money." She swept a hand around the hallway. "This place is a money pit, and with three children to put through college, he's afraid to make the move."

Gigi had already changed her mind about leaving and

was following Penelope out to her vast kitchen and family room. Penelope opened a cupboard and took out two mugs with red-and-white-striped candy cane handles. She filled them each with cocoa and handed one to Gigi.

The warm mug felt good in her cold hands.

Penelope took a sip then stopped abruptly and looked at Gigi over the rim of her cup. "Don't worry, it's sugar-free."

A thumping sound came from above.

"Just the kids. Hughie's having a nap and Mason and Ava are supposed to be resting in their rooms." She rolled her eyes. "Doesn't sound like they're getting much rest." She motioned toward the sofa. "Do you want to sit down?" She quickly picked up the sections of newspaper that were scattered across the cushions.

Gigi joined her on the couch.

Penelope turned toward Gigi suddenly. "Please don't think badly of George. He's just upset about this case that got dumped in his lap. Tiffany Morse was supposed to be handling it, but well"—Penelope rolled her eyes—"we all know what happened to her."

"Really?" Gigi tried to look innocent as she took a sip of her cocoa. "Is it a very complicated case?"

Penelope rolled her eyes again. "No, and that's what's really got George in such a snit. It's ridiculous to ask someone with his experience to handle this. But the orders came from Flanagan, and he's a partner so . . ."

Gigi nodded to show she understood.

"And of course partners' families get special treatment." She shook her head. "The problem is George isn't sure there's anything he can do. The police have really begun to crack down on traffic violations, especially anything involving alcohol. They even put up that camera on the corner of High Street and Elmwood. That's where Flanagan's grandson was clocked doing ninety-five miles an hour. Can you imagine? Even if it was late at night. Someone could have been hurt."

"Was he drinking?"

Penelope nodded. "Yes, he was over the limit. And underage to boot. And I guess he's not much more than a point away from losing his license. Apparently Tiffany had been trying to prove that the camera wasn't reliable, but she didn't get very far. Now it's up to George to determine what course to take. And it's making him very ornery. He feels the whole thing is beneath him." Penelope picked up one of the throw pillows on the sofa and began to run her fingers through the border of fringe. "Besides, he's afraid he won't be successful, and they'll can him." She laughed. "Well, maybe that would be the push he needs to join up with Oliver and get out of that rat race."

Gigi was digesting this bit of news when a pitiful wail came from above.

Penelope glanced at her watch. "Sounds like Hughie's up. That wasn't a very long nap."

"I'd better be going." Gigi took the opportunity to get to her feet.

The wail became louder and rose to an ear-shattering crescendo.

"If you don't mind seeing yourself out . . ." Penelope was already moving toward the back stairs that ran from the family room to the upper level.

"No problem." Gigi buttoned her coat as she headed toward the front door.

All the way home the only thing she could think about

was the information she'd gleaned from Penelope. It seemed likely that Flanagan's grandson's DUI was Tiffany's last case. Gigi thought back to the folder she and Madeline had found under Tiffany's rug. Did the dark blue Mercedes in that picture belong to the young man?

But then why had Tiffany hidden it? And was there any relation between that and her murder?

Gigi gave a groan of frustration as she pulled into the driveway of her cottage. She couldn't go to Mertz with what she'd discovered. That would mean admitting to having snooped in Tiffany's office. Gigi shuddered at the thought. That would not go over well at all.

Gigi spent a luxurious afternoon on the sofa curled up with a book. It had been a long time since she'd been able to relax like that. Pia had woken up and made a brief appearance—just long enough to burn a bag of popcorn in the microwave—before departing for her studio. Gigi had opened several windows, shivering under a throw on the couch, hoping to rid the house of the smell.

The shadows in the room grew darker until Gigi reluctantly left her warm cocoon to turn on some lights. She realized she was hungry, but for once, she did not feel like cooking. She poked around in the pantry until she found a container of mac and cheese Pia had purchased. It didn't look *that* bad. Gigi read the directions, popped it in the microwave and pressed start.

Reg looked at her with sad eyes as if he were embarrassed by her sudden and unexpected lapse in judgment. Gigi turned her back on him and stirred the mixture with her fork. She took a bite. The first words that came to mind were *wallpaper paste*. How could people eat stuff like this?

Her stomach growled, and she was sorry she hadn't saved some of her clients' dinner for herself, but one of the women wanted her husband to try Gigi's food so she had sent along the extra portion.

By the third forkful she was used to the taste and wondering whether there was a way to make a more flavorful, lower-calorie version. She was scraping up the last bits of macaroni when the doorbell rang.

Reg went into his usual paroxysms of barking, sliding the last few feet down the hall to the foyer. Gigi followed, still holding the container of mac and cheese. She pulled open the door.

Mertz stood on her doorstep. "Are you busy?" he asked as he stomped his feet and brushed snow from his coat.

"Not at all."

He stepped inside and kissed Gigi briefly on the cheek. He rubbed his hands together. "It's freezing out there, and the streets are beginning to ice up. I'm afraid the road crews will be busy tonight." Mertz gestured toward the container in Gigi's hands. "What's that you're eating?"

Gigi felt her face redden. "Macaroni and cheese," she admitted reluctantly.

Mertz shook his head. "That's the kind of meal I subsist on, but I never thought I'd see you eating it." He slipped out of his coat and hung it in the closet.

"Pia left it in the cupboard," she explained lest Mertz think she had actually gone out and purchased it. "I was hungry, so . . ."

"I guess that means you don't have anything for a starving detective?" Mertz draped an arm around Gigi's shoulders as they walked toward the kitchen. He peered into her container. "Not even a bite left. Must have been delicious."

Gigi gave him a playful punch in the ribs. "Let me see what's in the fridge."

She opened the refrigerator and poked around. "Would eggs and bacon do?"

Mertz's face broke into a smile. "Quite nicely. Far more nutritious than the granola bar in my pocket."

Gigi popped some bread in the toaster and got a carton of eggs and a packet of bacon out of the refrigerator and put them on the counter. "How do you like your eggs?"

"Scrambled would be great."

Mertz played with Reg while Gigi fried some bacon and whisked eggs in a bowl. She slipped the golden liquid into the pan of hot, melted butter, where it immediately sizzled and soon began to form soft curds. Gigi realized she was whistling to herself. Having Mertz sitting in her kitchen, relaxing with Reg, suddenly seemed just perfect.

She slipped the eggs from the pan onto a plate, added a few slices of crisp bacon, two pieces of toast, and placed it in front of Mertz. Reg's nose twitched eagerly as he planted himself at Mertz's feet.

Gigi made herself a cup of tea and slid into the seat opposite Mertz. He'd polished off half the meal before he looked up.

"I have a huge favor to ask of you." He swiped his napkin across his lips. "I talked to the chief, and he agreed. Probably the only way we're going to catch this lawn ornament thief is by setting up some kind of sting."

"Did you talk to Manny at the junkyard?"

"I did. He wasn't able to tell us much of anything. And his description was too vague to be of any use." Mertz ate the last bite of his toast and licked his fingers. "Which is why the chief agreed to go along with my idea of a sting."

"How are you going to do it?"

"Well, that's where you come in." Mertz looked away briefly. "I was hoping you'd let us put a lawn ornament out in your front yard. We'd have someone stationed here looking out. There's no guarantee the guy will come by, but it's worth a couple of man hours just in case. People are getting all riled up about the thefts—especially coming on top of the two murders. There wouldn't be any danger to you," he added reassuringly.

"Sure. I don't mind."

"Great!" Mertz pushed back his chair abruptly. "It's in the car. Let me help you with the dishes, and then I'll go get it."

Together they loaded the dishwasher, then Mertz went out to his car.

Gigi heard the front door open again, and Mertz stuck his head into the kitchen. "Come and see. I've got it all set up."

Gigi grabbed her jacket from the hook and followed Mertz outside, Reg at her heels. She got to the bottom of the front steps and stopped in her tracks, her mouth hanging open. Smack in the middle of Gigi's front lawn was a giant metal reindeer with a sack of toys slung over its back and a Santa hat on its head. A single spotlight, stuck in the ground, illuminated the whole thing with a glow as bright as the midday sun. Reg ran straight toward the metal ornament, stopped a safe six inches away and began barking furiously.

Mertz eyed it proudly. "Our thief won't miss seeing that."

"No one is going to miss seeing that," Gigi said when she got her jaw working again. She heard the sounds of a car coming down the street, its headlights sweeping the road. It slowed perceptibly as it passed Gigi's house.

"One of the guys on the force loaned the piece to me. Said he didn't need it at the moment."

"Really? That could be because it's not Christmas," Gigi said eyeing the deer in dismay. What on earth were the neighbors going to think?

"You're sure you don't mind?" Mertz asked somewhat hesitantly.

"No, it's fine." Gigi blinked several times but the apparition refused to go away. It was real, and it was on her lawn. "So, what's next?" She turned to Mertz and shivered.

"Come on, let's get back inside." He put his arm around her, and they walked toward the steps. Reg wove in and out between them, frolicking in the snow, stopping briefly to lift his leg on a snow-covered rhododendron bush.

Gigi was grateful to get back inside. She flicked a few stray flakes of snow from her shoulders. Mertz had some clinging to his hair, and Gigi beckoned him close so that she could brush them away. That led to a kiss that took away any remaining chill Gigi might have felt.

"What do we do now?" she asked, leaning against Mertz's shoulder.

"Wait. Police work is ninety percent waiting and ten percent action, I'm afraid." He glanced at his watch. "I'd best be getting outside to keep watch."

"Oh, no. It's freezing out there. Can't you keep watch from the living room window?" Gigi gestured toward the bay window that gave a clear view of her front yard, now complete with a heinous spotlighted reindeer sculpture.

Mertz looked doubtful. "I need to be able to take off after the fellow if he shows." He pursed his lips. "I suppose it won't be easy to get away with that thing. Ought to give me enough time to get out the door . . ." He still looked doubtful.

Gigi pulled over a straight-backed armless chair and placed it in front of the window. She patted the seat. "You can see everything from here. And you're right. It's going to take some doing to run with that thing."

Mertz stood bouncing from one foot to the other. "Oh, all right. I don't suppose it will hurt." He sat down on the edge of the chair. "But don't let me keep you from anything."

"I won't."

Mertz turned his back to the room and trained his gaze on the front yard. Gigi headed toward the kitchen to start the dishwasher. She left the light over the stove burning in case Pia returned home in the middle of the night. She really was beginning to worry about her sister working as hard as she was in that uncomfortable studio. Although other artists she'd known had talked about being in "the zone" and losing track of everything while they worked, from the time to their own physical comfort.

Gigi grabbed her book from her nightstand and went out to the living room to curl up on the sofa.

"Anything yet?" she asked, although she already knew the answer.

Mertz shook his head without turning around or taking his eyes off Gigi's front yard.

Gigi started to read and soon found her eyes drooping. "I'm going to go to bed, although I feel terrible leaving you here all alone like this. Can I make you some coffee or something?"

Mertz turned around briefly and smiled. "No, thanks. I'm fine. Dinner was delicious, by the way."

"I'm glad you've had something to eat." Gigi bent to kiss him on the cheek, but he turned his head so that their lips met.

Gigi got in bed still feeling vaguely guilty that she was leaving Mertz to watch alone. But he must be used to it, she reasoned with herself, as slumber overcame her. It was the policeman's lot.

# Chapter 22

When Gigi woke up the next morning, she momentarily forgot about the events of the night before. She had pulled on her robe and was starting toward the kitchen to brew some coffee when everything came back to her. She turned on her heel and headed toward the living room.

Mertz was gone, but the hideous reindeer sculpture wasn't. There was a note on the chair Mertz had vacated. It said he was leaving to catch a few winks before going to the office, and another officer would be stationed outside during the day.

Gigi peered through the window. Crouched behind the near bushes was a uniformed patrolman. She wondered if she ought to take him some coffee. He was wearing a heavy jacket, a hat with ear flaps and warm gloves, but she could see the tip of his nose was red, and he was clapping his hands together to keep them warm. As soon as she was dressed, she'd bring him a thermos.

Gigi took a quick shower and dressed warmly in her usual jeans and a sweater. She was delivering her clients' breakfasts, and then she was headed to Sienna's, along with Alice, to plan baby Camille's christening.

Gigi packed her containers and loaded them into the car. She could see Reg's nose pressed to the glass alongside the front door, but she didn't want to take him this time. The temperatures had dropped overnight, and he would be safer at home.

As she gave the thermos of hot coffee to the fellow standing guard over the ridiculous reindeer lawn ornament, she wondered what Pia would think if she came back and found the policeman crouching in the bushes.

The patrolman's eyes lit up when he saw the coffee. "Thank you, ma'am."

"How long will you be out here? Not long, I hope."

"No, ma'am. Someone is coming to relieve me shortly. We're taking short shifts on account of the cold."

"I don't suppose you've seen anyone approaching?"

He shook his head. "No, ma'am. Not yet."

Gigi said good-bye, got in the MINI and backed down the driveway. She now had a whole new perspective on the reindeer—from this side it looked even worse. She shuddered and sent up a silent prayer. *Please someone steal it, please!*

Gigi hoped to make her deliveries quickly. Penelope had Hughie in her arms when she answered the door and Gigi could hear Saturday morning cartoons blaring in the background, along with the sounds of Ava and Mason squabbling. Penelope grabbed her container and hurried to the family room to referee her two older children.

Madeline answered her door still in her pajamas and

robe. Gigi thought she heard Hunter's voice coming from somewhere in the town house and hastened to leave. When Gigi got to Barbara's, her car was in the driveway, but once again, it was a maid who answered the door. Gigi handed over Barbara's breakfast and was back out on the road in minutes.

The rest of her deliveries finished, Gigi headed toward Sienna's house. The roads were slightly slippery from the previous day's snow, but Gigi pulled safely into Sienna's driveway five minutes later. Alice's Taurus was already parked in front of the garage, and Gigi parked behind it.

Sienna threw open the door before Gigi had even climbed the front steps.

"So good to see you." She gave Gigi a hug. "Come on in and get warm."

Sienna took Gigi's coat and hung it in the closet. Gigi could hear Camille cooing from the kitchen, and Alice answering in surprisingly accurate-sounding baby talk.

Sienna had the table in the kitchen covered with a pale pink linen cloth and set with her best china plates and cups and saucers. A very impressive frosted tea cake stood on a stand, with a stack of elegantly folded linen napkins next to it.

"Everything looks so pretty," Gigi exclaimed.

"Doesn't it?" Alice said. She had Camille on her knee and was bouncing her up and down.

"Thank you!" Sienna's face blushed with pleasure. "I only hope it tastes as good as it looks. But this is a momentous occasion, and I thought I ought to do it up right."

"Well, you certainly have."

Gigi stared at the cake and the beautiful tea things set out on the table. Some wisp of a thought floated across her mind—something to do with the murders. But what on earth could a tea cake and pretty dishes have to do with murder? She tried harder to reel the thought in, but the harder she tried, the more elusive it became.

"Earth to Gigi," she heard Sienna say.

Gigi startled. "Oh, sorry. The cake reminded me of something, but now I can't think of what it was."

"Not something to do with the murders, I hope." Alice clutched Camille to her more tightly, as if protecting her from the very word.

"Yes." Gigi shook her head. "But unfortunately it's gone now."

"I find if you don't think about it at all, it will eventually come to you," Sienna said as she hastened to retrieve the kettle, which had begun to whistle fiercely, from the stove.

"You're probably right."

Gigi tried to pay attention to the conversation that flowed around her, but the kernel of an idea that had flashed across her mind as quickly as a meteor continued to plague her.

"So we're doing iced pink cupcakes, pink lemonade, Earl Grey tea and cheese straws for something savory," Sienna concluded.

"What?" Gigi said.

"Haven't you heard a thing I've said? And you haven't touched your cake." Sienna pointed at Gigi's plate. Camille was in her lap, and Sienna was feeding her a bottle.

"Sorry." Gigi ran a hand through her hair, leaving her auburn curls in even greater disarray. "I'm just a bit distracted, I'm afraid."

"The murders," Alice said knowingly.

Gigi nodded. "Mertz still thinks the obvious suspect is

Declan. He had a huge argument with Bradley the night Bradley was killed, and both of them were apparently having an affair with Tiffany Morse. More than enough reason in his book for Declan to want Bradley dead."

"It would be a terrible shame if that gorgeous man was guilty," Alice said, forking up the last bite of her cake.

"The worst of it is that my sister still has delusions about having a relationship with Declan. I don't want to see her hurt."

"If not Declan, then who?" Sienna cradled Camille against her chest, gently rubbing her back and urging her to burp.

"I was convinced that Tiffany was the culprit, but now that she's gone . . ." Alice licked some crumbs off her fingers and eyed the tea cake longingly.

Once again, the ghost of an idea teased Gigi, but once again, she was unable to grasp it before it slipped through her fingers.

"I've got to be going." Alice pushed her plate away and stood up, brushing some crumbs from her lap. "I have a bunch of errands to run this morning." She gave Sienna a squeeze. "This was lovely."

"My car is behind yours, so I'd better get going, too." Gigi stroked the top of Camille's downy head. "And it looks like it's time for Camille's nap." The baby's head was tucked into the crook of Sienna's shoulder, and a thin thread of drool dribbled from the corner of her mouth.

"No need to see us out," Alice said as she settled her purse on her arm. "You go put the baby down."

Gigi followed Alice to the foyer, where they retrieved their coats from the closet.

"I do hope you catch hold of whatever that idea was you

had." Alice slipped into her coat and wound a multicolored, hand-knit scarf around her neck. "I know how those things can drive you crazy." She patted Gigi on the arm. "Just relax, and it will come to you."

Gigi drove away from Sienna's trying hard *not* to think about whatever it was she was trying to remember. Of course that was like telling herself *not* to think about pink elephants. She was trying so hard, she almost missed the turn into her own driveway.

She didn't want to look at the yard and possibly see that the reindeer was still there, but it was impossible to avoid it. The reindeer continued to be on full display, and a different policeman was shivering in the bushes. Gigi promised him some warm coffee and went inside the house.

Reg skidded down the hall, trying to pretend that he'd been at the alert and ready, but Gigi could tell by the way the hair on one side of his head was matted down, that he'd most likely been fast asleep on either the sofa or the bed.

She crouched down, and he licked her face profusely, knocking her over at one point and sending her into a fit of giggles.

"Okay, that's enough, boy, I've got lunch and dinner to get ready."

Reg followed Gigi down the hall to the kitchen. On the way, she peeked into the guest room, where a lump on the bed suggested that Pia had come home and gone to sleep. Had she noticed the policeman guarding Gigi's newest acquisition—a gift-toting, Santa hat–wearing reindeer?

Before leaving that morning, Gigi had put the fixings for Tuscan bean soup in the slow cooker. Judging by the aroma drifting from the pot, it was almost done. Gigi had the fillings for low-fat chicken potpies already made and defrosting in the refrigerator. All she had to do was fill individual ovenproof dishes, top them with a small round of pastry each and include instructions for baking.

Gigi lifted the lid on the slow cooker and tasted a spoonful of the soup. It was perfect. She packaged a handful of croutons in with each container and added an individual potpie to each Gourmet De-Lite box.

She was wiping down the counter when she noticed a teacup in the sink. Pia must have made herself some tea before going to bed. That reminded her of the lovely feast at Sienna's and once again, that elusive thought began to tease the edges of her mind.

She finished cleaning up and was getting her coat from the closet when the doorbell rang.

Gigi pulled open the front door to find Mertz standing on her steps looking rather sheepish. He pointed to the lawn ornament. "My plan hasn't exactly been a resounding success, has it?"

Gigi opened the door wider, and Mertz stood on the rug in the foyer stamping the snow from his shoes.

"Perhaps you need to give it time."

"Well, the chief's given me another day, and that's it." He looked totally crestfallen. "I'd better go out and find a pair of good walking shoes, because I'm probably just a hair away from having to look for a job as a security guard."

"I'm sure it's not that bad."

Mertz pulled a face. "It's the combination of the murders and the thefts that has everyone up in arms."

The word *murder* brought Gigi up short. The thought that had been eluding her all morning suddenly swam into focus.

"It couldn't have been Declan," she burst out, grabbing Mertz's arm. "It had to have been a woman."

Mertz looked confused. "What do you mean? What's this about a woman?"

Gigi was thinking furiously. "It wasn't a man who killed Tiffany Morse. It was a woman."

A bemused look settled over Mertz's face. "And how did you come to that conclusion?"

"The tea set. Tiffany had arranged everything beautifully—her best china, linen napkins, fancy cakes. She wouldn't have done that for a man. She had to have been expecting a woman."

"Maybe her guest was a woman. And the murderer showed up afterward. Before Tiffany had the chance to clean up."

Gigi shook her head. She was trying to picture the scene. "No, there were two pieces of cake on the plates. They hadn't been eaten. She was expecting a woman, and it was a woman who murdered her."

She could tell by the look on Mertz's face that he was considering her idea.

"But who?" He finally asked after several minutes.

"I don't know." Gigi bit her lip, thinking furiously. "Maybe Cheryl, Bradley's sister-in-law. Or possibly Janice Novak."

Mertz looked blank so Gigi explained about Janice being fired from Simpson and West.

Mertz sighed. "There's no evidence pointing to either of them." He glanced at his watch. "I guess I'd better get digging if I'm going to save my job." He gestured toward the window. "We'll have someone outside for another twenty-four hours, then we'll move that monstrosity from your lawn." He laughed. "It really is hideous, isn't it? And Bob made a big deal about getting it back." He shook his head. "I can't imagine why." He pulled on his gloves. "I'd better be going. I just wanted to check on the situation and let you know what's going on." He kissed Gigi on the cheek, and she could feel the coldness of his skin against hers.

"I have to be going, too. I have my lunch and dinner deliveries to make."

Gigi stood by the door and watched as Mertz headed down the driveway; then she retreated to the kitchen to collect her Gourmet De-Lite meals.

"Come on, Reg, you're going, too." Gigi pulled on her coat and gloves.

Reg scrabbled to his feet and began to run between Gigi and the back door.

She peered over her stack of containers. "You're going to trip me, bud."

But she made it without incident and carefully stacked the containers in the backseat as Reg made himself comfortable up front. He had his paws on the dashboard and was looking out the window eagerly.

Gigi backed out slowly, and when she came abreast of the reindeer, Reg began to bark furiously.

"Shhh, it's all right, boy." Gigi reassured him. "It's fake."

He gave a brisk shake and settled down as the reindeer slowly retreated from view.

Gigi headed toward High Street. She passed the site of the upcoming gourmet store and nearly slammed on her brakes in shock. A large *For Rent* sign was propped in the window. So the new shop wasn't coming to town after all. She thought about the enormous mural Pia had been working on night and day. Would they still be buying it? Gigi worried her lower lip with her teeth. She knew Pia was counting on that sale. It was meant to fund her cross-country trip. Her sister was going to be horribly disappointed.

Gigi drove on with a knot that had suddenly formed in the pit of her stomach. She was sitting at the light at High Street and Elmwood when she remembered the traffic camera that had been installed. She glanced up at the post and saw what she thought must be it. Once again, she wondered why Tiffany had hidden that file under her rug.

The light changed and Gigi continued on to Penelope Lawson's house. Penelope's husband answered the door.

Gigi handed over the container.

"Thanks. Penny's having a soak in the tub. It's been a rough morning so far." He gestured toward the foyer where toys were scattered all over.

Gigi said good-bye and continued on with her deliveries. Barbara Simpson was her next stop. She pulled into the circular drive in front of the Simpsons' impressive house. Barbara's dark blue Mercedes was parked in the driveway, as it had been on Gigi's previous visits. This time, however, it was facing away from her.

Gigi was about to get out of the car when the license plate on Barbara's car caught her eye. It was a vanity plate with the letters *SNKMS* on it. When Gigi first bought the MINI she'd toyed with the idea of a vanity plate herself but had ultimately decided it wasn't worth the extra money. Besides, she couldn't settle on just what it would say. She looked at the letters on Barbara's again and wondered what it meant. Not her initials obviously. Gigi sounded the letters out in her head. Snookums. The pet name Barbara had said Bradley had given her.

The car in the photograph in Tiffany's hidden file had been a dark blue Mercedes. And Gigi was pretty certain the license plate was the same.

Suddenly, everything fell into place like the tumblers in a combination lock. She dug in her purse, found her cell and pulled it out. Her hands shook slightly as she punched in the numbers.

The phone began to ring. *Come on, please pick up.*

Madeline answered on the fourth ring.

"Madeline! Do you remember the photographs we found in the file under Tiffany's carpet?"

"Of course."

"The one of the blue Mercedes with the vanity plate?"

"Yes."

Gigi crossed her fingers. "The date and time were stamped on the photo. Did you happen to notice what they were?"

"No, frankly I didn't look at them."

"Is there any way you could find out?"

"Well . . ." Madeline drew the word out hesitantly. "I happen to be at the office at the moment. There are a few things I'd planned to work on over the weekend, and of course, I left the files here. I suppose I could go back down to Tiffany's office and check."

"Can you do it now and call me right back?" Gigi glanced toward the closed door of Barbara's house. How long before someone noticed her parked there?

"Okay. Give me five, all right?"

"Great." Gigi clicked the call off.

She leaned back in her seat, idly scratching the top of Reg's head. Reg sighed with satisfaction. Gigi's cell phone rang, and she jumped, barking her knee against the dashboard.

"Yes," Gigi said breathlessly.

"I'm in Tiffany's office now," Madeline said in a low voice.

Gigi heard the sounds of paper rustling.

"Oh my God," Madeline exclaimed. "The photo is dated the day of Bradley's murder."

"And the time?"

"Midnight."

"That means Barbara was in downtown Woodstone that Saturday night at midnight. When everyone else thought she was at home, passed out from having had too much to drink. She wasn't drunk or even sick. She was pretending."

The tone of Gigi's voice must have alarmed Reg because he sat up suddenly, his ears twitching left and right as if trying to locate what had upset her.

"And that whole business with her cashmere shawl being lost—it wasn't lost at all. She used it to protect her clothing then made it look as if the murderer was trying to implicate her."

A picture came to Gigi's mind. "One day I saw Janice Novak wandering around town wearing a sequined top. I thought it looked rather odd. But I think it was the one Barbara wore the night of the party. She must have been worried that the police would be able to find blood on it, and she tossed it in a Dumpster. Janice must have dug it out."

"What are you going to do?" Madeline's voice dropped to a whisper.

Gigi looked up and was relieved to see that the door to Barbara's house was still closed, and no one appeared to have noticed her car in the driveway. Reg was becoming impatient, so Gigi rolled the window partway down to give him some air and allow him to get his fill of whatever delicious smells were attractive to his canine nose.

"I'm going to call Mertz. I'll have to convince him I'm right. Hopefully he'll believe me."

"Be careful. That woman is a murderer. Who knows what she might do?"

Gigi said good-bye to Madeline and immediately dialed Mertz's number. He wasn't in his office, and she was leaving a message when she heard the crunch of gravel. Reg immediately stood at attention.

Gigi looked up to find herself facing the barrel of a dainty but deadly pearl-handled revolver.

# Chapter 23

The moment Gigi saw Barbara's gun, she realized that she had never truly appreciated the concept that surprise could cause your jaw to drop. Hers dropped so far she was convinced it hit her chest and bounced back again, causing her teeth to clang together.

"What . . . what . . ." was all she was able to articulate.

Barbara sneered. "Oh, don't look so surprised. I've been watching you from the upstairs window. You've put it all together, haven't you? And probably called your cop boyfriend as well." She gestured toward Gigi's cell phone. "When he gets here it will be too late. You'll be dead, and I'll be on a flight to the Cayman Islands, where Bradley was wise enough to open several bank accounts."

The tone of her voice set the hair on Reg's back bristling, and he began to growl deep and low in his throat.

"Tell that stupid cur to shut up or I'll shoot him." Barbara stuck the pistol through the open window and waved it around wildly.

Gigi's mouth dried up, and her tongue threatened to stick to the roof of her mouth. She put a hand on Reg to reassure him. "Steady, boy, everything's fine."

She could tell by the look he gave her that he didn't believe her for a minute, but after one last, rumbling growl, he fell silent, his head resting on his paws but his ears alert and twitching.

"Now it's time for you to get out of the car." Barbara gestured with the pistol.

Gigi was sorry she had turned the engine off. A hard stomp on the gas and she would have been out of there. She prayed that Mertz would return to his office soon and get her message. Hopefully he wasn't camped out on her front lawn guarding that useless lawn ornament. She had to stall as long as possible. She slowly reached for her purse, then retrieved her gloves from the dashboard compartment where she'd stuffed them.

Barbara waved the pistol in Gigi's face. "Quit stalling. No one's going to save you, so don't even think about it." She glanced at the watch on her other wrist. "I have to leave for the airport soon. The car is coming for me in an hour."

Gigi started to open the car door. "No, you stay here," she said to Reg as he attempted to follow her. If anything happened to her, she knew Mertz would take care of him. She bit back a sob at the thought.

"The dog, too. I don't want him to start yapping and alert the neighbors."

Gigi's heart plummeted. The thought of anything happening to Reg took all the starch out of her. Perhaps if she humored Barbara . . . She slipped out of the car, and Reg quickly followed, his nose to the ground. He was going in circles, sniffing furiously, but Gigi could tell his heart wasn't in it. Instinctively, he knew something was wrong.

"Come on, I don't have all day."

"Reg, let's go." Gigi called out as she navigated the paved walkway leading to Barbara's front door. Her foot slipped on one of the stones, and she stumbled clumsily, going down on one knee. The slate tore a hole in her jeans, and once again, Gigi stifled the sob that, had she let it, would have turned into a long, drawn-out wail.

Barbara ushered them inside and led the way to the conservatory where she had once served Gigi tea. Barbara sat at the table and motioned, with the pistol, for Gigi to take the seat opposite. Reg seemed to have momentarily forgotten his misgivings as he nosed around the room, sniffing furiously.

"I've only got a few minutes," Barbara said as she leveled the pistol at Gigi and leaned back in her chair. "I thought I had planned it all perfectly, but then you had to start sticking your nose into things."

Gigi hoped that if she could get Barbara talking, perhaps Mertz would get her message and put two and two together. "So you weren't really drunk the night of the engagement party?"

Barbara threw her head back and laughed. "People are so willing to believe the worst. I have to give you credit." She put a hand on Gigi's knee. "You were the only one who believed I was actually sick. That makes me feel really bad about . . . all of this." She brandished the pistol in Gigi's face. "No, I went to rehab, and I've been sober ever since. And that's where I started to develop some self-esteem. But it wasn't easy to maintain given the way that Bradley treats—treated—me." Barbara brushed at a tear that sat glistening on her cheek. "It wasn't always that way. Once we were young and so in love. I started drinking when he changed—when he began chasing younger women and putting me down all the time."

"But murder? Couldn't you have just divorced him?"

Barbara gave a bitter laugh. "He had me sign a pre-nup. And I wanted it all. I deserved it. He owed me."

"But why kill Tiffany Morse?"

Barbara made an impatient gesture. "She thought she was so smart. The night of the party I stole Bradley's cell phone and texted Tiffany that Bradley wanted to meet her. She had already gone home—Bradley was the last to leave since he had to settle the bill and see all the guests off. Of course she went flying back to Declan's. If Bradley thought she cared about him, he was a fool. It was the partnership she wanted. And the money. Miss Morse had expensive tastes."

"But why—"

"I had it all arranged that Tiffany would be the prime suspect in Bradley's murder. Everyone knew she was furious with him about the partnership. I figured the text coming from Bradley's phone would clinch it. Tiffany threw the phone in the Dumpster, but thank goodness for our local garbage monger, Janice Novak. Her finding the phone was a stroke of pure luck. And your handing it over to the police was even better." Barbara pointed the gun at Gigi. "But don't think I'm going to take pity on you because of that." She glanced at her watch again. "It's getting late. In a few hours I'll be soaking up the sun in the Caymans enjoying the money Bradley never had the chance to spend." Barbara gave a smug smile.

Suddenly a crash and the sound of breaking pottery came

from behind Gigi. She jumped. Was someone in the house? Would they call the police when they saw Barbara with the gun?

She spun around, but no one was there.

Barbara laughed. "It's that wretched dog of yours. He's knocked over one of my planters." Barbara gave a smile that sent chills down Gigi's spine. "Did you think someone was coming to rescue you? I assure you, there's no one here. I gave the maid the day off, and when she arrives tomorrow, the house will be empty."

Gigi put a hand over her mouth to stifle a sob.

"Where were we?"

"Tiffany . . ."

"Ah, yes, the lovely Miss Morse. I should really blame old man Flanagan for giving her that case. His grandson was picked up drunk and speeding through downtown Woodstone the night I killed Bradley. That camera on the corner of High Street and Elmwood got a crystal-clear picture of his Porsche doing ninety-five miles an hour through the red light. Flanagan was determined to get him off and gave the case to Tiffany. She may look like a piece of fluff, but don't underestimate our Miss Morse. She's a bulldog in the courtroom."

Gigi tried to follow what Barbara was saying, but by now her heart was beating so hard it was pounding in her ears and making it hard to hear.

"Tiffany insisted on reviewing the evidence. She had some idea that she might be able to prove the camera wasn't accurate. The police sent over all the photographs of cars taken that night. Unfortunately one of them was mine. Tiffany recognized the vanity plate. Back when we were first married, Bradley used to call me 'snookums.' It was his pet name for me." Barbara's chin wobbled slightly and so did the gun.

Gigi wondered if she would have a chance to grab for it. It was her only hope. Otherwise, Barbara was going to shoot her at point-blank range. Gigi was determined to not go down without a fight. This wasn't the first time she had faced a murderer.

"Tiffany realized I'd killed my own husband and was framing her for it. She threatened to go to the police with what she'd discovered unless I paid up."

"Blackmail?"

"Yes. But I wasn't having any of it. I didn't plan on spending the rest of my life looking over my shoulder, so Tiffany, unfortunately, had to go." Barbara smiled but there was no warmth in it. "And now, I'm afraid, so must you."

She raised the pistol and leveled it straight at Gigi. The only noise Gigi could make was a small squeak. She felt paralyzed from the neck down.

Finally she found her voice. "No," she protested.

Her tone must have caught Reg's attention because he launched himself at Barbara's leg. Reg was small but with a strong set of withers and a great sense of determination. He knocked Barbara sideways in her chair, and the gun fell from her hand and skittered across the table. Gigi grabbed for it but so did Barbara, and it went spinning to the floor.

Barbara lunged after it, hitting the floor with a loud *oof*, as if all the air had been knocked out of her. Gigi was younger and more agile and managed to kick out a leg, striking the gun with the side of her foot. For one horrible moment she was afraid the maneuver might cause it to discharge, but nothing happened. The gun disappeared under a large ficus tree in an ornate blue-and-white planter that was suspended several inches above the ground by a set of wheels.

Barbara scrambled after it on her knees, making tiny mewling sounds as she clawed her way across the stone floor. Gigi pushed the planter aside and reached for the gun. Barbara had collapsed onto her belly and had stretched her arm out at the same time. Gigi kicked the gun again, sending it spinning even farther away. She felt as if she and Barbara were locked in some bizarre field game with a gun instead of a ball. Reg thought it was a game, too, and went scampering after the revolver, sliding gleefully across the slick floor.

Gigi panicked. What if Reg caused the gun to go off? Any of them could be hit.

"Reg, no," she yelled firmly.

Reluctantly, Reg came to a stop and glanced at Gigi over his shoulder. His look clearly said he was not pleased to have been interrupted in his pursuit of this new toy.

Gigi watched in horror as Barbara managed to hook her fingers around the gun and pull it toward her. She was panting heavily, and sweat glistened on her upper lip.

"Don't move." Barbara held the gun pointed in Gigi's direction as she struggled to her feet, pulling down her top and brushing it off. She looked at her watch. "You've made me waste too much time. Now I'm going to have to hurry." She scowled at Gigi as she aimed the gun.

Gigi's knees wanted to buckle, but she forced herself to stand straight and look Barbara directly in the eye. "What kind of shot are you? What makes you think you're going to hit me?" Gigi was stalling, and Barbara probably realized it, but Gigi noticed her bristle.

"You're close enough. I won't miss."

Meanwhile, Gigi looked around. There was another large, tropical-looking tree in a wheeled, terra cotta planter within arm's reach. As Barbara brought the gun up, Gigi gave the planter an almighty shove, sending it careening into Barbara and knocking the weapon from her hands.

This time Gigi was prepared, and she dove after the gun as if she were doing a swan dive into the deep end of a pool and not onto a stone floor. She ignored the pain that shot through her knees and elbows as she hit the unyielding surface. She felt as triumphant as a receiver making a touchdown in the final minutes of the Super Bowl as she got to her feet.

This time she was the one aiming the gun.

Barbara's face was red with fury as she rearranged her top and brushed at the knees of her trousers.

Gigi held the gun trained on her and crouched down to pick up her purse. Using only one hand, she dumped the contents onto the wrought-iron garden table and dug through the mess for her cell phone. She was about to punch in 9-1-1 when she heard a noise coming from the front of the house.

Both she and Barbara swiveled in that direction. Four of Woodstone's finest, with Mertz bringing up the rear, barreled into the room, guns drawn. Gigi lowered hers and placed it on the table.

Barbara shot Gigi a venomous look as one of the officers put her in handcuffs and another read her her rights. "I'll be vindicated," she yelled as they took her from the room. "Just you wait."

Gigi watched her go before collapsing against Mertz's broad chest. As his arms came around her, she began to shiver uncontrollably.

"It's okay. It's all over," he whispered as he stroked her hair gently. "It's all over."

# Chapter 24

As soon as Barbara was taken away, Gigi began to shake. Mertz held her and rocked her until her teeth finally stopped chattering. Various aches and pains were setting in, thanks to her swan dive onto the stone floor. Her first order of business when she got home was going to be a hot bath perfumed with at least half a bottle of her favorite lavender bubble bath. And she wasn't getting out until there was no more hot water left.

Mertz insisted she wait until the shaking had completely stopped. He put a finger under her chin and tipped her head up. "Are you sure you're going to be okay?"

Gigi nodded mutely.

"I can have one of my men drive you home."

"No, that's fine. I'm okay."

"Let me see. Put out your hand."

Gigi held out her hand and was relieved to see that it was steady.

"If you're sure . . ."

Gigi smiled. "I am. I just need to get into a hot bath, and I'll be fine."

"I'll stop by later to check on you." Mertz scowled. "I can't leave the scene right now."

"Don't worry, I'll be fine."

"Promise?"

"Promise."

Gigi's first thought as she neared her cottage was whether or not Pia would be home. Her second thought was whether or not Bob's reindeer was still prancing around on her front lawn. Gigi sincerely hoped not.

Instinct made her want to close her eyes as she approached her driveway, but Reg gave her a concerned look so she kept them open.

"What are we going to find, boy?" She turned to him briefly and ran a hand over the top of his head.

Pia's rattletrap van was parked front and center so Pia was obviously home. Gigi sighed as she pulled in behind it. A quick glance at the lawn revealed that it was denuded of the lawn sculpture. Yay! She was one for one at least.

Gigi dragged herself up the two steps to the kitchen door and pushed it open. The kitchen was empty, although a package of cookies stood ripped open on the counter with a carton of milk sitting out next to it.

Reg made a beeline for the living room, and Gigi reluctantly followed. Pia was sprawled on the sofa, staring at the picture on the television with the sound off. Crumbs littered the front of her sweater, and there was an empty glass next to her on the floor. She grunted when Gigi said hello.

Gigi perched on the armchair opposite. "Is something wrong?" she asked even though she already suspected she knew the answer.

Pia groaned and rolled on her side, dislodging the cookie crumbs and sending them showering to the floor. "I had a call from Peter Werks. He's the guy who was opening that new gourmet shop in town. He's decided against Woodstone. They're going to build in Greenwich instead." Pia's lower lip trembled.

"Won't he be able to use your mural there?" Gigi asked hopefully.

Pia rolled her head back and forth. "No, the dimensions are different. He said it wouldn't work. He's letting me keep the deposit, but he's not paying the rest."

"Didn't you have some sort of contract with him?"

Pia flipped her head back and forth again. "No, it was a gentleman's agreement. Although some gentleman he's turned out to be." She turned her head and buried her face in the pillow.

"Maybe someone else will buy it?" Gigi's mind was half on the conversation, half occupied with wondering how long before she got her bath. She could feel her bruised muscles stiffening inch by painful inch.

"It's too big to go anywhere else. Who would have a wall that large?"

"Another store maybe?"

Pia snorted. "I can't see the Shop and Save being interested, or Abigail's or the Silver Lining."

Gigi felt bubbles of excitement stir in her stomach. "Maybe not, but what about Bon Appétit? Evelyn is redoing the shop in a sort of country French style. Your mural would be perfect."

Pia lifted her head from the cushions. "Do you think so?" Even she sounded slightly excited.

"I can ask her. Personally, I think it would be perfect with the changes she's already made."

Pia sat up abruptly. "Would you ask her? I won't charge her anything near what I was asking Peter Werks."

"I'll call her on Monday. It's too late now. Besides, if I don't get into a nice hot bath, I'm going to stiffen up like the Tin Man in *The Wizard of Oz.*"

Pia gave Gigi a quizzical look.

"I'll tell you about it later," she said as she headed toward the bathroom.

"Are you hungry?" Pia called after her. "I can throw together some vegetable soup. I picked up a crusty loaf of bread on my way home."

"Sounds great," Gigi said.

*Would wonders never cease?*

Gigi woke up on Sunday morning and stretched luxuriously. She didn't deliver food to her clients on Sundays, so there was nothing she absolutely had to do for the entire day. The idea was intoxicating.

Mertz called early to ask if he could bring over some bagels and croissants for breakfast. Gigi took a quick shower, pinned her damp, curling hair up on top of her head and donned her best pair of jeans and the sweater that brought out the color of her eyes. She had brewed coffee, set out a pitcher of orange juice and grilled some bacon by the time Mertz got there.

Reg jumped all over him trying to get his attention, but Mertz had eyes only for Gigi. He gathered her in his arms and stood with his head resting on top of hers.

"I spent a terrible night last night thinking about what might have happened if I hadn't gotten your message in time. That woman was determined to shoot you."

"And she almost got away with it," Gigi murmured against Mertz's chest. His coat felt rough against her cheek. "If it hadn't been for Reg disarming her, I would have been in big trouble."

"Good boy!" Mertz said, glancing at Reg, who sat patiently next to them waiting for his fair share of attention. Mertz waved the white paper bakery bag he had in one hand. "I've got some good things for us to eat."

Gigi pulled away. "And I've got coffee and bacon going. We just have to pour the orange juice."

"Sounds wonderful." Mertz followed Gigi out to the kitchen, where she'd set out woven mats, linen napkins and silverware on her small kitchen table.

The door to Pia's room was still shut, and Gigi imagined she would be sleeping in. She'd heard the television going until quite late last night.

Mertz put his napkin in his lap and helped himself to some of the bacon on the platter. "I'm still amazed that you made the connection between Barbara Simpson and the murders," he said as he spread cream cheese on his poppy seed bagel.

"I didn't at first," Gigi admitted as she stirred her coffee.

"She'd managed to convince me she was really sick at Hunter's party. Apparently I was the only one who was fooled—the others all thought she'd had a little too much to drink, which was what she wanted them to think—that she'd had a relapse."

"And that she was tucked up in bed at home when the murder occurred. Guardian confirmed that she turned off the alarm to enter the house long before Bradley was killed."

"And everyone assumed she was too inebriated to go out again." Gigi took a bite of her buttered croissant and chewed thoughtfully. "She'd stolen Bradley's cell phone earlier in the evening—I remember his complaining that he couldn't find it when he wanted to call a taxi for Barbara. Barbara, meanwhile, planned to use it to text Tiffany to get her back to the scene."

"And hopefully make her the scapegoat. Barbara had a lot of nerve; I'll have to say that for her." Mertz washed down a bite of bagel with a gulp of coffee. "She used that shawl thingy of hers to cover up her clothes when she committed the murder, having already established that it was missing. She could have thrown it away or burned it, but instead she brought it back to the scene, making it look as if she was being framed." He shook his head. "That was almost a little too clever."

Gigi nodded. "It was good luck for her that Declan was heard arguing with Bradley that night. It gave him motive as well as means." Gigi was quiet for a moment. "I couldn't bear the thought of it being Declan. It would have broken my sister's heart." She nibbled on some crumbs from her croissant. "I'm still worried about her. Declan's made it clear he isn't interested in anything long term."

"Well, you don't have to worry about that anymore."

They both jumped as Pia's voice came from the doorway.

"Declan and I had a long talk, and he made it clear he wasn't interested in me. No hard feelings though." Pia smiled. "He's commissioned me to do a mural to put behind his bar. He stopped by that day"—she leveled a glance at Gigi—"the day you also showed up, to see my work. He liked it, and I'm going to start on something for him next week."

"Oh," Gigi said in a tiny voice.

"I knew what you were thinking." Pia grabbed one of the croissants and leveled it at Gigi. "But I was annoyed with you so I decided it would serve you right to let you think the worst for a little longer."

"Oh," Gigi said again while Mertz turned to glance out the window, an amused look on his face.

"I'm heading to the studio so I'll leave you two lovebirds alone." Pia grabbed a piece of bacon from the platter and started toward the back door.

Gigi felt her face get red, and when she looked at Mertz, she could see his was doing the same.

"Barbara insisted she and Bradley were once lovebirds, too," Gigi said. "But then he became more distant and ultimately abusive until she felt the only way out was to kill him."

"She wanted his money, too," Mertz pointed out. "That was her ultimate revenge—spending Bradley's fortune and enjoying her life while he was dead in his grave."

Gigi shivered. "I just can't imagine it. It doesn't make any sense."

"Murder never does." Mertz had the last sip of his coffee.

"I hope you noticed that Rudolph is no longer gracing your front yard."

"I certainly did."

"I have to apologize because I know you'd become quite fond of him."

Gigi was about to open her mouth to protest when she realized he was kidding. "Was it Jimmy?"

"Yes and no."

Gigi gave Mertz a confused look.

"It was a young man named Jimmy but not the Jimmy who is Barbara Simpson's brother."

"Really?"

Mertz helped himself to another bagel. "It seems young Jimmy is a freshman at Woodstone High School. According to his mother, he suffers from something called OCD, or obsessive-compulsive disorder. He is supposed to take medication but doesn't always comply. He recently became obsessed with lawn ornaments and started stealing them and hoarding them in the family garage. His mother didn't know what to do—she made him take that frog and violin piece to the junkyard, others she's taken to consignment shops in other towns. She was afraid that if anyone found out, Jimmy would go to jail."

"Will he?"

"No, I doubt it. It's out of my hands, but I suspect the court will recommend further psychiatric treatment and insist he stick to his medication regimen."

Mertz stood up and began gathering the dirty dishes. Gigi threw the empty bakery bag in the garbage can and wiped down the kitchen table.

Dishes done, Mertz put his arm around Gigi. "What do

you say we adjourn to the living room sofa?" he asked with a twinkle in his eye.

The snow had melted and the sun was out the day of Bon Appétit's grand reopening. It was also the launch party for Branston Foods' new line of Gourmet De-Lite dinners.

Gigi chose her outfit with care. Reg watched from the bed as she pulled various garments from the closet. The look on his face clearly registered his approval or disapproval. Gigi tried to ignore him as she went through her clothes.

In the end she chose a wool sweater dress in a soft sage green that was nipped in at the waist with a wide, brown suede belt. She had a pair of matching brown suede boots that would go perfectly with it. She spent some time washing and styling her hair into soft waves that framed her heart-shaped face. She didn't usually wear much makeup but she added a little eye shadow and mascara to her everyday routine and finished it off with a slick of peach lip gloss. When she stood back from the mirror to admire the effect, even she had to admit that she looked pretty good.

The glance Mertz gave her when he picked her up confirmed that she was definitely at her best. His hands lingered on her shoulders as he helped her into her coat, and standing behind her, he leaned forward and kissed her on the cheek. Gigi sighed with satisfaction and snuggled against him briefly. Her life had truly taken a turn for the better.

Mertz had recently acquired a new car and he ushered Gigi into the front seat with a flourish. She pulled the seat belt around her and settled back into the comfy seat.

"This is quite a big day for you," Mertz said as he got

behind the wheel. He glanced at Gigi quickly, giving her a big smile.

"Yes, I guess it is."

"You look gorgeous." Mertz leaned over and brushed Gigi's lips with his.

The contact sent a zing through her that set fire to her confidence. She raised her chin a bit higher. "I think everything is going to turn out okay."

"I know it is," Mertz said as he put the car in gear. He stopped suddenly. "Is Pia coming? Does she need a ride?"

Gigi shook her head. "She drove over earlier to check on the placement of her mural. I told her we would meet her there."

"Okay." Mertz shifted into reverse and backed down the driveway.

Bon Appétit was packed when they got there. Earlier Gigi had delivered several boxes of light hors d'oeuvres for Evelyn to serve—bread sticks wrapped with prosciutto, bruschetta topped with tomato compote, leaves of endive tipped with goat cheese, and plenty of other delicacies. Evelyn had arranged them beautifully on tables she had rented for the occasion.

Gigi did a quick check to make sure everything was in order. Branston Foods had sent over the company chef, a supply of frozen Gigi's Gourmet De-Lite dinners and a microwave. He was busy heating up a selection of the dinners and setting them out in bite-size portions.

Sienna came up to Gigi with one of the samples in her hand. "These are delicious! I know what I'm making Oliver on nights when I don't want to cook."

Evelyn bustled over as soon as she saw Gigi. She had a

jeweled headband holding back her customary bob and was wearing a bright turquoise cashmere cardigan over her black dress.

"Everything has turned out so wonderfully." She enveloped Gigi in a big hug. Gigi could smell the faint notes of Chanel No. 5 contrasting with the scent of Ivory soap. "Even if I no longer have to worry about the competition, the renovation is going to completely revitalize Bon Appétit." Evelyn clucked her tongue. "I had no idea how complacent I'd become until now." She gestured around the shop. "The new décor is just what was needed and your sister's mural!" She clapped her hands together. "It's a masterpiece and is absolutely the finishing touch."

Gigi glanced past Evelyn to where Mertz was standing surrounded by several women. She felt a sudden sharp jolt of jealousy, but then Mertz looked up and smiled at her, and the feeling dissipated just as quickly as it had arrived.

Pia stood in front of her mural, her short hair becomingly tousled and her leggings and long, hand-knit sweater making her look every inch the artist she was. Three or four people stood with her, gesturing toward the large painting that now dominated one wall of Bon Appétit.

Several more people came up to Gigi exclaiming over her frozen dinners, and soon, Evelyn's new freezer case was completely emptied. Victor Branston and his wife breezed in at the last minute, coats unbuttoned and faces red from the cold.

Branston pumped Gigi's hand vigorously. "What a success," he exclaimed as he smoothed his silver mustache with one hand and held Gigi's with the other. "Georgia," he called to his wife, who was hovering over the hors d'oeuvres table, filling her plate. "We must get going." He turned to Gigi. "I apologize, but we have another commitment for the evening. It must seem terribly rude to you, but I'm afraid it can't be helped." He leaned closer to Gigi and whispered in her ear, "Invitation from the chairman of the board."

Gigi assured him that she understood completely, and he rushed toward the door, pulling the protesting Georgia along in his wake.

Noise swirled around Gigi's head. The room was warm and suddenly felt oppressive. She eased her way through the crowd toward the front door. She caught Mertz's eye as she went past, and he quickly excused himself from the middle-aged blonde in the designer outfit who was bending his ear and followed Gigi outside to the sidewalk.

The moon was full and the inky black sky was clear and sprinkled with twinkling stars. Gigi wrapped her arms around herself as the brisk air washed over her.

"Cold?" Mertz took Gigi in his arms and steered her into the shadows under the bright canopy with *Bon Appétit* written on it in script.

Gigi relished the cool air on her face and the warmth coming from the secure circle of Mertz's arms. She felt him digging in his pocket and backed away slightly.

He pulled a black velvet box from his jacket and handed it to Gigi.

She stared at it quizzically. "But," she protested, "you've already given me a beautiful Valentine's Day present."

Mertz ducked his head. "Open it," he encouraged her. "This is something else."

Gigi lifted the lid on the box. Nestled inside, on a white

satin cushion, was a sapphire ring surrounded by diamonds. Gigi didn't know what to say.

Mertz dropped to one knee and took Gigi's hands in his. "Will you marry me?"

His voice cracked slightly, and Gigi's heart went out to him.

"Yes. Oh, yes."

Mertz sprang to his feet. He plucked the ring from the box, and Gigi held out her hand. "I hope you like it. It belonged to my grandmother." He made a face. "I'm afraid a policeman's salary—"

"It's perfect." Gigi cut him off. "Just perfect."

She would have said more, but Mertz's lips enveloped hers and they stood like that until the cold sent them scurrying back to the warmth inside.

# Recipes

## Gazpacho

*Gazpacho is a lovely, light soup to serve in the summer, although it's delicious any time of year. I like to think of it as "liquid vitamins" because of all the nutrient-rich veggies in it. You can leave out the olive oil garnish to further reduce the calories, but the oil does add a note of "silkiness" to the soup.*

1 small red onion
1 small green pepper, seeded
2 cucumbers, peeled and seeded
1 or 2 large cloves garlic, peeled (depending on your taste)
2 large tomatoes
2 cups tomato juice or V8 juice

Salt and pepper to taste
2 tablespoons balsamic vinegar
2 tablespoons extra virgin olive oil

Cut all the vegetables into small chunks and place in a food processor. Process until desired consistency. Pour into a large bowl and add the tomato juice or V8, salt and pepper, balsamic vinegar and olive oil. Stir well and refrigerate until completely chilled. Taste for seasoning and add more salt if necessary.

*Approximately 8 servings, 70 calories each*

## Curried Chicken Thighs

*This slightly exotic dish is a whole meal in one pan.*

1 tablespoon olive oil
1 onion, diced
1 garlic clove, minced or pressed
4 skinless chicken thighs
½ cup chicken broth
½ small cauliflower, microwaved two minutes
4 small red potatoes, in large dice, microwaved two minutes
3 teaspoons curry powder
1 teaspoon cumin
1 teaspoon garam masala
1½ 14.5-ounce cans diced tomatoes

Preheat the oven to 350 degrees.

Heat the olive oil in sauté pan over medium heat. Add the onion and garlic and cook, stirring occasionally, until the onion is wilted. Add the chicken thighs and cook 3 to 4 minutes, until slightly browned. Add the chicken broth and scrape up any browned bits from the pan. Add the remainder of the ingredients and cook in a 350-degree oven approximately 45 minutes, until temperature of the chicken thighs reaches 165 degrees on a meat thermometer.

*4 servings, 350 calories each*


## Lighter Chicken Tetrazzini

4 tablespoons butter
½ pound mushrooms, sliced
1 tablespoon dry sherry
4 tablespoons flour
1½ cups chicken broth
½ cup 1% milk
Salt and pepper to taste
2 cups cooked chicken breast, diced
1 cup frozen peas
½ pound linguine, cooked al dente
¼ cup grated Parmesan cheese

Preheat the oven to 350 degrees.

Heat 1 tablespoon of butter in a skillet over medium heat. Add the mushrooms and sauté 2 to 3 minutes, until mushrooms are cooked. Add the sherry and cook over high heat until evaporated.

In a saucepan, melt 3 tablespoons of butter, add the flour and cook, stirring, for 1 minute. Whisk in the chicken broth and bring to a boil. Cook, over low heat, stirring occasionally, for approximately 4 minutes or until the sauce has thickened. Remove from heat and stir in the milk and salt and pepper to taste.

In a large bowl, mix the white sauce, mushrooms, chicken and peas. Combine thoroughly. Spray a casserole dish with nonstick spray. Layer half of the pasta, half of the mushroom/chicken mixture and repeat. Top with the grated Parmesan and bake for 45 minutes or until bubbling slightly.

*6 servings, 360 calories each*

fere. I don't need you to keep me from disgrace. Rogue or no, I'm capable of holding my own without some drab little tight-lipped American nipping at my heels. Frankly, I would rather haul a tiger around on a bridle than cart you through a Season."

Hands fisted at her hips, she faced him squarely. "I'm glad we have an understanding, then, Mr. Blackwell. Especially since I am the one with the unhappy task of holding *your* bridle, which from here makes you look less and less like a tiger and more and more like an ass!"

She turned on her heels, her spine ramrod straight, and crisply left the room, the sound of the library door shutting in a most unladylike manner behind her that made his jaw drop open in astonishment.

Women blushed and fluttered at the sight of him, and generally yielded to his every whim, he reminded himself. *Hell, and that's the ones I don't pay! Damned if my grandfather hasn't found the one woman on this planet I believe I can genuinely confess to loathing at first sight—and who apparently shares the sentiment when it comes to me!*

Ashe's eyes narrowed as he considered his petite opponent in the upcoming game. The stakes were too high to underestimate her. Whatever his grandfather had promised her, the sooner he could find it out and match the offer, the better. Not to break his word, but to eliminate at least one miserable element from the Season ahead.

Though he had a sinking feeling the petite terrier was not going to be amenable to a bribe. His grandfather's business ventures had been very successful, and he'd heard him mention Townsend's phenomenal success across the Atlantic. The little chit had no doubt inherited enough to make her impervious to any offer he might make.

*If she's incorruptible, then I'm trapped unless I can find another way. But no matter what, I'm not going to be outdone by an upstart American and forfeit my pride and abandon my family's honor into Yardley's sweaty hands. If I have to cart the chit around, I will—but I'll be damned if she doesn't regret every minute that she thought to hold the whip hand with me.*

He lifted his glass in a quiet salute to the closed library door. "You'll wish you'd stayed home, Miss Townsend, for this is one favor you're going to beg me to release you from before the month is out."